The First Year

Andy Furillo

To Deb

1. ELECTION NIGHT IN SACRAMENTO

Twenty times a day, the train whistle blew and the bell clanged and the crossing gate dropped. Three, sometimes four locomotive engines pulled freighters loaded with lumber and steel and rice and oil. They stopped traffic from east to west. They made athletic young women running their dogs wait. They made muscle boys playing catch with medicine balls running up and down the street wait. They made aging millennials with asymmetrical haircuts biking to midtown tattoo shops wait. They made political consultants hurrying to downtown coffee meetings wait, strategizing their manipulations. They made homeless people mining trash cans wait. They made construction workers building multistory apartment buildings all over the downtown-midtown grid wait. They made happy hour beer drinkers and afternoon coffee sippers scurrying to brew pubs and sidewalk cafes beneath gigantic spreading elm trees wait. Moms and dads taking kids to school, lobbyists cutting backroom deals, professional basketball players, amateur hustlers, aspiring street musicians, do-gooders aiming to reduce human suffering, Democrats, Republicans, obtuse Libertarians, utopian socialists, cops, Black Lives Matter activists, firefighters, industrial arsonists, pedestrians, motorists, the unemployed, the 1 percent, single-room occupants, Victorian mansion dwellers – they all had to wait, until the 60, the 80, the 100 cars rolling north or south up or down California's 400-mile Central Valley completed their crosstown runs through the heart of Sacramento's midtown-downtown grid.

The rumble and the roar of the Union Pacific lured Lincoln Adams out of the bar on Q Street, right next to the tracks that ran between 19th and 20th. Every time a freighter shook the walls, the bartender rang a train bell from an old Southern Pacific locomotive and the house dropped the price on whiskey shots to two bucks.

Link didn't drink whiskey, or at least not very much of it. He preferred pints, two to a sitting.

He also liked to stand next to freight trains.

They drove everybody else in town crazy, the way they disrupted cross-town traffic. But they brought joy to Link. He'd go out of his way to be inconvenienced by them. They did something to his mind and soul. They slowed his heart rate. They smoothed and calmed his brain waves. They made him breathe slower, easier, deeper. They took him back in time. They made it go slow.

What they did was put Link in a trance. They infuriated everybody else in town, keeping them from where they wanted to go. They mesmerized him.

Link reacted differently for an easily explainable reason: he never had to be anywhere. He was an artist. He sculpted logs for a living, and he had hit the big time. He had become fabulously rich. It didn't matter to him if the train held up municipal commerce for an hour. He didn't mind if he had to stand there all day. The longer they ran, the deeper he fell, the more truth he discerned.

He'd been living and working and doing pretty damn well for himself for nearly a quarter century, carving logs and selling them out of a little statuary store on Q Street that the owners sold out from underneath him and turned into the railroad bar. He made more than a good living. His stuff got picked up by a few refugee chefs who flooded into town from New York and Buenos Aires and San Francisco, in search of a place that needed to be put on the map. One of them discovered Link and filled his jam-packed restaurant with his totemic stuff. Word got out to the art critic at the local paper, who wrote Link up real nice. More reviews followed, all the way up to a profile with a picture in *People* magazine. That brought in the celebrities, who flew into Sacramento and stayed an extra day to check out his shop. They liked the bigness of his old-growth cutouts, animism on a stick. You took one of his originals into your home and you better be careful what you say around it. These things had a way of making you feel them, of making you think they were about to join the conversation.

Link didn't mind being known for his work. He liked the printed word. He liked it a lot. He appreciated his local standing as an artistic raconteur.

He did not like his depiction in *People*.

"The Michelangelo of the Redwood" was the nickname coined in the profile that did it, that rubbed Link the wrong way. "He can impose on a tree what the Renaissance maestro imposed on marble."

Once the *People* piece ran, Link trended among celebrity eaters. He became more than a beloved local with an artistic trick. He became adulated.

He did not like being adulated.

Link viewed himself as just a regular guy, a true Native American native of California, Nisenan on his mother's side, born in the foothills east of Sacramento that rose unobtrusively from the valley's bottomlands. He spent his adult life adhering to the principle of balanced detachment. He had fashioned a semi-Buddhistic mindset for himself that sought to distance himself from his emotions, to look at them objectively. He never had to work harder to apply it than after the publication of the ridiculous *People* magazine story. It made him pretty fucking mad. He fought off disgust. He fought to regain his center. He strived to prevent the publicity from having an effect on him. In a world of illusion, publicity was one of the great deceivers. Publicity deceived nobody more than the public. Now, the rich and famous, chasing others rich and famous, hounded Link almost daily. The rich and famous in the hunt for style points hounded him to sculpt for huge sums of money. The rich and famous, who knew nothing about him or his art, pressured him, stifling his creativity. The adulation of the rich and famous made him question his self-identification as an artist. The rich and famous turned him away from his craft. The rich and famous with no center to their soul sapped him of his energy. The rich and famous made him want to vomit.

The rich and famous killed his inspiration.

Link stood on the sidewalk outside the bar, next to the tracks, as the steel wheels of the train cars roared past him along their 18-inch gauge, cutting through the mist of the cool autumn night. The mantra of motion and sound did its thing. It lulled him into the middle of himself. It shattered the illusion that someone in his circumstance ever had to be anywhere on time. It told him the truth. It moved him into a state of abject clarity. He realized this was true: his artistic impulse had been destroyed. He stared straight ahead, into the blur of a train speeding by at 55 miles per hour. The question entered his mind: why not jump into it? Into the blur. I've given everything that I've got. I'm incapable of giving any more. So, what's the point? Am I just going to watch the Kings on TV for the rest of my life? Engage in meaningless chit-chat in coffee bars and breweries?

With maybe 15 cars to go, Link sensed, as he always did, this moment of mindfulness coming to an end. The clanging stopped to the south. The train whistle faded to the north. His brain returned to its more frequent consciousness, and another harsh reality jolted him all the way out of his locomotion meditation.

Oh, yeah, that – the election.

Minutes before, in the railroad bar, it had felt like everyone there, everyone in the whole country, was in a panic. Link had been knee-deep in grim conversation before the roar of the passing train made it impossible. Before this year, he'd followed politics in the months leading up to presidential elections and almost never once they were over. He'd had his points of view. He viewed himself as your basic wishy-washy liberal, an advocate for peace and prosperity. He held stronger positions in support of environmental protection. His number one issue: race relations. "Race relations have been America's number one problem since 1492," Link had been opining to another wan patron in the bar, "and they remain unsolved." Link did not know if they could ever be solved, but he did know that the day America stopped trying to solve them, the idea of America would die.

This election had that kind of end-of-world feel for Link. For the first time in his life, he felt America at a crossroads, with one path leading to regression. He felt that the outcome could set America back more than 50 years. He felt that the outcome could sharpen America's tribal divisions in a way it had not experienced, maybe ever. He felt for the first time in his life that the outcome of this election could set people at each other's throats. The tension meant politics were never far from his mind, like the sound of trains crossing Sacramento, almost constant enough to tune out, but almost impossible to ignore.

Politics usually didn't rile Link. In his practice of balanced detachment, nothing demanded a separation from his feelings more than the governing art. You get too close to them in this game and it'll make you crazy, Link always thought. And mostly, in his lifetime, politics usually stayed within their 18-inch gauge, just like the trains. He was too young in the 1960s to fully absorb the tension of the era. He didn't have to register for the draft until three years after Tet. Debate over the Vietnam War did not roil the neighborhood where he grew up, a poverty-stricken Native American mini-reservation, which in California they called a "rancheria." Where Link grew up, people were too busy trying to survive to worry about their young men being killed, much less whether it was a worthless waste of a nation's life force.

In the decade or so before the emergence of Donald J. Trump, there were occasions when politics slapped Link upside the head. He didn't like it when George W. Bush got elected. He didn't like it when the country blundered into Iraq on misinformation. He liked it when the Hawaiian kid took the baton. He didn't like it when the recalcitrant right waged endless war to thwart everything the Hawaiian kid tried to do.

He lived throughout all of it, though, without great trepidation, with balanced detachment. The country was still on the rails.

But now it felt like the country was about to go off them.

Link, like many of the like-minded drinkers in the bar he'd just left, found many reasons to despise what he viewed as the misogyny and the racist narcissism of a despicable candidate, as well as the incoming first family of phonies, and a surrounding cast of goofballs. He believed "blatherskites" was the word he had used. Link viewed Trump a thief, a cheater, a failed businessman, a liar, a lunatic, a sower of discord in a sewer of hate, a sexual assault artist, a daddy's boy, and a horrible father by the looks and actions of his children.

Politics to Link were in many ways personal. They were about the politician, and even if he disagreed with a George W. Bush, he had a feel that the two of them could hit it off over a plate of huevos rancheros.

"Trump wouldn't even know what they are," was one of the last things he'd said, as he heard the bells clanging to signal a coming train. He pushed his stool back from the bar and signaled to pay his bill.

Not necessarily at the bottom of Trump's long train of injuries and usurpations, in Link's at times Jeffersonian way of thinking, was that the Republican candidate was a teetotaler.

There were people in our society who had a reason to give up the drink. Low-bottom drunks, parolees whose condition of freedom included abstinence, a few others with their own unique circumstances that barred them from partaking in the sacrament of sociability. Link could understand their reasons to stay dry. But he never totally trusted people who gave up the drink when they didn't have to. He viewed you with suspicion if you gave up drinking as a fashion statement.

He took Trump's refusal to drink as a sign of weakness. A man who could not trust himself with a pint of a decent double IPA could not be handed the nuclear codes.

What was he trying to hide?

Only problem was, it looked like Trump was the night's winner.

Politics had taken over again from Link's train trance. When the last car ran past the railroad bar, Link crossed the tracks on his way to another bar. This one was across the street and a half-block down.

In a world where little seemed to stay the same, there was always Benny's.

The place was run by the Thai immigrant community in Sacramento and it initially catered to Americans interested in moving to Chiang Mai. The bar's location down the street from the town's daily brought in the newspaper reporters. Benny, himself a Thai immigrant and a compulsive gambler, brought in the bookies. The friendly clientele brought in Link, from across the street, who had been going to Benny's for 25 years by the time he walked through the door on this disastrous night. Benny's had been a first-rate working-man's bar in a quadrant of town with blue-collar joints on almost on every street. There was the Zebra at 19th and P, the Press Club on 21st and P, the Round Corner on 22nd and S, the Old Tavern on 20th between P and Q, the Starlite on 21st a half block off Q, and, of course, Benny's, on Q between 20th and 21st. The only place in the neighborhood that didn't seem to fit in these days was the railroad bar, even if it did do as much business as all the old neighborhood joints combined. Blame that on the millennials. Young people fell for the gimmicks; it was the way of the world. New places dished gimmicks out by the dozens in order to become the old places. The railroad bar gimmicked shot-cost reductions. All the old places did was open at 6 a.m., or cater to gays, metal heads, crank dealers, pool hustlers, or, in the case of Benny's, back in the day, gamblers and newspaper reporters and anybody wanting to move to or from Chiang Mai.

Friday nights in the fall, in the days before sports gambling went offshore, the little place with the green awning that displayed the founding owner's name filled with degenerates from all over town who stopped in for a few pops and a few plays on the football cards. A Japanese bookie brought the cards in every Wednesday and paid off the following Tuesday for the few who beat the biggest sucker bet in the country. The bookie with the cards eventually died, but Benny's compulsion to bet baseball did not. First, he lost his wife, then his girlfriend, and then, sadly, his liquor license. Three of Benny's regulars bought him out. He disappeared into oblivion.

Benny's looked as it always did at about a quarter-to-8 on a Tuesday – mostly empty. In a couple hours, a younger, harder-drinking night crowd would come in and shut the place down at 2 a.m. Link, filtering in from across the tracks, caught the back end of a sparse happy hour crew mostly made up of a half-dozen guys in blue, grease-stained work shirts who held down the corner of the bar closest to the front door. They worked in the body shops sprinkled throughout the neighborhood. They slammed dice cups on the mahogany and boilermakers down the hatch. They seemed unconcerned about the political sea change taking place on the flat-screens above them. Link knew them all by name and sensibility, the consequence of coming into a place two or three times a week from the beginning of its time, and more than a third of his own. He also knew a couple other characters seated a few scoots down, where the bookie used to collect. He pulled up a stool next to them.

"Good evening, boys," Link greeted them.

Between them, Mike Rubiks and Frankie Cameron accounted for several thousand pours at Benny's. They had worked at the Beacon, or what was left of it, for about as long as Link had prowled the neighborhood. The paper once circulated from the Mokelumne River to the Oregon border, and you could get it in every town from Forbestown to LaPorte, Nubieber to Hayfork,

Yreka to Markleeville and Rackerby to Loma Rica. Now, you were lucky to get it in Land Park, the lovely leafy neighborhood just south of Broadway. The Circulation Department had been shipped off to the Philippines. Service got so bad you couldn't even cancel the damn thing.

Link loved the Beacon crowd of the old days, loved it when he walked in on Thursday or Friday night any time of year and there'd be 15 of them dancing to Muddy Waters on the juke box. He'd sneak in behind the bar when Benny wasn't looking and turn the music way up. Late at night, he'd sneak the women home to his apartment next door. Now he lived on the other side of the grid, in a little place he owned on D Street between 13th and 14th, but there were no more Beacon women to go with him. They'd all left the paper and were replaced by new ones who didn't hang out at Benny's. Not many of the Beacon men did anymore, either. Mike and Frankie were about it these days, steady as rain, although Tuesday usually wasn't their night.

As the results came in on TV, it didn't seem to be anybody's night, certainly not Frankie's or Mike's, the two of whom shared Link's instinctive apprehension about a Trump presidency.

They'd just called Florida for Trump, and North Carolina looked like it would be next to fall. Virginia was in danger, and so were Michigan, Wisconsin and Pennsylvania.

"Can you believe this shit?" Rubiks said to Link, without looking up from his Budweister longneck. Rubiks spoke in a controlled outrage, trembling observable in his narrowed, angrified eyes, pouring off his reddening, furrowed forehead that was exposed in greater detail by the recession of his hairline.

Link shook his head.

"The early returns do not appear favorable," he said.

"No shit," Rubiks said. "All I can say now is they better not fucking call the election for at least another 15 minutes."

Link nodded again, thinking of 1980, when eastern prognosticators called the election for Ronald Reagan hours before the polls closed. It cost the Democrats dozens of seats in Congress and in state legislatures.

"If Trump is as bad as the pundits think, I would think that a few seats in Congress would be the least of our problems," Link said.

Rubiks stood four inches shorter and several wider than Link. He favored Pendletons, blue jeans and work boots in winter, short-sleeve shirts and blue jeans and work boots in summer, spring and fall – never a tie, and never shorts. A thick six-footer, he grew his beard wild enough to hide a wandering army. He used to be in the army himself, during the Gulf War, where he took one in the face during the Battle of Medina Ridge. He got over it, and he expected everyone around him to get over whatever their problem was, too. If you didn't, he'd get in your face, especially in a bar. One thing Rubiks was not getting over, however, was this election. He did not take well to Link's detached downplaying of the significance of an early call on the outcome.

"It all matters," he said. "Every seat, every vote, every person. Every district. You're going to need everything you can get to stop this guy. If he wins, we'll need to fight back with everything we can get. So yeah, they better not call any fucking election until everybody votes."

Link nodded once more and ordered a Sierra Nevada Pale Ale. The old reliable, the Tommy Heinrich of the craft beer movement, still standing after 30 years of publication. He of course shared Mike's concern. He was appalled as anybody when Trump launched his campaign with an attack on Mexico. Those were partially Link's people, after all, just a little further along in their migration.

"The yakkers totally fucked this thing up," Rubiks went on, in reference to the huge majority of television commentators who thought Hillary Clinton would cruise to victory. "I always gave the motherfucker a puncher's chance. The TV people all said it was over when the pussy-grabbing story broke. Fuck, man – it was just the opposite. That's what his people needed to *hear*. They were part of his *demographic*. It fired up his *base*."

In no particular order, Rubiks identified the Trump constituency as climate change deniers, advocates of open carry, off-road vehicle drivers, urban motorists who made right-hand turns before pedestrians stepped off the curb, southern San Joaquin Valley farmers who believed the Dust Bowl was a hoax, old Birchers, young alt-righters, Rush Limbaugh listeners, contributors to the Joe Arpaio Defense Fund, Fox News watchers, construction subcontractors who cheat their workers out of overtime, white meth heads over the age of 50, young Birchers, older alt-righters, small-town southern Baptist preachers, girlfriends of Aryan Brotherhood prison gang members, Saturday Night Special manufacturers, Cliven Bundy, advocates for mentally ill gun purchasers, border agents, police officers whose grandparents voted for George Wallace, retired New York City hard hats who beat up antiwar protesters in the 1960s, all living Democrats for Nixon, Confederate Civil War reenactors who were really in practice for the real thing, supporters of the Dakota Access Pipeline, contributors to the George Zimmerman Defense Fund, football fans who stopped watching when Colin Kaepernick took a knee, abortion clinic bombers, and, mainly, people who hated Hillary Clinton more than they loved their country.

"It was a segment of the electorate that the pollsters never quite corralled," Rubiks said, finishing his impressive litany with this modest summary.

The declaration of North Carolina for Trump pushed Mike Rubiks to his limit, and the announcement Michigan would follow hurled him beyond it.

"That is fucking it for this country," he bellowed to nobody in particular. "That phony fucker wouldn't know Elvis if he ran into him in a phone booth."

"I think he does lack some basics in regards to human decency," Link agreed.

On the other side of Rubiks, Frankie Cameron sat quietly, hunched a pint of Racer 5. He wasn't exactly happy with the apparent outcome, but he seemed to be less bothered by it than Rubiks.

"We survived the Civil War," he put in quietly. "We will survive Trump."

"That's what I'm afraid of," Rubiks said. "He's going to normalize all this crazy fucking right-wing racist alt-right horseshit. Fuck, man – you talk about the Civil War. This is like the bad guys won. The fucking confederacy has taken over the entire country. They didn't surrender at Appomattox. All they did was buy some time."

Frankie had been at the Beacon about as long as Rubiks and in the newspaper business a few years longer than that, up and down the California coast. He'd spent most of his career covering crime

and punishment and had just recently been assigned to the federal
courthouse. Frankie had always kind of wanted to be a city side
columnist like Mike Royko or Jimmy Breslin. The problem was,
he only kind of wanted it. He didn't have the passion that is a pre-
requisite for the job, the one that requires you to place the column
above everything else in your life, the way Link did with his logs.

"How are you, Frankie?" Link asked.

"Ask me in about a week," he replied.

The polls in California closed on schedule, and by 8:30 p.m.
Link had enough. It was over. Trump won, and he had to get
home.

Rubiks stewed hopeless and out of his mind, his eyes wet and
red. He slammed his empty beer bottle into the counter.

"Don't mind me," he announced. "I'm going to go jump off the
Tower Bridge."

"That won't do you much good," Link said. "You better go to
San Francisco where the fall is longer."

"There's always Foresthill," Frankie Cameron contributed,
referencing the 730-foot span across the North Fork of the
American River. "It's closer, and higher."

Mike gave them both dirty looks and shot out of Benny's
without another word.

Frankie's long-sleeve shirt was rolled above his elbows, while
his Jerry Garcia tie dangled loosely at the neck. He washed his
khakis only after he spilled beer on them. He'd been in the
newspaper business a long time, and he wondered how much
longer he'd stay in it, now that it no longer referred to itself as the
newspaper business. The paper still came out, but the bosses said
to forget about the print product, that reporters needed to get their
heads around the new future: search engine optimization. Every
story for itself, every reporter for him or herself. Buyouts, layoffs,
the changing habits of readers, the merging of retailers, the
emergence of different advertising platforms – it all reduced the
Beacon newsroom from about 300 in its prime to less than 65 on
the eve of Trump. He had a long way to go to the finish line of
retirement, but maybe it was time for him to take a buyout. The fun
had gone out of the newspaper game. He got into the business not
so much to change the world with his discovery of truth and facts,
but because the newspaper world that he thrived in was fun and

attracted fun people. He'd have gone crazy sitting in an office all day or dealing with clients or serving for the pleasure of a boss. He knew that if it wasn't for the newspaper business, he'd be selling pencils on the street. He had to get out and roam, meet and interview priests and scoundrels and inmates and captains of industry. Like Mike, Frankie did not fit in the corporate world, and it had been nice of the newspaper business to give him a comfortable landing spot.

Frankie stayed with his beer and watched the yakkers try to explain why they'd been so wrong about everything.

"They never got to the bottom of Hillary's emails," he deadpanned.

Link stroked his chin and shook his head.

"Time to go," he said.

He said his goodbye to Frankie. He said goodbye to the bartender, a Thai émigré, a sweetheart, name of Om, by getting Om's attention, bringing his hands together at his chest as if he were saying a prayer, and bowing. Om did the same, back at him. Then they shook hands like a couple of good old boys, a native person from Northern California and an indigenous Thai from Chiang Mai.

Outside Benny's, beneath the soft pink neon haze shining off the nighttime mist, Link saw a friend of his sitting on the sidewalk, smoking a cigarette, his back rested against a brick planter that mostly served as an ash tray.

"Scrounger," Link greeted the youngish man in dirty ripped blue jeans and a jacket off the third-hand rack. "What brings you over here?"

"What do you think," the disheveled fellow said, his voice slow and his speech slurred, as if he'd been drinking for a few hours. Which was in fact his everyday goal.

"My guess is, a drink," Link said.

"You guessed right. Now, are you going to help me out or what?"

Link had known the Scrounger for a few years, knew him as a regular on the city's robust panhandling scene. People like the Scrounger had become increasingly unavoidable in Sacramento. Heavy winter rains had flooded the lower American River, driving the homeless off the river banks. The high water drove the homeless into downtown. The high water drove the homeless even more under the eyes and foot of the non-homeless. The homeless panhandled the non-homeless, urinated in the non-homeless's bushes, shit in the non-homeless's streets.

For his part, Link had no problem with the homeless. He kept his left front pocket filled with Susan B. Anthonys. He gave them to any homeless who asked. Sometimes he went to the wallet and pulled out a fiver. Sometimes he yanked out a twenty. Sometimes he yanked out multiple twenties.

The homeless bestowed honorary human status on Link.

Beyond the money, Link liked to engage the homeless. He liked to hear their stories. He liked to pry into their lives. They were the best story-tellers, maybe because they had the best stories to tell, stories from the road, outside the confines of workaday existence, true stories of survival, of coping with their crazy or their failure to make it in capitalism's collapse-or-expand competitiveness, of their desperado lives on the run away from the hounding of the law, of their surrender to the constant party and the attendant hard drugs and fire water.

He needed to know how they became homeless, whether they liked it, whether they were conscious of their status, whether they even cared. He himself had been on the edge of homelessness many times in the years before his tribe's casino deal, and he always wondered how he would have made it. Art as a means of life support was a hit-or-miss proposition.

Some of the homeless didn't like it when he worked them, some of them spent all night in all-night diners, talking to him. Sometimes, the homeless stayed up with him until the bars opened at 6 a.m. Then he'd buy them an eye-opener before heading home and going to sleep.

Link knew that among the homeless legions, the Scrounger held a reputation for surliness. Usually, he had an explanation: that he'd been drinking. That he'd become drunk. That he'd been cut off. The Scrounger's public learned over time that they could easily rectify his bad manner, by buying him a drink.

Nobody judged him less for his shortcomings than Link.

Seeing the Scrounger's miserable condition, Link reached for his wallet and found five $20 bills that he bestowed on his friend.

"That'll do the trick," the Scrounger said, staggering to his feet.

He didn't say thank you.

When the ungrateful and surly Scrounger made it upright, Link saw an open gash over his right eye. It was not uncommon to see the Scrounger's face mashed. He lived on the streets. When he ran out of drink, he grew unruly. He tended to take his displeasure out on other members of the species, especially those within his own socioeconomic status.

"You might want to get that looked at," Link said.

Link leaned in to get a better look at his battered eye. It was in the process of closing shop behind a curtain of purplish blue.

"Precisely why I'm here," the Scrounger said.

The Scrounger opened the door to the bar and saw Om hustling drinks.

"The doctor is in," the Scrounger said, sounding happier as he walked inside without as much as a look back at his benefactor.

Link had seen this scene before, from the bars around the Beacon to the midtown millennial spots to the places around the Capitol where the swells cut deals on cocktail napkins. He thought about following the Scrounger back inside and calling for a real medical professional, not the one who sold booze at Benny's. He knew that interventions never worked with the Scrounger. He also knew that somehow the Scrounger would make it through the night.

So he felt comfortable rolling home.

He made a right to the railroad tracks and another toward home. He walked in the dark between the rails, like he always did. At 6-foot-4, he was tall enough to land on every other railroad tie with each step. He found his stride. He created a perfect rhythm. It took him back in time.

Thinking backward usually made things easier, but as Link walked home, he felt like progress had been set back maybe a century or more, like the past was all gone and the future had been placed on indefinite detention. All that was left was the here and now, and the here and now looked pretty damn bleak.

Pounding every other tie with every step, Link's mind went blank. He steered off the tracks at J Street, into the heart of midtown. The neighborhood had changed over the previous 25 years, just like the world, only more so. Heroin dealers used to sell junk out of buckets they lowered on a string to the desperate addicts below. Hard-core bikers used to gather at Java City at 18th and Capitol, and the neighborhood was OK with it – it kept the crack dealers off the block. Now there were coffee joints on every block where the young business and artistic elite that had moved in from the Bay Area conducted their affairs in the open. Methadone clinics had converted into yoga studios. The younger crowd paid higher rents, and there were a lot of them taking in the cool November evening air, a lot more than the usual Tuesday night foot traffic.

Link eavesdropped their conversations. They conveyed hopelessness. They metastasized despair.

2. THE UBER RIDE

Late one Friday night very early in the New Year, Link walked alone in the darkness along a dirt road in the middle of nowhere. Here, nowhere is defined as the campus of Deganawidah-Quetzalcoatl University.

The public knew the school as DQU, the little Indian college on the plains of Yolo County, just east of the Vaca Hills that separated the Central Valley from Northern California wine country. DQU used to be a communications installation of the U.S. Army. Native American activists on the campus of the nearby University of California at Davis did not think that using the place as a cell tower for the military represented the best and highest use of the acreage. In 1971, they invaded. The Army surrendered without a fight – finally, something for the native peoples to put in the win column. It wasn't exactly Little Big Horn, but with their victory, the occupiers established DQU.

The Army left its fortress intact for the occupiers. The white man's government considered the transfer of the half-dozen barracks-style buildings a sign of good faith that the two nations could get along. DQU officials turned them into an administration building, a library, two lecture halls and a couple of dormitories.

Over the decades, students found DQU to be too isolated for their increasingly metropolitan tastes. They needed more extraneous intellectual enrichment. They needed better places to eat – even a McDonald's would be an improvement. They needed fun and entertainment. To get it, they drove 15 miles to Davis.

The spirit of '71 fizzled. Enrollment at DQU dwindled. DQU lost its accreditation. DQU shut down.

Tribal elders hung onto the property. They used it for celebrations and retreats and powwows. They used it for a mid-winter appreciation of Native American art, and who better to invite for a regular seminar than the local dignitary Lincoln Adams? They asked. He accepted. His seminar became an annual early January thing.

On environmental principle, Link refused to own a car. Making it out to DQU was a huge hassle. School officials always offered him a ride. Link always refused to accept. He told them it would defeat the purpose of his principled opposition to individual automobile consumption.

Obstinate as well as principled, Link took the bus. It was an exercise in inconvenience. He made it out there all right. Getting home was another story. The last return bus stopped at the dirt road leading down to DQU at 4:30 p.m. His seminars never ended any earlier than 8 p.m. He followed his teaching with his drinking. He was always good for a couple pints of Berryessa Double Tap and a lengthy conversation about the liberation of animist spirits from dead trees.

As usual, Link's first-Friday-in-January seminar at DQU ran long.

The elders offered him the 25-mile lift home.

"No, thank you," he told them. "I do not want to send anybody out of their way. I can just call for an Uber."

He poked the app on his cell phone. He could see his call was being picked up by a driver on the western edge of Davis. He saw her as an attractive, blond-haired little picture at the bottom of the screen. The name next to the picture was Angelina.

He knew she would have difficulty finding the DQU campus. All non-native peoples did, and a few native ones, too. He called and told her he'd be waiting where the DQU dirt road meets the main highway that connected Davis to the little town of Winters to the Napa Valley beyond. She said it should take her about 15 minutes to get there.

"Can we at least drive you to the highway to meet your ride?" one of the elders asked.

Again, Link politely declined. He would walk the one-mile distance.

"I have to tell you, I do not get out as much as I used to, or as much as I should," Link said. "This is a chance for me to enjoy the darkness and the night in a way that I normally cannot during the daytime."

The elders looked at each other and shrugged.

"Whatever," one of them said.

"I, too, find it difficult to enjoy the darkness during the

daytime," another said. "And I am not an artiste."

They all got a laugh out of that one. Even Link.

Rocks from the dirt road crunched beneath his feet as Link made his way toward the highway. He got there just as a pair of headlights slowed down. Then, they passed him by. He watched as the car headed toward downtown Winters. He was used to being missed. Most Uber drivers said they mistook him for a dead tree.

His wardrobe made him easy not to see.

His height stood out and he carried it over a medium build, but you'd never see him across four seasons wearing anything other than what he wore to DQU – all black, all of the time. Black cowboy hat, beaten. Black leather jacket, dulled. Black tee shirt, concealed in winter. Black jeans, faded. Black cowboy boots, scuffed.

Back home on D Street, he kept his closet full of black tee shirts pressed to perfection and hung on hangers. His chest of drawers contained three or four more pairs of Levi's 510s, in different degrees of fade. He kept just the one jacket and the one pair of boots. Each lasted for years, down to the studs. Link wore the same uniform, every day, although he did give up the jacket for summer. When he was young, he topped himself off with a full black beard and hair parted in the middle and braided down to his waistline. Ten years ago, a revolution of grey gained the upper hand on his face. He defeated the intrusion by slashing it off, except for the mustache goatee. It sprouted an inch below the corner of his mouth. It shagged two, maybe three inches beneath his chin. The mustache/goatee combo stayed more grey than white. He unfurled the braids and chopped them into layers. They dropped below his cowboy hat to his shoulders – the darker strands still holding a commanding lead over the advancing greys. The cheekbones were high, the skin smooth, the nose Roman, the eyes showing slight traces of his people's emigration from the Asian land mass. In his youth, if he wasn't such a damn good artist and a bit snotty about it, he would have made a fine male model, although that thought never entered his head. There was no questioning his retention of rugged handsomeness as he passed the turn into his sixties.

Link waited patiently for his Uber driver to call.

In a couple of minutes, Link's phone lit up.

"I am your Uber, Angelina," the voice said. "I cannot find you."

"Hello, Uber Angelina," Link replied.

He redirected her to his spot and said he would be waving his arms when he saw her headlights approach the DQU road.

She pulled up and Link slid into the back seat of Angelina's Toyota Corolla.

"You said you were at college," Angelina told Link as he got into the car. "Where? Where is college?"

"Oh, it's down this road about a mile," Link said.

He turned and pointed toward the half-dozen barracks-style buildings in the distance. Only one was illuminated. The others were harder to see, hidden in the dark, like Link was at night.

"College, bah," Angelina said. "Go to Russia. Go to St. Petersburg. Go to Novosibirsk, in Siberia, where I went to university. There, you will see what college looks like. Your college, it looks like barn."

In Angelina, Link sensed irritation in search of an argument.

He was right.

Uber Angelina had barely wheeled a U-turn back towards Davis before she steered the conversation to the news of the day.

"Your president," she said, with a sneer.

"Trump? He's still got a few weeks before he begins to destroy everything," Link joked.

"No," Angelina said. No indication she noticed the humor. "I am talking about your Obama."

"Excuse me?"

"Your great Obama, your genius from Africa, your savior, your elite leader of international world order of liberal democracy. He should be impeached."

It had been a long day, and this was quite a load for an Uber driver to be dumping on him.

The day began as they all did with Link, with him walking the two blocks to his neighborhood cafe. He jacked himself up on dark roast and, on most days, read the *New York Times* cover-to-cover – a measure of leisure that came with his having attained international artistic stardom. On this day, the big story was about the Russians stealing the American presidential election and throwing it to Trump. He decided he needed to dig deeper into the story. Like he did whenever something of this magnitude challenged credulity, he flipped out his laptop and clicked into his browser. In a few seconds, he had before him the document referenced in the story as the Intelligence Community Assessment. It was entitled, "Assessing Russian Activities and Intentions in Recent US Elections."

The bold type on the first page of the report had hit him like a punch in the nose: "Putin Ordered Campaign to Influence U.S. Election." Words like "unprecedented" and "longstanding" bounced in front of his eyes.

For months, he'd been reading the newspapers and watching MSNBC and getting familiar with the suspicion that Russia had snuck into the country and made some plays that put Trump in the White House. He didn't know exactly what to make of the allegations. He didn't know whether to trust the shock and awe of the news.

Now, the CIA, the FBI, the NSA and every other alphabetically identified snoop and spy outfit all were saying that it was all true, that the nation's most recent presidential election had been hijacked by Russia.

And goddamn if he hadn't just gotten in the car with a Russian woman who talked so mad she might even have been in on it.

In this context, her remark on Obama was a direct challenge to his balanced detachment.

"Impeached," he said. "You know he's only got two more weeks in office, right?"

"I do not care if he has two minutes in office. He should be in jail."

"Because?"

"Your assessment report in news today. It is all Obama's fault. He put out report to hurt Mr. Trump. He should be impeached and prosecuted."

"Did you read the report, Miss Uber Angelina? It says that Russian operatives hacked the Democratic National Committee's computers. They put them on WikiLeaks. To throw the election to Trump."

"And you believe?"

Link didn't see why all the alphabets would make up something like that. Such a possibility never occurred to him. Why would they lie about some Russian-created social media persona that identified itself as Guccifer 2.0, whose job was to make sure everybody knew that, hey, somebody stole the emails from the Democratic National Committee, and from Hillary's campaign manager, and now you can read all about it on WikiLeaks. Why else would Roger Stone, the long-time Republican political hatchet man who had been buddied up with Trump for a couple of decades, do Guccifer's PR for free? Why else would Trump tell his followers 137 times in the final month of the campaign to check out WikiLeaks?

There was a lot he did not understand. There was a lot he needed to find out.

It occurred to Link that for years – more like for forever – he had not been paying attention. Now Trump was forcing him to.

In the meantime, his Uber driver was pissing on the kind-of-black guy that he thought was the coolest president in the history of the white man's America.

"Your Obama," she growled again, as they approached the Davis city limits.

Link found most Uber drivers overly solicitous. He found their solicitousness to be a major turnoff. He preferred to sit in silence rather than talk to them about their lives. If they were such interesting people, Link thought to himself – silently, so as to be polite – why were they driving for Uber?

Angelina, on the other hand, was contentious, humorless. She seemed borderline vile. He sensed a viciousness in her, just beneath her surface. Her unusual I-don't-give-a-fuck approach engaged him. She disagreed with him, and for some strange reason he did not quite understand, in this he found her agreeable. Curious. She flashed open hostility, and, separating himself from his emotion, somehow he found that attractive. She seethed with contempt, and he wanted to know more.

He'd known her for about nine minutes.

Sitting in the back seat, he began to notice her – truly notice her, in a way he never did with his Uber drivers. He noticed she had a lot on her mind. He also noticed her creamy blonde hair and how it dropped from her shoulders and covered the collar of her own black leather jacket. He might have had an artistic connection to the essence of being that emerged in his sculpture, but when it came to how women looked, Link fell for the illusion. Balanced detachment had a tendency to go out the window. He was no better than the vast majority of his gender, and he wanted to see some more of Uber Angelina.

Maybe this classic failure of detachment was why the species continued to propagate.

"What a fake story he puts out, about election," she went on. It was like she was baiting him.

This could be fun.

"You mean," he said, "the one that Donald Trump stole, in collaboration with the Russians?"

"You and your fake news," Angelina replied. "*Nyet.*"

Link hesitated a moment before deciding to go all in.

"I think the I.C. has plenty of evidence to go on," he said steadily, then realizing he'd slipped into the kind of pretentious familiarity with the news that would suggest he knew what he was talking about. "The Intelligence Community, I mean. The assessment lays out enough information to keep reporters busy for years. Investigators have enough to go on in this case to keep them working for the rest of their lives. You have to understand. The FBI, in our experience, generally does not go out of its way to rile up our people."

Angelina repeated the one word of her native language that all American idiots understood.

"*Nyet,*" she said.

She went on:

"Of course it is your CIA who say this election had problem. Same CIA who kill Shah of Iran and Diem of Vietnam. Same CIA that lie about Hussein Saddam, who tell your George V. Bush – "

"That's 'W'," Link corrected.

"Your George W. Bush, how Hussein Saddam..."

"Saddam Hussein," Link broke in again.

"...how Saddam Hussein play role in 9/11. Is this CIA so stupid? Now, they tell you Americans our president is bad guy, when all Vladimir Putin do is lead world against terrorists. You don't even know terror in your country. You must have airplane bombed by Chechnya, children killed in school, to know terror. You have one bad day. We have 20 years of Chechens. We need bring back gulag, you know. Now, you have Obama. We have

Obama. You try to give us Hillary Clinton. He is bad. She is worse."

It sounded to Link as if Angelina had some strongly held opinions on the Russians' alleged political scheme, even stronger than his own.

He believed she'd read something about it, too, although not in the *New York Times*. Maybe the Russia Today website. Or Fox News.

"I take it you don't believe the assessment?" he asked.

"*Nyet.*"

"You don't believe the Russians hacked the DNC?"

"No evidence."

Link was no huge fan of the CIA. His Native American ancestry meant the agency's participation in the publication of the assessment detracted from its credibility, in his view. Link viewed the CIA's existence as antithetical to the embrace of democracy and contrary to the flourishment of the human spirit. Yet in this instance, he had to admit, on that morning, that he found the CIA to be acting in defense of the all the principles of American self-government. He knew that the American system was not perfect. He knew that the American system could be abusive, even genocidal. Take his own people, the Nisenan, and all the tribes of California. There had once been 300,000 of them, before Spanish missionaries came to save them from their natural spirituality, before the Gold Rush, before the general slaughter of the native peoples and the theft of their way of life. Now there weren't enough full-blooded California-born Native Americans to fill AT&T Park. Yet he'd come to appreciate and extol the American system's ideals, if not its practical application. He knew that the American system had made a few mistakes, especially if you were red, brown, yellow, black, or pinko. They'd break your back, steal your land, hang you from a tree, run you off the ancestral migratory routes that took you north of the Rio Grande in winter. Yet, somehow, as they stumbled and fell, the Americans mostly fell forward, and decade by decade they made incremental progress. Link's reading of history told him that you could make an argument that there had never been anything in human history that tried to do what the American system purportedly sought to accomplish – a belief that all men, and, presumably, women, were created equal. A chicken in every pot. A stew of all peoples from all nations in one land, alive and prosperous, in harmony. Peace on earth. An attainment of the general groove.

He didn't think Uber Angelina was into this kind of vibe. He decided to lighten the mood.

"Are you a troll," he asked Angelina. "Or are you a bot?"

Uber Angelina flashed a little humanity. She chuckled at the question.

"Trolls," she said. "No such thing. Of course CIA say there is such thing. CIA must know trolls live in your California. I see them each day, in your seat. I pick them up at bar. They cannot walk. Of course CIA say 'Russian troll, Russian troll, Russian troll.' This is joke. You think Russia is only country in world with trolls? This is fake news."

"I take it you believe that Hillary's campaign manager ran a child molestation enterprise out of a Washington, D.C., pizza parlor?"

"More than I believe news today, about your 'assessment.' "

"What about 'influence cutouts'," Link prodded. " 'Front organization'. 'False flag operations'."

"*Nyet.*"

"The assessment says the Russians did the same thing in Ukraine in 2014," Link said.

"The assessment say lot of wrong things. Wrong on everything. My country cares nothing about your American elections. Russia not care. President Putin not care."

"It said that Russian hackers made intrusions into the state and local election operations across the United States," Link said.

"*Nyet.*"

"The assessment says the Russians penetrated the DNC computer network more than a year before the election."

"Assessment is wrong."

"Russia's General Staff Main Intelligence Directorate – I think you call it the GRU – swiped huge volumes of data from the DNC, is what it says."

"Assessment is lie. Why does nice man like you believe such assessment?"

"Our intelligence agencies say with 'high confidence' that your GRU created Guccifer 2.0 and DCLeaks," Link said.

He threw around the names as if he knew what the hell they were after a morning of amateur research. He knew more than the average American about this shit, but the nature of the information was such that even the most diligent news junky couldn't fully pull himself out of the dark.

"Guccifer 2.0, Guccifer 2.0, who knows Guccifer 2.0," Angelina said, waving it off with her right hand. "Nobody in Russia know Guccifer. Guccifer is American make-up."

Despite the antagonism, Link was starting to dig this. He'd spent two months obsessing on this subject, and now he found someone with more than average knowledge of this stuff. So what if she disagreed with him.

She seemed to be having a good time, too.

"What about Julian Assange," Link said. "Is he a fabrication?"

"Who cares about him," Angelina said.

He could almost see her smile. He sure felt it.

She dismissed the self-imprisoned WikiLeaks founder with another flip of the hand.

It was after midnight by the time Angelina stopped in front of Link's house on D Street, in Mansion Flats, a Sacramento neighborhood just north of downtown that got its name from the multi-level gingerbread job where the governor lived.

Darkness prevented Angelina from fully admiring Link's own single-story, high-water Victorian with the grey and blue paint job and red detail work along the moldings beneath the roof line. Link had splashed the colors across the house himself over two weeks the previous summer.

"Do not blame us for your Trump," Angelina told Link.

He opened the car door to get out and never see Angelina again. Before making his escape, Link pulled a $10 bill out of his wallet, a tip because he'd actually enjoyed the conversation.

She refused to accept it.

Stuck with his hand reaching out, Link for the first time came face-to-face with Angelina. She looked sharp, angular. In the darkness, it looked to him like she wore some sort of weird, mysterious, engaging, possibly flirtatious smile. Link discerned through the dim street illumination that Uber Angelina looked like she sounded – gorgeous. Thin lips, smooth milky skin, high cheekbones, eyes slightly slit.

"No tip," she said, through the devious upward curvatures of the corners of her mouth. "But maybe we talk more. About your stupid politics. Maybe you convince me Russia is so bad. I don't think so. Maybe I convince you CIA story is hoax."

She lifted an eyebrow. With purpose.

Link put the money back into his wallet.

He pulled a business card out. He handed it to her.

"Call me anytime," he said.

She accepted the card, and she smiled.

"Time for me to go. American trolls need ride home."

3. FRANKIE'S BIG STORY

Groundhog's Day, as usual, arrived with a thud in Sacramento. Nobody cared about the holiday or what Punxsutawney Phil saw or didn't see. Spring would arrive when it arrived.

Nobody needed a rodent to tell you that.

America's long winter, however, had just begun.

Lincoln Adams strongly adhered to the Baba Ram Das credo – Be Here Now. But, man, it was getting tougher and tougher to be anywhere, anytime, let alone in the present. It appeared he was not the only one who felt this way. Two weeks into the Trump Administration, millions took to the streets in protest the day after his inauguration, demanding his arrest, or resignation. A week later, they jammed every airport in America demonstrating against his Muslim ban.

Trumpism disgusted Link, that was for sure. Just as troubling, he could not pull himself out of an artistic stall. It was almost as if one reality contributed to the demise of the other, and he couldn't tell where the one ended and the other began.

This wasn't the first time that Link felt artistically gassed, that some kind of funk sapped him of his creativity. Sometimes you pick up the chisel and you look at the log mounted on a pedestal in front of you and, boom – nothing. No big deal. You just walk away, up to McKinley Park or something, maybe go get drunk at Benny's, take a bike ride up the American River Trail, hop on the Capitol Corridor over to San Francisco, catch a blues band at the Torch Club, yak it up with a couple of the musicians, come back the next day or week and give it another shot. Still no luck, you step back again, a couple times. Eventually, the spirit fires. Or so it used to go.

This time, things were different. Just nothing was happening. He felt spent. Bereft. He wondered why. He felt too attached. He wondered if Trump was to blame.

Link had never been one to blame anyone for anything, in a life that proceeded with a steady, upward pace, from the semi-rural poverty of his beginning to his current standing in the community. He grew up the only child of a single mother. They lived in the relative poverty of an Indian rancheria, the uniquely Californian byproduct of Native American suppression. Californian white men didn't think the reservation thing would work in their state – too much land was too cool to go to waste. Instead, after running the indigenous peoples out of their homelands and massacring them nearly out of existence, state authorities leaned on the feds to dispense with the natives' tribal designations. They devised the "rancheria," which confined the Indians to tiny plots of land in the rocky hinterlands. The placements virtually guaranteed they would not prosper.

Try as they might, neither tribal decimation nor education nor criminal justice (with which the young Link was only tangentially familiar) could dampen the boy's artistic impulse. From the time he could hold a pencil, his mother saw his knack for capturing nature on paper. She framed his drawings and put them on the walls of their two-room trailer. His teachers made him for a genius. He took a wood carving class in high school. His work wound up as an exhibit in the county courthouse. His mother helped him apply for a grant. She advised him on how to spend the money. On her advice, he fled the western slope of the Sierra for the Pacific. He enrolled in the Mendocino Art Center, where he came under the tutelage of a mentor – a crazy Indian wood sculptor who everybody knew only as "the Witch Doctor," whose artistic instruction included a long reading list – Alan Watts, Carlos Castaneda, H.P. Blavatsky, Jack Kerouac, The Electric Kool-Aid Acid Test, articles on UCLA basketball coach John Wooden's "pyramid of success," The Gospel of Thomas, *The Agony and the Ecstasy*.

"These will help you figure things out," the Witch Doctor told the student.

"Figure what out?" Link responded.

"Whatever you think *needs* figuring out."

Soon enough, Link found his rhythm. The way he explained it, he achieved the liberation of animal and other natural spirits that somehow became entrapped in sacred redwood logs that could only be provided to him by the Witch Doctor. His stuff was good, and in his early years he produced it at a fairly prolific clip –

several dozen pieces a year, every one of them an original. His forays into the logs were something like reverse exorcisms. To extract the spirit from the wood, he had to inject his own into it. The two would converse. He'd find out what form the spirit wanted to take. Then he'd jump out and carve it.

Simple stuff. Anybody could do it.

People liked his work and bought it. He sold out of a studio in Mendocino. He made damn good money.

About the time Bill Clinton became president, money stopped mattering to Link.

Meanwhile, the elders back home on the rancheria had caught the gambling fever. Tribes around the state showed them the way: become a tribe again. Do what's right for your people.

Open a casino.

The gold rush hit. Money men from Nevada swooped into Link's ancestral lands. They sought out rancheria residents who could prove their Nisenan lineage. Tribal elders signed up. Tribal elders signed deals with the casino people, the banks, the lawyers. They rounded up all verifiable Nisenans. They rounded up Link. They told Link he could join in and fight for the casino. They told him it could take years to win the politics, longer in the courts. There was no guarantee they would win jack shit. They told him they would pay him $1 million if he signed away all future casino rights and profits.

It was a no-brainer.

He put his name on the dotted line and cashed a check for $1 million.

Link knew that if he held out, he could have eventually been paid 40 times what he got. The tribe in soon time opened a 300,000-square-foot casino on Interstate 80 exactly halfway between San Francisco and Reno and right in the middle of a metropolis of 2.5 million people. The casino smashed past every projection of profitability. The rancheria folk haven't stopped fighting with each other since. Not so much for the loot – everybody got plenty – but for the ability to control and direct the future of their people. It was pretty much the same thing that the American invaders had been wrestling with since they snipped the umbilical with England.

Link stayed out of it. He did fine with his million. He moved

home and set up shop in Sacramento. He rented a building next to
the railroad tracks and turned it into his combination studio and
statuary shop. He carved logs day and night. He sold them in his
little storefront. A few years after he opened his shop on Q Street,
the city started a once-a-month, Second Saturday art walk. Folks
checked him out. Folks bought his stash. It helped that he knew a
few people in blues bands and that he let them jam inside the store
on Second Saturdays. Art and music fans jammed the store. He'd
sell enough stash on the one Saturday night to pay the rent for a
month.

The town's weekly alternative newspaper wrote him up. He
rented an apartment across the street from his store, next door to
the neighborhood bar, Benny's, where a bunch of degenerates who
worked for the local newspaper hung out. The bar fed him a steady
stream of customers. The paper's art critic interviewed him at
Benny's. Then she slept with him in his apartment next door. She
gave him a nice review.

He liked the local publicity. He liked being known on the
streets. He liked never having to buy a drink, although he always
insisted on picking up the next round. You also had to wrestle him
for the dinner check.

Speculators drove up the cost of land in Midtown and bought
his store out from under him. They raised his rent. He could have
paid it but refused, on principle. They evicted him. It made for a
stink in the papers: to paraphrase the headline, "Rotten bastard
developers run out cool Indian spiritual artist dude." But the
speculators wanted that building. Someone was dead set on turning
it into a bar that would sell whiskey shots every time the train
passed by.

No biggie. Link found a studio a block over, on R Street. The
street used to be nowhere, an industrial zone evacuated by business
and left to waste. Artists moved into the warehouses. They lived in
lofts for nothing. The lofts became trendy. The street became
fashionable. Link bought his own building, a one-story,
nondescript former state office building, a former hideaway for
state welfare fraud investigators. He liked the big windows, the
front door with the metal bar with "push" on one side and "pull"
on the other. He loved the high ceiling. He could get a 25-foot tall
log in there, if he wanted. The place was perfect. It was authentic.

Before he knew it, the developers came in and repurposed all the warehouses on the block into new "lofts" for city-subsidized artists. With its bland nondescript 1950s style, his studio now stood out as unique.

Link never sought international fame. He never thought he was anything more than what he was – a guy who had a sense of nature, an appreciation for the spiritual world, and a gift for being able to see forms in the seemingly inanimate mid-sections of dead, felled trees.

He grew into late middle age and he didn't mind when he got a call from a freelance writer in San Francisco who wanted to do a story on him for the *Chronicle*. Sure, Link said. He'd always had good relations with the press. The *Chron* story came out well. You could tell that the writer genuinely liked Link. The problem was that the piece cast him in some kind of otherworldly glow. Non-human, almost. Link didn't like that aspect of it. But other writers did, and then they descended on him from papers like the *L.A. Times*, and then the *New York Times*.

And then, *People* magazine with that "Michelangelo of the redwood" crap.

The stories boosted business. He sold in the Bay Area. He sold on street corners in New Orleans, in galleries in SoHo.

The celebrities found out about him, and they crowded into the comfortable little world he had created for himself on the banks of the Sacramento.

The first was a versatile, blonde-haired, Academy Award-winning actress who Link met on the natural, through a lawyer friend in town who stopped into Benny's regularly. The lawyer's daughter worked as a personal assistant to the actress who flew the daughter and her boyfriend and her father around the world on her movie shoots. The lawyer took the actress to Link's original shop on Q Street, and she damn near bought the place out. She commissioned her own piece. He was honored that she asked. It would be easy to do a piece for her. She commissioned several other pieces over the years, after the eviction, and she visited him at his R Street studio. He had never charged more than a thousand bucks for a special request, but in her judgment his work was worth a lot more. About a year earlier, she insisted she would pay him $250,000 for his next project for her. He told her he wouldn't charge anything more than $5,000.

They settled at $125,000.

Rich people drove very hard bargains.

Big money carried the consequence of pressure. All of a sudden he was no longer producing for himself, out of a spirit that ran through him from universe. All of a sudden his work became a job. All of a sudden he lost touch with the natural world. All of a sudden he couldn't find the essence that he sought. The piece for the actress worked, probably because she was a decent person. Her money wasn't evil, didn't render the piece evil. It just made him feel weird. In time, he would feel even weirder.

He completed the actress's piece on Feb. 2. Coincidentally, or not, it emerged as a groundhog.

Link celebrated the completion by himself at the railroad bar. He took them up on the $2 shot when a freight train rolled past. He jacked the blast of Wild Turkey straight down. He hit the street into the cool, wet, enjoyable evening air. It had been pouring in Sacramento for four months, and the rivers were rising. That was a good thing in the midst of the most recent of California's recurring droughts. But the rivers were rising a little faster and higher than the hydrologists could accommodate, and there also was the problem of a reservoir a hundred miles to the north topping its dam and forcing a quarter-million people to flee when an emergency spillway crumbled. The constant ebb and flow of oppositional crises in California always amused Link.

Outside the railroad bar, he hoped to catch the train. He just missed it.

The elm trees that canopied the city were devoid of leaves. They were stark and spare.

Across the street, the pink neon of Benny's invited him over. He checked in on his pals.

Om spotted him as soon as Link opened the door. The two indigenous peoples exchanged their ritualistic bow. Looking down the bar, Link spotted two other natives, Mike Rubiks and Frankie Cameron. They inhabited their ritualistic perches. He took a seat next to them.

Link ordered a Sierra Nevada Pale Ale, in the bottle. Om popped the cap and slid the beer in front of Link on a coaster. Link raised the bottle high:

"To Frankie," he said.

Mike and Frankie clinked glasses. So did Om, who had filled himself a shot glass of Racer 5 for the toast.

The paper that day carried a story by Frankie on a trial that had been underway for a few days in federal court. The story had a few elements.

Four years earlier, a computer hacker broke into the server at one of the local high school districts. The intrusion yielded the names and Social Security numbers of approximately 200 students. The hackers used the numbers to set up bank accounts in the names of phony businesses. The same hackers also hit up American Express and stole the account numbers of 119,000 customers. The hackers rang up $10 million in bad charges – none of them for more than $19.99. By the time the victims noticed that they'd bought stuff they never ordered, the crooks had closed out the business bank accounts. Then they used the other ones to steal more money from other Amex customers. They ran the scam for three years before the feds caught up.

They busted up the operation in late 2014, at the peak of its profitability. They made a few arrests.

All of the suspects shared an interesting trait in common: they all were members of Sacramento's Russian community, which numbered close to 100,000 strong.

Frankie's story told about a useful idiot named Mikhail Mazmonyan who sat accused and alone at the defense table. The story identified Mazmonyan, once a grunt in the Soviet army, who'd been living in Sacramento for nearly 25 years at the time of his arrest. The story said Mazmonyan never made anything of himself, that he mostly worked as a day laborer who fought Mexicans and El Salvadorans on street corners to obtain construction jobs during the downturn in the economy and routinely got screwed out of his pay. An embittered Mazmonyan took up auto theft, Frankie reported, and discovered that he had a natural skill for taking automobiles apart and preserving their parts for shadowy resale. Thus Mazmonyan got to know people who had their fingers in other pies, such as mortgage fraud. The story said he knew people who got rich ripping off the subprime market. By the time Mazmonyan got into the game, the financial crisis hit. The downturn in the economy ruined the mortgage fraud scheme.

Mazmonyan looked for other opportunities. Russian organized crime kingpins in town knew of Mazmonyan's history of service. When the next racket – computer hacking – came into play, they put him to work as a mule.

The case broke when the FBI tracked Mazmonyan, 60, and two other men to a motel room in Sacramento, the story read. *Inside the room, agents found a large, black plastic trash bag stuffed with $249,000 in cash. Before trial, federal prosecutors offered an immunity deal to one of the other suspects. He took it, and it was his testimony in trial this week that laid out the contours of the Russian computer hacking and identity theft operation in Sacramento.*

"I remembered this case from back when they first made the arrests, before I'd even gotten onto the federal beat," Frankie told the boys at the bar. "I got roped into it a little bit, to help out with some legwork. Then I forgot about it – until I see it on the docket last week, and I've got nothing to do, so I stumble on into the courtroom when this guy is testifying, and he lays it all out. Great story. Stumbled right into it."

"Timing is everything," Link said.

"Luck also helps."

The story continued:

Officials identified the third man in the room as Nikita Maslov, 55. Like Mazmonyan, Maslov is a Russian national who also had been enlisted in the Soviet army before the country's break-up. Maslov's case, however, was severed prior to trial due to his lack of mental competence to assist in his own defense. Maslov has since been hospitalized and will be re-evaluated in three months.

A fourth defendant, Anton Karuliyak, 53, was taken into custody in Los Angeles the same day as the raid on the Sacramento motel room. The FBI said that Karuliyak was returning home to his residence in the Brighton Beach neighborhood of New York City at the time of his arrest.

Authorities said in a search warrant affidavit that they believed Karuliyak masterminded the operation. Still, a federal magistrate in Los Angeles allowed Karuliyak to post a $25,000 unsecured bond. Karuliyak made all of his pre-trial court appearances, but he failed to appear for jury selection last week, and sources believe that he has since fled to Moscow.

The unsealed search warrant affidavit said the Moscow computer hacker responsible for stealing the Social Security numbers of the students from the San Juan Unified School District, as well as American Express numbers from people across the country, was recruited by Karuliyak. According to the affidavit, Karuliyak arranged for still-unidentified persons to open bank accounts, and it was also Karuliyak who arranged for Mazmonyan and the two other men to withdraw the cash from the banks and bag it up for delivery to him.

"I just have one question," Link said.

"What?" Frankie asked.

"How did this guy get such a low bail?"

"That," Mike Rubiks said, "is a very good fucking question."

"Nobody has a good answer," Frankie said. "He had been making all of his court appearances, before trial."

"And now he's gone," Link added.

Link finished his beer and said goodbye to the boys.

As usual, he walked home alone along the railroad tracks, the same ones that the Robber Barons installed about a hundred and forty years earlier. The only thing the tracks separated from the city in those days was another kind of track just northeast of downtown, where thoroughbreds raced on a mile-and-a-half oval and bookmakers took action from the state's political elite. Those were the days long before Sacramento declared itself a "Farm to Fork" capital and the politicians and lobbyists needed to bet on horses to make life so far away from San Francisco interesting.

Link stepped off at Capitol Avenue for a bite to eat at Jack's, an urban diner in midtown with the best French fries on the planet, when his cell phone beeped.

He recognized a voice from the recent past.

"Mr. Lincoln Adams?"

"Yes."

"I am Angelina."

The voice recalled blonde hair and black leather on an Uber ride home from the middle of nowhere. He greeted her politely.

Angelina seemed to still be pissed off. She asked:

"You read story today? In *Sacramento Beacon* newspaper?"

"I did," Link replied. "I found it very intriguing."

Link told her that the reporter who wrote it was a drinking

buddy.

"I've known him for 25 years," he said.

Angelina was not impressed:

"All lies in American press."

Link took this remark as a direct assault on Frankie Cameron. He felt compelled to defend Frankie's honor. He told Angelina that Frankie was incapable of telling a lie, let alone writing one.

He was explaining the workings of the American press to the best of his ability, until another impulse surged through Link's general lower area to the tip of his tongue.

"Where are you right now, Uber Angelina?"

"I am on Uber."

"What part of town?"

"Near your house, riding drunken Americans from bar to next bar."

He asked if she could meet him at Jack's.

Four minutes later, she sat across from him in a booth. They shared a hot chicken wing salad and a large plate of the aforementioned fries in a mixture of spicy oil and ranch dressing.

Now Link got the full frontal on Angelina. Her leather jacket opened to a white blouse tastefully buttoned above the cleavage. The blonde hair parted down the middle decorated a collection of attractive features highlighted by electric blue eyes that shot darts through slits proportioned nicely above a pair of sharp and smooth cheekbones. She strode in tall: Link could see she stood just a few inches shorter than himself. It looked to him like she had the wingspan of a condor.

He could see her in a tennis outfit.

Across Angelina's fine features, Link also discerned a layer of wear.

Dipping a fry into the dressing, he wondered aloud why she called him.

Traces of a blush told Link that there was more to Angelina than a straight shot of Siberian ice water. She actually kind of smiled when she told him, "You are only real American I know. And you are very tall."

Tonight it appeared to Link that Angelina was signaling an interest that transcended talking politics. She seemed borderline friendly. He smiled. Discussing the story in the paper that day became easier than it had been on the phone, less combative.

"This report came right out of court testimony and court documents, the way I understand it," Link said. "Witnesses swear to tell the truth. If they lie, they can go to jail. Same with the people who present the court documents."

Angelina's brow furrowed.

"Your witness tells lie," she said. "Your justice systems work only for American police. Police make lie. Russian go to jail."

Before Link could respond, Angelina continued: "I know too of these men in story today. I know too what story say about them, that it is wrong."

The blush was gone from her cheeks.

"Your story, it mentions a man not in trial, who could not be competent to help his American lawyer."

Link recalled the detail.

"Nikita Maslov, he is uncle to me."

Angelina told Link that her Uncle Nikita emigrated from the old Soviet Union to the greater Sacramento area with his friend, Mikhail Mazmonyan, during the chaos of the Yeltsin years. Uncle Nikita, too, had fought in Afghanistan. Uncle Nikita, Angelina said, could no longer hear – he had his ear drums blown out as a heavy artillery gunner.

"I think it affect his mind, too," Angelina said. "Never same again."

She explained that Uncle Nikita lived off his Soviet army pension and the few rubles he earned part-time as a janitor in an office in suburban Folsom, out near the prison made famous by Johnny Cash, before her cell phone exploded in pink light.

"Darn," she said. "I forget to sign out of Lyft."

Like most ride-share drivers, Angelina worked for Gimbel as well as Macy.

"I must take call," she told Link.

He stood as she slid out of her seat.

"We will talk more, about bad American reporter stories – maybe other things, too," Angelina said. "I will call you."

4. DETAINED

Link went dark after initiating the piece for the Oscar actress. A couple weeks later, he received another request from another Academy Award-winning blondie. This one wanted a turtle: she'd gone swimming with schools of them in the Galapagos. She offered $150,000. Link turned her down. He tried to do it politely.

Later in the year, right before the election, one of the better known Hollywood lefties got Link's cell number. He demanded nothing in particular; he had no concept of a sculpture in mind, and told Link to set his price.

"Just do your thing," the actorvist said.

Why weren't all these people so damn reasonable?

Link gave the guy his pre-*People* rate: $5,000. Deal.

Link loaded up the pedestal with an old log he had hanging around the studio.

He waited for the spirit. The spirit never came. The spirit, it seemed, was taking the day off.

Late in the afternoon, Link plopped into the pull-out sofa he kept along the far wall of his sparsely-furnished studio. Bereft of energy, he questioned his self-worth. He thought again about taking a dive beneath an oncoming freight train. He tried to picture the result. He couldn't see himself lying there in bits and pieces. Such a decision would carry consequences. Never again would he be able to see raindrops from hit-and-run thunder storms light up on the leaves of cottonwood trees along the Sacramento River, in the slanting late-afternoon fall sunshine. He would also miss Friday nights in summer sitting out by the left field foul pole at Raley Field, watching minor league baseball at major league prices.

Visible through the windows to the street beyond, a visitor approached.

Link got up to greet the Scrounger, who pushed on the metal bar across the front door, just like the sign said. Only problem was, the door didn't move. Link had fashioned it so that if people wanted to get in, they had to pull on the metal bar, sign be damned.

The Scrounger pulled on it, out of frustration, and it opened easily.

"Why do you do that to people?" the Scrounger asked, as he walked in, and as Link got up from the sofa to greet him.

"Do what?"

"Put up a sign on the door that says 'Push,' but then make it so that you have to pull?"

"Just trying to keep folks on their toes," Link said. "How are you, Scrounger? What's going on?"

The young vagrant looked quite a bit better than the last time Link saw him, on election night outside Benny's. For one thing, he wore clean clothes. Surprisingly, he also appeared to be sober. And he wasn't bruised or bleeding.

"Nothing, my man," the Scrounger replied to Link. "Carrying a light agenda today."

It was another cold, rainy day, in a time of year when the moss and fungus could really get going on sidewalks and trees and in the dark corners of town. Nobody worried too much about it. They knew the summer would burn it all away soon enough.

The Scrounger wore his green, military-style jacket open, revealing a red tee shirt with a black-stenciled likeness of Che Guevara on it that caught Link's attention.

"Don't move," he instructed.

The artist made it to his feet a little quicker than most dispirited 60-somethings, and he quick-stepped it to his drafting table.

"Turn towards me," he instructed the Scrounger, who complied.

In a few strokes, Link roughed out the project he would carve for the actor. It would be a man, looking homeless, wearing a couple of coats with pajama bottoms sticking out from the bottom of his pants. He would have the body of the homeless, and the face and hair of Che.

"It's a start," he told the Scrounger.

"Start of what? The beginning of the end?"

"No," Link said. "Maybe my next piece. This means we may be spending more time together. I may need you to model."

"Don't know if I want the job," the Scrounger said.

Link smiled and further assessed the Scrounger.

"Yes, sir. I think you will do."

He pulled out his cell phone and snapped a picture.

"Wait a minute," the Scrounger said.

"Don't worry," Link responded. "Your face will remain undisclosed. I am only stealing your build, and I will add to your wardrobe, and I definitely have to have Che."

"Man oh man," the Scrounger complained. "I come over to see my man and now you're stealing my identity."

"You will achieve anonymous immortalization."

"Do I get paid."

"I did give you a hundred the night of the election."

"Yeah, I was a pretty popular guy for about an hour."

"Oh, that reminds me," Link said, pulling his phone out of the front pocket of his black Levi's again. "Frankie and I are going to the Kings game tonight, and we've got an extra ticket. You want to go?"

Link had extended the invitation reflexively, and did wonder for a moment about its wisdom. It was one thing for him to spend a few hours in the bar with a street person, maybe even hang out with them for a while on a street corner, sharing a beer or smoking some weed, which he'd been known to do when he first moved to Mendocino. This was different. Ask a vagrant to a basketball game? Besides, Frankie couldn't stand the Scrounger.

What the hell. Things were different for Link lately. Like, it was one thing to kibbutz with an Uber driver. It was a whole other thing to give her your business card. Maybe he had grown more impulsive, the result of his lack of artistic inspiration, and the takeover of the White House by a foreign power.

No matter. It was too late to retract the invite.

The Scrounger stroked his chin.

"Well," he said. "Yeah. I haven't been inside the new arena yet."

Link called Frankie at work and they agreed to meet at 6 p.m. at the Coin-Op, a bar on the K Street Mall that featured Berryessa Double Tap, on tap.

The reporter and artist signed off and Link and the Scrounger ran over for a quick warm-up to the Federalist, an indoor-outdoor place off a midtown alley with an entrance fashioned out of a shipping container.

Link ordered up a couple pints of Ubah Dank, a new IPA just out of the tank from New Glory Brewery, down in Sacramento's industrial belt.

"Not bad," the Scrounger said. "My first sip in, oh, about 16 hours."

"Abstinence will get you nowhere," Link chided.

"I was just testing Humphrey Bogart's line about his afternoon of sobriety being the worst of his life. I'm feeling him."

Link had known the Scrounger for a couple of years, mostly seeing him panhandling up and down the K Street Mall, never really stopping to talk to him for more than a few minutes, inviting him in for a pop once when he saw him sitting up against the brick planter that people used for an ashtray outside of Benny's. Mike Rubiks and Frankie Cameron didn't exactly appreciate it; they didn't exactly appreciate the Scrounger's aggressive style. They didn't know that the Scrounger was a professional. They didn't know that he knew who was a soft touch and who wasn't. They didn't know that he had a plan for dealing with the obstinate types like Mike Rubiks and Frankie Cameron who wouldn't give him a nickel. Only way to deal with fuckers like that, Scrounger decided, was to make them take notice, and it usually came out something like, "Hey, you self-important asshole. Give me a hundred dollars so I can get drunk and piss on your sidewalk."

Link sought to understand all sides of every story, and this pregame beverage was a welcome distraction from the situation in the studio. It was time to get to the bottom of Scrounger.

"So, tell me," Link said to the Scrounger, after a few silent minutes of enjoying their pints of Ubah Dank IPA. "How does a bum like you get to be a bum like you?"

The Scrounger seemed to be savoring his drink more than usual after his extended dryout.

"Well, for me, I've always had a problem with authority," the Scrounger said with eyes closed.

The Scrounger told a story of being the oldest son of a cop, a pretty tough, hard-headed dude, who wanted to make an example of him for the two younger boys in their Denver suburb. They skirmished on a daily basis. When the Scrounger graduated from high school, the old man kicked him out of the house and The Scrounger headed straight to the railyard, with a pal who was just as shiftless as he was. They took up hoboing for a living, wound up in Sacramento, and kind of liked it.

"I'm trying to set down some roots," the Scrounger said.

"It just occurred to me," Link said to the Scrounger, "that I don't know your real name."

"No need to get into those details, for now."

"Are you wanted?"

"I would hope. By somebody. Doesn't everybody want to be wanted?"

"I mean by the police."

"Maybe. Maybe not. My father's a policeman, but I don't think he wants me. Maybe that's my problem."

"How about your mother."

"She's a policeman, too. Or a policewoman. Or I should say a dispatcher. Or that she was a dispatcher, until she married my dad."

"Don't you miss her?"

"I give her a call every once in a while."

The Scrounger, in his mid-20s, already seemed to have seen the entire country a couple times over, from the skid rows of L.A. to Pittsburgh and railyards from Seattle to Charleston. "About a year ago, we're in North Platte," the Scrounger said. "It's got to be the widest railyard in the country, probably a hundred tracks across, and our train comes to a stop right in the middle of the whole damn place. We jump out of a box car and a couple railroad cops see us. We take off running, and we jump on a train that is just beginning to roll, and my pal steps into a coupling, right when the fucking train hits the brakes. The train slams to a halt while my buddy's foot is inside the coupling. It cuts his foot off right at the ankle. Me and a couple other guys managed to get him out of there without getting caught. Got him to a hospital."

"Did anybody grab his foot?"

"Didn't have time. But that's not the worst I saw. Another time, we're rolling out of Anniston, about six of us, and it's hotter than hell and damn if we're going to do the ride in a box car. Those fuckers get pretty hot, you know. Noisier than hell on the inside. Deafening. So we sit on the rack on the front of a hopper, and we're having a great old time, bouncing toward New Orleans, drinking whiskey, when one of us bounces over the side. His shirt sleeve gets caught, and he's dangling along the side of the train at 70 miles an hour and he's screaming at us to cut him free. Fucking shirt was too tough, wouldn't just rip off at the shoulder. Well, I pull out my knife and I cut it off. He's got a 50-50 chance. But doesn't fall out and away from the train. He goes under the wheels."

The Scrounger took a longer sip of his Dank.

"You get tired of this shit," the Scrounger said.

"Call your mother," Link answered.

"OK."

The two were halfway through their pints when a couple of beer bikes rolled into the alley. These pubs on wheels had become very popular in recent years in midtown. They carried about 20 drinkers each as they pedaled from bar to bar. The beer bike people thought they were the most important drinkers in town. On the beer bike, the beer bike people forgot they were just as doomed as everybody else. When the beer bikes stopped at a place, all of a sudden you had 20 beer bike people taking over a joint and they were loud and preposterous and the service went to hell and all other conversations more or less stopped.

"Our cue to leave," Link said.

Link and the Scrounger departed for the Coin-Op, down K Street, toward the arena. At one time it was the busiest street in town, the heart of the commercial district with a Kress and a Woolworth's and a Weinstock. When the department stores died, when people didn't think they had to come downtown anymore to buy a dress or didn't want to put up with homeless drunks on their way to the five-and-dime for a sandwich, they stayed in the suburbs. The city thought the best way to bring the street back to life was to turn it into a pedestrian mall with a trolley down the middle. From a transit point of view, the trolley was great. As for urban renewal, the city got zilch, even more of a zombie zone. Still, you had to love the sycamores that lined the half dozen blocks from the Convention Center to the arena, especially when they lit them up during Christmas time. It still had some decent restaurants up toward the top, and they were redeveloping the last block before the gym into what could become the life of the city.

Lobbyists and legislative staffers who crowded the mall by day had given way to a night shift of the homeless. Link, with a pocket full of gold dollars, distributed them to anybody who asked. His generosity made him a very popular fellow on the strip.

He and the Scrounger beat Frankie to the Coin-Op. They ordered three Double Taps. Frank strolled in with his soup-stained tie flapping beneath a Levi's jacket, his thinning, sandy hair in need of a cut. His press pass dangled from his neck. Working in the federal courthouse, Frankie wore khakis to look semi-respectable. In the old days when he covered cops, it was always jeans. He didn't get out of the court building much, but he still wore a comfortable pair of walking Keens, just in case he had to spend a lot of time on his feet. You never knew if you'd get called out to a fire and have to put in few miles with no place to sit down.

It took Frankie a few seconds before he realized that the Scrounger was a member of their party of three.

"You," is all Frankie said to him.

"Hey, man – it's cool," the Scrounger said. "I get what you guys do, you and that scary-looking Rubiks fucker you drink with at Benny's. I'm just pulling your chain, man. I love what you guys do."

" 'Pulling our chain'. You know you've threatened to have us both imprisoned for war crimes dating back to the eighteenth century."

"I must have been drunk. Seriously, I've got nothing but mad respect for you guys who try and find out what the fuck's going on. Sometimes I get a little carried away. It's nothing personal."

The Scrounger was in a good mood today.

"Like the time you told me that I was on the take from the gun lobby when I didn't report who the manufacturer was of a gun that was used in a double murder in a trial I was covering?"

"Did I say that?"

"You also told Rubiks that Elvis was only a secondary figure in the history of rock n' roll."

"I'm lucky he didn't murder me."

"He tried. You were lucky the auto-body guys were in the house that night."

"Another reason I love Benny's."

Link sat on the other side of the Scrounger who sat at the corner of the Coin Op bar. Frankie took up the other edge of the corner. He and the Scrounger were close enough to strangle each other and mean enough to do it in the right circumstance – which this was not, due to Link's presence.

"I've got something to tell you," Link said to Frankie, by way of changing the subject.

"For a change," Frankie replied, taking advantage of the pint that the Scrounger shoved in front of him. "Usually, you've got nothing, which is why I love you."

"Seriously," Link continued. "I haven't told you about this Russian woman I met."

"No, you haven't. Russians are a timely topic for me these days."

Link told Frankie about his ride from DQU and the Groundhog Night's phone call and late-night dinner with Angelina Puchkova.

In typical fashion, the first thing Frankie asked was whether Link got laid.

Link had expected the query. He shook his head no, and told Frankie that Angelina displayed a rooting interest – against – in the story about the hack on the school kids and the credit card customers.

"She said it was all lies," Link said.

"They all do," Frankie responded. "Especially when they know every word of it is true. But tell her I'd be happy to go over the details with her."

"I will pass that along," Link said. "If she calls me again."

The artist, the bum, and the reporter finished their Double Taps and went to the game. It was the team's first since they traded their NBA All-Star center, DeMarcus Cousins, and damn if the Kings didn't come out of it with a 116-100 win. Link and Frankie enjoyed it as much as any game they'd been to in years. It looked the same way for the players, too.

Coming out of the arena, the Scrounger asked if the other two wouldn't mind going back to the Coin-Op. The dryout was over.

Frankie and Link declined. Frankie took off on foot, back to the Beacon. He said he had to return some phone calls from sources on what he described as "a very hot tip."

"Tell us," the Scrounger said.

"I can't right now. But I will give you a hint."

"Tell us," the Scrounger repeated.

"It's right in there with the one I had in the paper a couple weeks ago."

"On the credit card trial?" Link asked.

"Only worse."

"Tell us!" the Scrounger pleaded once again.

"In time," Frankie said, before saying goodbye and taking off at a fast clip.

Link slapped a twenty on the Scrounger. The Scrounger thanked him and said goodbye before slinking off to find a couple pals on K Street who might want to share a bottle.

A light rain began to fall.

"Wait a minute," Link called to the Scrounger. "Where you staying? You need a motel room?"

He pulled out his wallet. The Scrounger waved him off.

"No, man. I'm good. I've got a place at the Sterling."

The Sterling Hotel was a classy bed-and-breakfast not far from where Link lived in Mansion Flats. The 123-year-old Victorian used to be the home of a late-19th-century department store magnate. It had since been repurposed. Rooms went for about $200 a night.

Link's confusion at how the Scrounger could afford it must have shown on his face

"C'mon, I'll show you," the Scrounger said.

They reached the hotel at 13th and H streets, and the Scrounger walked Link to a clump of hydrangea bushes that grew along the side wall of the hotel next to the alley. The Scrounger opened a gate and led Link into the bushes that concealed a small dome tent, completely concealed from view.

"There's a buddy of mine, used to sleep on the streets," the Scrounger whispered. "He cleaned up just enough to get himself a job here as the night clerk. He lets me stay. Same with the groundskeepers – all ex-homeless. They're cool."

Link nodded his approval.

"Decent set-up," he said

Link and the Scrounger snuck out of the bushes. The Scrounger headed back toward K Street looking for a bum party. Link headed home.

"Big day tomorrow," he told the Scrounger. "I've got to go up to Mendocino County, to pick up a log."

Link sounded ridiculous even to himself. He knew he didn't

need a log. He knew he'd never be able to pierce it. He couldn't get his mind off this inner hollow. It was not a feeling conducive to artistic performance. He'd had a good time hanging with the Scrounger and with Frankie. He had a great time at the game. But it all covered up the reality he knew he had to deal with: he felt dead inside.

He came to life, however, when he spotted something in front of his house on D Street – a pair of headlights, pointed right at him.

When he got to his front gate, Link saw that the beams belonged to a black-and-white police cruiser. He couldn't find the cops that went with the vehicle, until he walked up the stairs to his porch where they greeted him at the front door.

"Are you Lincoln A. Adams?" one of them asked.

"Yes, officers."

"We need you to come to the station with us."

Link found the request confusing, but he'd learned years ago it was never a good idea to argue with cops.

They appreciated his cooperation.

"It's probably nothing," one of the policemen said, "but we're working a missing person's report on a woman you may know."

He hadn't been so active recently in his interactions with other genders. So it didn't surprise Link when the cops identified the victim as Angelina Puchkova.

5. AN INTERROGATION

The officers told Link that for appearance sake it would be OK if he drove to the police station on his own.

"You never know what people might think if they see you getting in a car with us," one of them told him. "We're really bad PR these days."

Not having a car, Link said he'd just as soon ride with them. Unlike many people he knew, he did not mind being seen with cops. He knew, though, that they had one major flaw: they were, in fact, people. That made them suspect, just like everybody else.

He also found they had a wry sense of humor, when they were not stressed.

"I know it might be difficult for you," he told the officers, ducking into the back seat. "But please don't shove my head down."

They laughed.

The older of the two cops shoved Link's head into car anyway.

"You want it to look legit, don't you?" the officer said.

"Just don't waffle me," Link responded, waffling of course being the old trick where cops cuffed a disagreeable into the back seat but did not fasten his seat belt. Then they'd tap the brakes, hard, at every stop sign. The stop-force shot the guy into the iron-grated screen that separates the back seat from the front. The impression on the passenger's face left him looking like a waffle. The cops got a lot of kicks out of the tactic until it figured in the death of Freddy Gray in Baltimore. Then it wasn't so clever anymore. This joke didn't get as much of a laugh from the officers.

His ride in the back was short. A few minutes after his detention, Link was in a chair beside the desk of an old acquaintance, Detective Andrew Wiggins, an investigator with the Police Department's crimes-against-persons detail. That meant he mostly investigated homicides.

Link and Wiggins went back about 18 years, to when Wiggins, who was then a rookie-in-training, responded with his partner to a bar fight at the Flame Club on 16th Street. When the cops got there,

Wiggins found Link sitting on the chest of a white supremacist. The white supremacist, the investigation revealed, had sucker punched one of the regulars, a black guy who played piano at some club over on Broadway.

"Would you like me to give you a statement, officer?" Link said to Wiggins as the cop walked up and asked him why he was sitting on the chest of the scuzz ball with the swastika tattooed on his forehead.

Wiggins had laughed in an inappropriate fashion, which resulted in a letter to his file from his sergeant. It turned out no statement was needed. The supremacist was just out of Folsom and drinking on his $200 gate money. The parole violation meant he was sentenced to way more than you get for your average bar fight: he was returned to prison for a year, which turned into a death penalty. He got stabbed to death on the yard at Tracy after yelling a racial slur to a Vietnamese with a sharpened toothbrush stuck up his ass.

Wiggins kept Link appraised of the compelling turn of events and their palpable dramatic irony, so they stayed in touch, though the cop was not a big fan of Benny's – too many reporters. He and Link used to hook up at the old cop bars up on Del Paso Boulevard that later went to hell. The two hadn't seen each other five times since the neighborhood went bad and they all shut down. Cops didn't drink in public like they used to, but Link knew a couple out-of-the-way bars where they hung. He made a point once or twice a year of searching them out.

He bought them rounds. They appreciated it.

"Mr. Adams," Wiggins greeted him. Friendly, smiling. No pressure.

It was getting pretty late. Detectives, if they weren't in the early stages of a murder case, had usually cleared out by this time. Link began to wonder if Angelina was more than missing.

"Detective Wiggins. You are looking well," Link said.

He was tanned and good looking, attired in a brown tweed sports coat over brown slacks. Besides the touch of grey around the temples punctuating his otherwise brown hair, Wiggins looked the same trim, 6-foot 180-pounder who pulled Link off the chest of a Nazi.

"I'll tell you what's working well with me," Wiggins said. "A homicide rate that's less than a third of what it was 25 years ago. Not so many late nights. Allows me to get my rest and exercise. What's with you?"

Link laughed.

"Everything is fine, mostly, except once in a while when I get home at night and the Gestapo grabs me off my doorstep and drags me downtown for the third degree," Link said. "I suppose the plan now calls for you to beat a confession out of me."

Now it was Wiggins' turn to laugh.

"I apologize for the inconvenience. Hey, I see you got a write-up in *People* magazine."

Link rolled his eyes.

"Not you, too."

"What do you mean, me too? You're a big fucking celebrity, man."

"That's the problem," Link replied. "Everybody thinks I'm a something now, when I am no more different today than I was different before that article was published."

"You can't deny it, my friend. You are different."

"Indian artists' lives matter."

Wiggins laughed as he got up from his desk, a bit apprehensively, like a doctor about to perform a digital rectal exam. Not something he really wanted to do, or that the patient wanted done, but something necessary for the good of all mankind.

"So, you know why we violated your civil rights by bringing you down here," Wiggins said.

"Yes, Detective." That was all Link ever called Wiggins. "Your henchmen informed me that a minor acquaintance of mine has somehow fallen out of pocket."

"Oh," Wiggins said, laughing again. "There goes the element of surprise."

"You are surprising me in another respect, Detective."

"And that is?"

"Missing persons. I thought you worked murder?"

"You need to stay up to date on our efficiency protocols. If you came to Scott's more than once a year" – that was the cop bar *de jure*, located at a riverside seafood restaurant – "you'd know that we combined the Missing Persons and Homicide details years ago, once business decreased. It took a consultant to tell us that sometimes a missing person turns into a dead person. Management experts then deduced that we could get ahead of the game if we merged the units."

"I could see the possibility of you even saving a life."

"An unintended side benefit. Listen, I could talk all night long about how the Police Department could benefit from a top-to-bottom reorganization," Wiggins said. "But for now, I do have work to do."

The detective paused for a second, and with a hint of seriousness said to Link:

"Tell me about Angelina Puchkova."

Link provided the detective with the details of his two encounters with the woman. He told him about the Uber pick-up, the open hostility Angelina exhibited within minutes of his getting into her car.

"It was different than my usual Uber experiences," Link said. "It must be in their employment manual for them to be as obsequious as possible. This woman, she came right at me."

"About?"

"Trump. Russia. The FBI. She thought the whole theft-of-the-election thing was a fake story. Then, a month or so later, the night that the Beacon comes out with that story about the Carmichael kids' Social Security numbers being ripped off on that credit card scam, she calls me up to say it's phony, too. As if I could do anything about it."

Wiggins cradled his chin in the crook of his right thumb and index finger.

"Interesting," he said.

Link sat in a chair shoved up against Wiggins' metal desk in the detectives' squad room. Link felt more like a guest on a late-night TV talk show than a witness or a subject in a missing person's investigation. Wiggins told Link that if he were in charge of the world, he would continue the interview right there at the desk, over sipping whiskey. Departmental general orders, however, called for all official interrogations to be conducted in an authorized interview room where the questioning could be videotaped. The videos made for great courtroom comparisons of the interviewees' lies in the interview room with their lies in the courtroom. Off they went to the interview cubicle, exactly like the ones Link had seen on the reality police TV shows.

The detective left Link alone for a while. The five beers over the previous seven hours caught up with him. Link laid his head on the table. He might have conked out for a brief time. He snapped back to consciousness when Wiggins walked in with a hot cup of coffee.

"Straight from my French press," the detective said.

Link accepted the cup with two hands and sipped gingerly.

"You should open a shop," he told the detective.

"Just what Sacramento needs," Wiggins deadpanned. "Another coffee place."

Wiggins finally dispensed with the chit-chat. It was late, and he'd been working all day. He wanted to go home.

"OK, I'll be straight up with you," he told Link. "This woman Puchkova has been missing for three days, and her family thinks you know something about it. Now, to be perfectly honest, I believe that is total bullshit. But we have to respond and conduct an official investigation, and act on the information that was directed to us by members of the public who are reporting a crime. Which they have done. So here we are."

Link nodded, as if he knew the drill.

"What can I do to help?"

"Did you kidnap the woman?"

"No."

"Did you kill her."

"No. And aren't you forgetting something?"

"What's that?"

"You forgot to read me my rights."

"Oh, fuck."

"No biggie. I'll waive them."

"That won't do me any good."

"Why's that?"

"The tape is running, dammit."

"Start a new one. Then read me my rights, and we'll take it from the top."

"It's not that easy." Wiggins turned the camera off. "This will be the second written reprimand you've gotten me."

Wiggins grumbled and started the interview over. He pulled out an index card to read Link his Miranda warning, which ended with him asking:

"Do you consent, then, to this interview?"

To which the interview subject replied, much to the surprise of the detective: "I want a lawyer."

Off camera, Wiggins flipped Link the middle finger of both of his hands and very clearly mouthed: "You...fucking...asshole!"

Link cracked up.

"No, Detective. Just joking. I hereby waive my right to have an attorney present."

Wiggins, still out of the lens' range, mouthed to Link something to the effect of, "You motherfucker" and rubbed his hands down his face. Taking a few moments to recover, he restarted the interview.

"Mr. Adams, do you know an Angelina Puchkova?"

"I've met her a couple times, yes."

"Did you kidnap Ms. Puchkova."

"No."

"Did you murder her?"

"I refuse to answer that question on the ground that it may...."

Detective Wiggins damn near spit up his coffee.

"Just joking, detective. No, I did not murder Ms. Puchkova."

"Thank you, Mr. Adams. This interview is concluded."

Link and Wiggins departed the interview room, the witness chuckling and the detective steaming.

"I did not realize you could be such an asshole," Wiggins said. "This is going to cost me days."

"I'll make it up to you," Link said.

"I didn't hear that," Wiggins said, looking up at the various security cameras that caught on tape virtually everything said or done on the police premises.

Back at his desk, the detective had lightened up some. He began to see the humor.

"One other thing, off the record, for now," Wiggins said. "Were you fucking her?"

"I would have told you that in there," Link said, nodding back toward the interview room. "The answer is no."

Now it was Wiggins' turn to nod. Apparently, he was satisfied with Link's story.

It was the shortest bracing in the history of American policing.

"All right, we're good here," Wiggins said. "Just one other thing. Did she ever mention anything about her own business affairs? What she did for a living? Anything like that?"

"I didn't know she had an occupation other than being an Uber driver, so, no, not precisely," Link answered. "But she did say something about her being offered some other kind of job. Something about the mortgage business."

He recounted how Angelina told him about the woman who ran some sort of an office in Folsom, how the woman had given Angelina's uncle a janitor's job and how the same woman had offered Angelina a job, too.

"That should do me," Wiggins said. "I apologize for disrupting your evening. If you like, I'll have a couple of uniforms run you home."

"Don't worry about it," Link responded. "I'll get an Uber."

"You sure?"

"On second thought," Link said, just before he punched up the app on his phone, "I think I'll call a cab."

6. A READING FROM CHRISTOPHER STEELE

The morning after his detention, Link changed his plans. He put off the trip to Mendocino County for a day, to recover from the two hours he spent in police custody. His sense of balanced detachment had been challenged: meets woman, argues politics with her, she calls him up a month later, they eat out of the same dish of Urban Fries, she turns up missing, and her people blame him for the disappearance? And tell the police about it?

He didn't have the slightest idea of what to make of it. As he got older, he figured out how to deal with things he didn't understand: ignore them.

In the meantime, he would tuck his *New York Times* and his laptop under his arm and he would walk the couple blocks over to Shine, his neighborhood coffee joint.

He read the newspaper there just about every morning. Today, he needed to put in some laptop time, on a research project he'd been putting off. He pulled up a chair at one of the high tables and typed the words "Christopher Steele Dossier" into the search engine. Sipping a tall cup of dark roast, Link watched "COMPANY INTELLIGENCE REPORT 2016/080" load on his computer screen. The first heading: "US PRESIDENTIAL ELECTION; REPUBLICAN CANDIDATE DONALD TRUMP'S ACTIVITIES IN RUSSIA AND COMPROMISING RELATIONSHIP WITH THE KREMLIN."

One paragraph in, enough flew over his head that he put in a call to Mike Rubiks' office.

"Mike? Do you have a minute?"

"For you, an hour. But what's this I hear about you getting run in last night?"

"Excuse me?"

"Yeah. One of the photogs was listening to the police scanner last night, and you got a mention."

"A mention."

"Yeah, by name, on an APB or something like that, 'be on the lookout for a wild-eyed Indian chief in a black cowboy hat.' It busted them up on the picture desk. Except we don't have a picture desk anymore. But yeah, you got a description and an ID, the whole thing."

"I'll have to thank the dispatcher," Link said, only slightly perturbed. These days, in his mind, any publicity was bad publicity.

He filled Mike in on the circumstances of his interview with Detective Wiggins, without getting into too much, or any, detail about Angelina.

"So, what's up?" Mike asked. "You usually don't call me unless it's to hurry me over to Benny's."

"I have become interested in politics," Link admitted.

"You've become interested in politics. I thought you were an artiste. Several steps removed from the hurly burly."

"I like to think of myself being more in the middle of the hurly burly."

"But you're too busy contemplating the human condition, to have time for things like politics."

"You could say that the events of the last several months have brought me into a new awareness of an existential crisis we are all now facing."

"You mean that Trump is the fucking asshole of all time and that democracy as we know it is about to come to an end?"

"I choose not to personalize it to that extent."

"I think you're beginning to get it."

Link sighed. He usually didn't like to talk about himself, especially concerning his personal artistic crises.

"All I know is that I've got all these logs in my studio, and I look at them, and I can't see anything inside of any of them," he told Mike.

"You're in a slump, pal. You'll snap out of it," his friend responded.

"Stuff all of a sudden gets into your head and it roils the mind. If you can't separate yourself from it, it's probably better to try and understand it. So I am conducting an investigation."

"What do you mean, your 'work?' You don't work."

"I love you, Mike," Link said. "But I do not find that crack to be very funny."

"C'mon. You know that I know what you do. Lighten up."

"Apology accepted."

"I didn't apologize for shit."

"The Muslim ban. The press as 'enemy of the people.' I've got to admit, I'm a little off my game. I need to understand better what's going on. I thought you could help me."

"I'd be happy to bring you up to date."

"I don't want to just complain about this Steele dossier everyone's talking about. I want to know what I'm talking about."

Mike Rubiks had read through the dossier, had looked up every name laid out by the British spy. He probably knew the thing at least as well as most D.C. reporters whose job it was to flesh the thing out. But Mike Rubiks could not cover politics, at least not for the *Beacon*, or any other mainstream news organization. His beliefs were too firmly held. Besides, he didn't like the people in politics. He thought the mainstream party guys were too quick to abandon a good cause for a good paycheck. He thought the true believers – the people who agreed with him, or who just as adamantly opposed his take on the world – were raving lunatics. And there was so much more going on in the rest of the world, so much more that was in line with his real interests. So, he worked in what used to be the Features department of the *Beacon*.

Rubiks came to the paper as a 29-year-old intern, his first and only newspaper job, attained after a long hospital recovery from his war injuries and earning a Bachelor's in philosophy from UC Santa Cruz. Within a year, he was one of the *Beacon*'s biggest stars.

He was a child of refugees orphaned during the last years of World War II and raised in Southern California by neighboring families who took him when he was an infant. He became obsessed with the conflict that destroyed his parents' ancestry. He was consumed by the concept of war. By the time he was 14 he was an expert on military history, and early American rock 'n roll. He joined the Army at age 18 and was on his way to becoming a lifer until an Iraqi sniper shot him in the face, and he got sidetracked from the art of war by questions pertaining to the meaning of life. There's not a whole lot anybody can do with a philosophy degree, except hook on with a newspaper that looked to diversify by hiring military veterans.

Once they made him a full-timer, Mike Rubiks brought a crazy man's energy to the job and dispatched himself wherever news was hot, or at least wherever something that interested him happened, whether it was happening now or happened a hundred and fifty years ago. He chased Barry Bonds when the steroid-implicated slugger was chasing Babe Ruth's record. He tracked the Rolling Stones on tour. He interviewed blue hairs at Graceland on Elvis's birthday. He convinced the bosses to send him to Nome in the dead of winter. He wrote a feature on buying large-size Italian suits in Hong Kong. He wrote up gamblers who descended on Dallas for the armadillo races. He also took a tour in Iraq in 2003 as an embed, and he cajoled the sports editor to send him over to Stanford when Notre Dame made its every-other-year visit to Northern California.

The Beacon was flush in those days, but those days ended about 10 years ago when newspapers stopped printing money. In the era of search engine optimization, Rubiks was lost at sea. He generated little traffic. He racked up some hits with his appreciation for the craft beer scene, but that was about it. His style was niche. People didn't understand his concepts anymore. Young people didn't get him. They couldn't capture his crazy on their cell phones. It didn't translate into bullet points. He didn't do "what it means." If you didn't get Rubiks the way Rubiks presented Rubiks, forget about it.

So, nobody clicked Rubiks. The Beacon would have laid him off years ago if he wasn't a war hero.

"Are you busy right now?" Link, who didn't care about clicks, asked. "I don't want to intrude."

"I don't know if you'd call it busy, but I am working on a story – a restaurant just got shut down on 18th and I, for health code violations. It was popular with Millennials, so this is a national crisis."

"The Millennials must be served," Link said.

"I'd rather talk about the Steele dossier."

"I knew you were the right guy to call," Link said. He turned back to the document, reading and parsing at the same time. "So help me understand this. Putin's regime 'cultivating, supporting and assisting' Trump for five years, maybe more, 'to encourage splits and divisions in the western alliance.' 'Sweetener real estate business deals.' Russians offering dirt on the Dems, and Hillary

Clinton. The Russians bugging her phone. Putin's press secretary holding watch over the dossier *they* had on Hillary. If this is true, it's the crime of the century, the crime of the two and a half centuries of the United States. I mean, do you believe all of this?"

"Every word" he said.

"You seem to have been programmed to expect the worst."

"I was. And I mean, you read this thing through, and if it doesn't shake you to your bones on what it is Putin wanted and how he went about getting it, how they set Trump up with the oldest trick in the book, and how all the rat bastards around him tried to get rich off the fucking thing – if it doesn't make you want to throw up…"

Link scrolled down to the famous paragraph about Trump's so-called "conduct in Moscow."

"These of course are the prostitutes who pissed the bed that the Obamas slept in at the Ritz Carlton, while the asshole watched," Rubiks informed Link.

"I don't see how this could have really happened," Link said.

"Who am I to question four sources who supply information to a reputable, top-level British spy?" Rubiks answered. "But if you ask me, everybody is focusing too much on the hookers. They're not the real story. They're a distraction, if you ask me. You want the important stuff, go back to the first page, the part that is not highlighted in yellow, the part you never read about in any of the newspaper stories or see them talking about on CNN. The part about the aim of the Putin operation."

"'… to sow discord and disunity within the US itself, but more especially within the Transatlantic alliance…,' that part?"

"Exactly."

"'…PUTIN's desire to return to Nineteenth Century 'Great Power' politics'?"

"That's the whole thing," Rubiks said. "It didn't matter whether Trump won the election. Putin's primary goal was to tear this country apart. I think you'd agree that he accomplished it. It's going to be decades to put us back together – if it can ever be done."

"It's still kind of hard to overlook the allegations that pertain to the prostitutes," Link said, his attention still stuck on the salacious like many of his fellow Americans. "If they're not true, then the whole report is to be held in suspicion. And there are other sections in there that are pretty questionable too, like the parts about Michael Cohen. He claims he wasn't even in Europe when the dossier had him meeting with Russian operatives."

"The fucking media," Rubiks said, said, in a tone of disgust. "Why do they always have to focus on the obvious?"

"I suspect that is what their audiences expect."

"Sometimes readers don't know what's good for them."

"What do you make of this 'extensive programme of state-sponsored cyber operations' that Russia had going on?"

"Since you asked, I'll tell you," Rubiks said. "Keep in mind that Russia is pretty much run as an organized crime operation. They've got more organized crime groups than we do baseball teams. Christopher Steele mentions a few of them. 'Anunak.' 'Buktrap.' 'Metel.' There are dozens of them. They're the smartest in the world. They're Russia's number one industry. So what do they do after the communist system collapses and the country goes to shit with democracy?"

"I was not paying attention," Link said.

"They see the future," Rubiks said, "and it is right in that thing that you're looking into right now."

"My computer?"

"They schooled themselves in the art of hacking the motherfuckers. They were the best in the world. They won the gold, they won the silver, they won the bronze. They won it all. Their first targets – their guinea pigs – were their fellow Russians. They ripped them off from Moscow to Vladivostok. They did so well, they up-targeted foreign corporations that poured into the new Russian Federation. You know they sought out American businessmen who went to Russia, looking for investors. They buggered their computers like holy hell. Planted malware in their game zappers. Then they moved on to foreign countries, through Russian nationals who had moved abroad and were living in former Soviet republics. Such as Latvia, where my people are from. Pretty soon, the cyber crooks get expropriated by the government. It's all right there in the report, man."

"That's another thing," Link said.

"What is?"

"Like Frankie's story in the paper other day, with the school kids and the credit cards. Do you think it's part of the Putin plan?"

The thought caught Mike upside the jaw.

"Never even thought of that."

"You had Russians operating here, hacking into computers and stealing money, right about the time that this report says that the Russians were beginning to feel the pinch from the sanctions related to the Ukraine."

"Now that you mention it, you can't say that what Frankie wrote about was not part of Putin and Trump stealing the American presidency."

"This is something else that is troubling me," Link said.

Link scrolled down further into the report and pointed out to Rubiks the dossier's discussion of an " 'extensive conspiracy between TRUMP's campaign and the Kremlin'."

"They wanted each other," Rubiks said. "They needed each other. They got each other. You see this 'pension disbursement' deal? I mean this is really interesting."

This was the technical term for how the Russians snuck money into the United States through pension payments to its emigres, to get around the sanctions the Americans imposed on Russia after its invasion of Ukraine and the takeover of Crimea.

"Our paper picked up on this a month ago," Rubiks said. "Did you know there are 259,000 Russian pensioners living in the U.S.?"

"I did not," Link said.

"The suggestion is that they laundered money into the country through the pensioners," Rubiks said. "Now why would they want to do that?"

"You tell me."

"Somebody had to pay for all those Facebook ads."

"Dubious, at best," Link responded.

He sipped his coffee and moved further into the report, to the discussion of one-time Trump campaign manager Paul Manafort and how he ran the money operation on the U.S. side, how the Russians sank moles into the Democratic National Committee, how an odd-looking fellow named Carter Page acted as Manafort's intermediary to Putin, how Page "conceived and promoted" the idea of weaponizing the hacked DNC emails.

"The guy looks like such a doofus," Rubiks said. "Maybe he

wasn't so stupid, just stupid looking. If he really was the guy who had the idea to turn the Bernie Sanders supporters against Hillary, then – shit, you've got to give the motherfucker his due. Jesus, he looked so pathetic in those TV interviews, he had me feeling sorry for him. Then they lather up the Berniecrats with lies and emails and shit and they get enough of them to sit out the election or vote for Jill Stein or Lyndon Larouche or some other goofball, or Trump, or anybody but Hillary, and boom – Trump wins Wisconsin, Michigan, and Pennsylvania."

Rubiks took a deep breath.

Link changed the subject to the report's recount of how Trump allegedly did a little whoring on the side while in Russia, in St. Petersburg, between failed business ventures in the imperial capital.

"I see Trump may have been on the prowl," he said to Rubiks.

"So was Carter Page," Rubiks said. "I think the whole doofus thing was an act. He's going over to Russia and he's meeting with the CEO of their top oil company, this fucking Sechin, and he's hanging out with Putin's political director, Diveykin. The oil guy offers Page a 19 percent brokerage of the entire fucking state-run oil company if he can get Trump to lift the Ukrainian sanctions. The fucking company is worth $60 billion. Imagine if you get to sell off $12 billion of it? You've got to think that would bring in some fairly substantial brokerage fees. So maybe we should stop with the doofus take on this guy. Diveykin, he just wants to make sure Hillary doesn't win, which is kind of important for Page, too, if he wants to score on the oil brokerage. All of these guys, the bottom line with all of them – they're all about money. They'd sell the country out in a second."

Rubiks spun so hard Link didn't even have to read the dossier. He tried hard to stay mindful about who he was talking to, to keep taking in the facts without getting sucked into the politics.

"June, 2016 – the Washington Post breaks the story that the DNC computers had been hacked. The Dems hire a computer security firm to find out who did it. The firm identifies Russia as the intruder. A month later the FBI confirms it's investigating. Moscow gets nervous. So does Trump. Have you gotten to the Michael Cohen part?"

"Not yet. Give me a second."

"Cool. Let me make a quick call on this restaurant story. The bosses are on my ass like this is hot fucking shit."

Link, meanwhile, got to the part about Cohen, Trump's personal lawyer for the past decade. According to Christopher Steele, Cohen had consorted with Kremlinites in Prague. Cohen denied all of it. Cohen pushed an alibi. Cohen said he'd never been to Prague.

"I'm saving lives here," Rubiks said when he picked up his cell phone again. According to the county restaurant cops, there'd been a report of listeriosis at The Wonderful Curd, a gourmet cheese joint. Two customers, it appeared, had taken ill on bathtub cheese.

As for Cohen, Rubiks insisted the Trump lawyer lied for sport, lied for drill, lied for the sake of lying. Rubiks was adamant that Cohen somehow met with the Russians, no matter the denial, no matter what anybody's passport said. There was money to be made, Rubiks said, and Trump and everybody around him would stop at nothing to make it.

"Assume first with Trump, and with everybody who has ever worked for Trump, that they all are lying motherfuckers – it is in their DNA," Rubiks said. "Automatically assume that everything that comes out of Cohen's mouth is a lie. He had been directly soliciting business from Russia. He is the single strongest direct link between Trump and Russia. He has spent 10 years in service to the lowest calling in life, which is service to Trump. Even if he's never been to Prague, or the Czech Republic, you know that Michael Cohen still met with those bastards. Maybe it was at Trump Tower. Or the Café Prague on West 19th Street."

"The Café Prague?"

"Yes. It's in New York. I think it's since shut down. You ask me, Cohen is the main motherfucker, besides the number one asshole."

"You mean Trump himself."

"Yeah. Remember, Trump only ran for president as a for-profit operation. He never expected to win – he was only pursuing new business opportunities, in Moscow. So they set up the Cohen-Kremlin connection, soon as they were forced to get rid of Manafort when the *New York Times* busted him for the secret ledger."

"I don't want to believe any of this," Link said.

"Well, that one looks like a documented fact," Rubiks said, of the *Times* story that detailed the deposed, pro-Russian, Ukrainian government's accounting of $12.7 million in under-the-table payoffs it made to Manafort over the years for the illegal political work he did for them.

"That must have pissed Trump off more than anything" Rubiks said. "He hired Manafort because of his experience dealing with Russia. Manafort had been doing his thing over there for years. Manafort was the perfect guy to get Trump set up in Moscow after the election. Now Manafort's out of the game – he didn't last five days after the paper got him. They sub in Cohen for the Russia play. It made perfect sense – Cohen had been Trump's bag man for years."

"That is conjecture," Link broke in.

"True," Rubiks said. "But I'd put its likelihood at a level of 'high confidence,' as they say in the intelligence community."

The two got through most of the dossier with some laughs, but things got more serious when Link ran through the report's accusation that Cohen in August or September of 2016 held "secret discussions with Kremlin representatives and associated operators/hackers," employees of the so-called "troll farms." The topic was reportedly how to pay off the social media professionals in secret, with nothing coming back on Trump, or the Kremlin, in case Hillary Clinton won the election.

"Maybe it's better that she lost," Link said after they'd been through most of it.

"What?"

"She would never have investigated any of this. She would have thought that it would tear the country apart, just like it's doing now, and it would have gotten in the way of her agenda. I also believe, now that we're talking about it, that *she* would have been the FBI's target if she had won the election, for her emails and who knows what else. Then, if she would have pressed the FBI to investigate the Russians for trying to throw the election to Trump, it would have been a real bad look. We never would have found out the stuff we're finding out now."

Link's take took Rubiks aback, for about a second.

"You're right. But goddamit! I damn near got killed fighting for this country. It pisses me off that whatever ideal we stood for is getting shit on every day that this motherfucker is in office. So what if they never would have gotten to the bottom of it. We'd still have a country. By now, we'd be over the election and moved on with our lives. You think I like staying up 'til midnight every night to watch Brian Williams?"

"I wouldn't," Link said. "But I don't like politics. I don't follow politics. At least not like this 'Day 97 of the Trump administration' coverage. You're the political junkie. You're the one who watches politics like a spectator sport."

"I do," Rubiks admitted.

"Me, I just want to go back to being able to cut my logs. It just isn't happening for me anymore, and I think this is a part of it. I'm not finding the essence. I'm wondering if there even is an essence to anything. Who would think that the election of an American president could do this to people."

"I feel you," Rubiks said. "But you better strap in for a long ride. I'm not sure now if we'll ever be over it. It'll take 20 years, at least. Maybe 40, maybe 50. Maybe not until everybody who is alive today is dead."

7. AT THE BEEKEEPER'S BENCH

Link checked his voicemails the next day before he hit the road. The recordings spun bad news. Representatives of a conservative TV pundit, a hip-hop artist who made it big in the 90s, and an up-and-coming National Football League quarterback all put in orders for his work.

This was getting out of hand.

He fired up the rental truck. It was one of the few times a year that he ever got behind a wheel. It was the only way to get his logs back from Mendocino County.

He'd finally came up with an idea worth pursuing, inspired by his encounter with the Scrounger in his studio – Che, as a bum. He called his mystery man up in Mendocino, the Witch Doctor, and arranged to pick up a fresh canvas.

They would meet at the usual place, in the little town of Covelo in Mendocino County, almost all the way to Laytonville.

Only the Witch Doctor could provide the mystically-charged logs Link needed for his work. Only Link could pick them up, one at a time.

Link pulled out of the rental car shop. He popped in the Bluetooth. He punched up Frankie on the cell.

"So," he told his pal, "I had a very weird experience the other night."

"I heard."

"I guess it must be on the Internet by now."

"I'm sure it is, somewhere. But we didn't do anything with it. It was just the one shooter who heard it, and he didn't tell anybody, except for Mike."

"Which photographer?"

"José. He actually did try to check it out, to see if it was a story. Nobody in dispatch told him shit, and the watch commander never got back to him. Lucky for you our night cops reporter goes home at 9 p.m. Back in the day, they'd hold the paper until after midnight."

70

"God bless the early deadlines. Do you really think this would have merited a story?"

"Maybe. Depends on what they wanted you for. The fact you didn't get arrested took it off the board, in my book. So what was it all about, anyway?"

Link told Frankie about his session with Wiggins. Link told Frankie how the detective questioned him about the disappearance of the Russian Uber driver, Angelina Puchkova.

"That is pretty fucking weird," Frankie said. "I guess there is a lot of crazy going around these days."

"Tell me."

"I can't right now. My kid's got Little League tryouts. Can we meet up tomorrow night? I'd do it earlier but I've got some FBI types who want to talk to me in the afternoon."

"Like you say, there's a lot of that going around. What do they want to talk to you about?"

"A follow-up on the story I did on the Russian hacking of the kids' Social Security numbers."

"Is this the one you were taunting me and the Scrounger with the night we were coming out of the basketball game?"

"That's the one," Frankie said. "They say they're ready to fill in some of the blanks."

"Be careful, or you might wind up on TMZ. Me, I'm thinking about retiring."

"From the logs?"

"Yes. I need time away."

He told Link about the requests from the rap stars and the actresses and the rest.

"Would you believe I also got an email this morning from a representative of Angela Merkel?"

They agreed to meet the next day.

Link unplugged the Bluetooth from his ear. He drove north 60 miles on Interstate 5 to Williams, west 90 miles on Highway 20 to Ukiah, and north 65 miles on U.S. 101 and Highway 162 to Covelo. Link swerved the final 45 miles along the Eel River to the capital of the stunningly gorgeous Round Valley.

The place had once been home to 20,000 members of the Yuki tribe. Multiple massacres took the tribe population down to nearly nothing. The white man repopulated the valley by force-marching five other tribes into it with the Yuki whether the Yuki liked it or not.

Link found the Witch Doctor – himself a Yuki – in his usual spot.

It was a red bench on the wooden front porch of a store that had the valley's most reliable supply of paraphernalia for beekeepers. It looked to Link like the beekeeper business had taken a hit in Mendocino County. It looked to Link like the beekeeper business in Mendocino County was dead, along with all the bees.

The business was gone, the store vacated – but the Witch Doctor sat as usual on the red bench. He waited for Link, and he rose to give his protégé his usual welcoming hug.

"My uncle," Link greeted the Witch Doctor, his usual greeting.

"My son," the Witch Doctor responded.

The Witch Doctor wore blue jeans and a red flannel shirt and cowboy boots. His white hair rolled out in a braided ponytail from beneath his white straw cowboy hat. His stringy white goatee reminded old timers from the Vietnam antiwar movement of Ho Chi Minh's. Link took the Witch Doctor for 80 years old, but he didn't really know his birthday. Hell, he didn't even know his real name, didn't know a thing about him. He never asked. He never investigated. He just learned what the master had to teach.

Link's mother brought him to the feet of the Witch Doctor almost 45 years ago. Somehow, she came to the knowledge that the man knew a thing or two about carving. When her boy showed some knack, she brought him up to the Mendocino Arts Center for a tryout. The Witch Doctor agreed to take on the kid, and they'd been in touch ever since.

"I see that the bee store has closed down," Link said.

"I noticed that," the Witch Doctor replied, in his typically calm, slightly-slower than normal cadence, rhythmic, a contra tenor who sang falsetto when he sang, which was often, although usually only to himself. "The man who had operated it was one of the last Yuki who preceded me in this valley. I believe he was more than 90 years old."

"What do you think happened to him, my uncle?"

"Dead, would be a good guess."

"Did you know him?"

"Not well. I could never relate to his fascination with the way of the bee. I assume he held the same disinclination toward wood sculpture. I'd been seeing him in this valley for 50 years, at least. His death represents part of the passing. This valley will soon take on a very different feeling."

"Why is that, my uncle?"

"Legalized marijuana," the Witch Doctor said, matter-of-factly. "Many of the young people, your age and below, had made good livings during the days of the marijuana bootlegging. Now that you can grow it and smoke it freely, nobody around here can make the kind of money they used to. They are leaving by the hundreds. I suspect that vintners will be arriving at any moment to clear cut the bottomlands and plant them in wine grapes. That is a much more profitable crop than the cannabis, or so I'm told. I wouldn't know about those things."

The Witch Doctor winked before breaking into screeching laughter, hyenic in pitch. The truth was, he'd been part of the marijuana underculture from the beginning, when the light separated from the darkness in the late 1960s, when suburban kids who fled to San Francisco to turn on and drop out ran up against the cops, the tough black kids from the Fillmore District, the society freaking out around them, and they fled for the hills. Mendocino. Humboldt. The Santa Cruz Mountains. The San Juan Ridge in Nevada County. They didn't like conflict, which is why they blew out of town when the Summer of Love turned into the Altamont Winter. When they couldn't escape the tension of San Francisco, they communalized an alternative. This move worked well for the Witch Doctor, a leader of sorts, with youngsters a decade younger than himself following him into the mountains, where they built lean-tos in the side of mountains, among the redwoods. They built compounds around the lean-tos, acquired open lands on the cheap, and planted crops. The one that set them up was marijuana. They fiddled with the soil and created purple buds – "Killer Purple," they called it, and the DJs on the underground radio stations gave it four-star ratings. Mad money gave the Witch Doctor time to work on his hobby – wood sculpting. He made some sense with the chisel. His stuff sold from Garberville to Hopland. It got him noticed over on the coast, where he got an invite to teach at the Mendocino Art Center, and in the foothills east of Sacramento, where a single mom on a rancheria halfway to Auburn got word of the one they called the Witch Doctor and made a note to introduce her son to him when he got old enough to know better.

Link knew the old man to be a regular pot smoker who liked an occasional sip of a fruity cab – who didn't? The Witch Doctor had a very poor tolerance, however, and he knew to watch himself. He could not handle beer a bit – made him feel too full. So Link never took him to the breweries that flourished in the inland Mendocino valleys. They would, however, occasionally take a single puff together of the local crop, produced by the departing cannaculturalists.

One hit was it for Link. One hit brought him brilliance – not so much from within himself, but certainly from without everything around him. The wind was a bit softer, the trees slightly greener, the groove to a live band a little deeper -- but only if they were any good. Any more than the single puff and he could forget about things like conversation and critical thought. He knew not to smoke more than a couple of days out of a month. He'd been a daily smoker for years, way back when, and everything seemed fine and he carved his logs and made a good living and lived a nice and fun life. It wasn't until he was in his early 30s and decided to go a couple weeks without as much as a puff that he realized he'd been living in a cloud. As it lifted, the same kind of brilliance he now enjoyed with the occasional single puff emerged, contradictorily, from the center of his unimpeded brain. It was then that he did his best work.

As usual, the Witch Doctor broke out a three-inch, hand-carved wooden pipe loaded with Killer Purple. The Witch Doctor struck a match and offered it to his younger friend, who declined.

"I'm trying to figure things out, Uncle. I think the cannabis would impede that effort."

"Hmmm," the Witch Doctor said, as he filled his lungs with smoke. He gasped through his inhalation, "It clears things up for me."

He exhaled a cloud with the sweet but pungent fragrance that smelled so good it made Link want to take a hit.

"So, what's on your mind?" the Witch Doctor asked.

"Politics."

The Witch Doctor threw his head back in what Link thought to be an almost inappropriate laughter.

"These are the times we live in," the Witch Doctor said. "If you look at them right, they can present you with an opportunity. You have options, you know."

"Options, Uncle?"

"You can accept the present reality. You can withdraw from it. You can detach yourself from it, which would be completely understandable. Or you can get off your ass and do something about it."

"I am not following."

"My son, what have I always told you in these situations?"

" 'You'll figure it out.' "

"And what have you always done?"

"It seems to me, Uncle, that I keep coming back to this bench."

Link and the Witch Doctor had been meeting at this bench on this porch for more than 40 years.

A few weeks before Link completed his residency at the art center, the Witch Doctor stopped showing up for class. He gave no notice. Most of the other students felt abandoned. They left the art center and roamed the world in search of additional instruction. Link launched an investigation. He needed more of the Witch Doctor. He learned of the Witch Doctor's connection to Covelo, to Round Valley. He found his way to the red bench on the bee porch. He found the Witch Doctor, who found a student in search of himself.

Early on in their relationship, the Witch Doctor furnished Link with the logs that eventually made him an international master. He never told Link exactly where they came from. The Witch Doctor only said that they were from "around here," that the logs were cut from a forest that had deep spiritual meaning to the Yuki and Yana peoples.

From the red porch, for the past 40 years and more, the Witch Doctor climbed into Link's truck. They drove to the eastern end of the valley, 10 miles beyond where the paved road ended, where the old Round Valley rancheria gave way to a national forest. Rich white college students also favored the forest, as did the marijuana growers. The natives knew to keep their distance from the two groups, especially the pot farmers, who harbored some of the same traits that marked the white invaders of the nineteenth Century:

they would shoot you on sight if you interfered with their business.

"So tell me," the Witch Doctor said, on the ride into the forest, "how everything is going in the world of Sacramento."

Link told him there wasn't much new, "although I did get a visit from the police the other night."

"That can never be good."

"No, it was not. They wanted to know what I knew about a missing woman."

"A woman?"

The Witch Doctor listened attentively. Link ran down his encounters with Angelina and her Russian nationality and her obsession with the Trump-Russia investigation.

"Are you interested in her?"

It wasn't a trick question.

"I believe I am," Link said.

They rolled along the gravel roads east off Covelo not cognizant of posted signs warning them of risk of death in the event of trespass.

"I did find her compelling," Link said.

"Compelling?"

"I mean all women are compelling, and every compelling woman I've ever known felt compelled to turn up missing at one point or another, usually because they had had enough of me. But the cops never came knocking on my door because of it."

The Witch Doctor lapsed into thoughtful silence. Forty-five minutes into the ride, with no more discussion of the woman who had come into his life, Link and the Witch Doctor arrived at an isolated cabin on the edge of the forest. This is where the Witch Doctor stored his logs and turned them over to Link, free of charge. Link tried to offer him money – big money, thousands of dollars. The Witch Doctor never accepted it.

"I'm fine," he said every time Link offered the cash. "I've got way more than I need."

Link had no idea of the source of the Witch Doctor's income. Link knew that it was none of his business. Link just picked up the logs, took the Witch Doctor back to the red bench on the beekeeper's porch, thanked him for his time, and headed home.

"I'm just happy that you have turned out so well," the Witch

Doctor told him. "Your success amazes me. Your ability amazes me."

"It's not easy, my uncle."

"Of course not," the Witch Doctor replied. "Greatness comes with great difficulty. Everybody has it within them. You know better than anybody the work it takes to bring it out."

Link anguished at the thought of injecting himself into the log to bring out the essence of Che.

"It's getting more and more difficult. I'm not sure I can do it much longer. These people who want them..."

"Yes, I've been reading the magazines."

"I think I'm done with them."

"For now," the Witch Doctor said.

"And then there is Trump."

The Witch Doctor paused.

"He is no worse than Nixon," the old man said. "You'll get past him. But like I told you, he won't just go away. You're going to have to work to get him out."

"Mainly, I think I need to slow things down," Link responded.

He told the Witch Doctor of the sensation that had been surfacing in his head in recent months that the world that spun faster and faster and left him feeling as if he'd been centrifugally ejected.

"You'll figure it out," the Witch Doctor told him, as he got out of the rented truck at the bench in downtown Covelo, leaving Link to himself and his log in the back of the U-Haul.

He ruminated on the long, quiet drive home about the possibility of retirement. Then he realized he didn't have anything to retire from.

8. HELLO, *VOR V ZAKONE*

Link spent the night in Ukiah, had a nice dinner at the local brewery where he caught a jam band headed by the former lead guitarist of It's a Beautiful Day, the San Francisco group that almost got invited to Woodstock. Heading home the next day, right about when he hit the Woodland city limit in Yolo County, he stuck the Bluetooth back in his ear and called Frankie.

"Where are you?" Link asked.

"Home," Frankie replied.

"This a good time?"

"I was about to crack a 22-ouncer and turn on the Kings."

"I'll be there in a half hour."

Twenty-five minutes later, Link pulled into Frankie's neighborhood in East Sacramento. Clean, safe, so-so schools. Frankie's house fit him and his wife and two kids, even if they had to add a bedroom when their second came in female.

Frankie had been living in the same unpretentious house in the same unpretentious neighborhood in the same unpretentious city for 25 years. He moved there after one paper he worked on in Los Angeles folded and another one in San Francisco was about to go under.

Mostly, Frankie covered crime. He figured he was good for several hundred murders, maybe a thousand, between the cops and courts beats he covered over his nearly 30 years in the business. Mostly, the unfortunate endings of the dead were just that – unfortunate. Mostly, to Frankie, they were just unfortunate stories. Mostly, he exercised his journalistic objectivity when it came to writing about the murdered. Mostly, he knew that a circumstance here and a circumstance there and they'd be alive and the accused instead of mourned and dead.

He dug into a few lengthy investigations. He won a couple of awards. He liked the work. It beat selling pencils on the street.

He met his wife on the newspaper in L.A. She had the good sense to get out of the business 15 years ago. She became a legislative staffer. Now she ran the state senate's Education Committee. She made good money. She'd have a pension. She'd have health care for life. She played backstop for his newspaper career that looked to be on its way to the showers.

Like Rubiks, the transition in the business from print to search engine optimization angle wasn't a good one for Frankie Cameron. Clicks lied. He was a newspaperman.

Medium height, medium build, medium intelligence, medium energy – that was Frankie Cameron as he moved into his mid-50s. Medium length sandy hair, neither light nor dark. Unremarkable features. Glasses. He wore button-down shirts frayed at the collar, and only because he felt like he had to wear ties, he only wore the colorfully loud Jerry Garcias, a testament to his musical preferences. His shoes lasted him three years a pair, and he wore them until he could breathe through his soles. Gin blossoms flowered each cheek – weird, Frankie thought. He didn't drink gin. Or anything hard. Only beer, and never more than 15 to 18 a week.

He only got on this federal court beat about a year ago, when the guy who had been doing it forever retired. The editors offered the opening to Frankie. He demurred. He owned the county courthouse. He knew everybody there – the judges, the DAs, the defense attorneys, the bailiffs, the clerks, the crooks, the vics. Got along with most of them. The feds? He had no sources. Hadn't spoken to a federal agent in more than 20 years. Didn't know federal procedure.

What the hell. He eventually took it. Change was good. Change kept him young. Change kept him invigorated. Change kept his mind from ossifying. Change kept him from being bored. Frankie lived for good stories to discover and write – he was pure newspaperman. The county courthouse spouted stories like they were coming out of a firehose, so fast and so furious and with such force that it was almost more than any one reporter could corral. Just the way he liked it. At the fed, they'd come slower, but deeper, more complex, presenting more of a challenge. Not that he was slowing down. Not that he ever had a problem motivating himself, driving himself. It was a constant in his newspaper career, re-motivating himself every day to find the best story and turning it as quickly as possible, no matter where he was or what he covered. To keep it fresh, he moved around within the paper to different beats, different challenges, wanting everybody to know that when it came to any comparison of the swinging dicks in the newsroom, his would be in the conversation. If only the business could hang on. If only the focus could remain on putting out this incredible product that presented the world to the customer every day.

He'd barely found his way to the federal court men's room before he stumbled into the Mazmonyan trial. He'd read the online filings. He went up for the opening, then the first witness – the snitch. The snitch laid out what he knew, how Anton Karuliyak recruited him from a mortgage fraud wind-down in a strip mall in Foothill Farms, how the snitch basically sat on the money that Mazmonyan withdrew until Karuliyak came around for the pickup.

Nothing too hard about that. Write down what the dude says. Put it in the paper.

His story got a little boost from the backdrop from the Russian hack on the election as well as their hit on the school kids' Social Security numbers and the theft of the credit card numbers belonging to 119,000 oblivious Americans. The backdrop gave his story some legs, and now Frankie stood at the curb when Link pulled in from Mendocino with a log in the back of his rented truck.

They headed to the Starbucks on 59th Street, close to the Sacramento State campus. Frankie sniffed the U-Haul's interior air.

"Smells like a forest," he said.

Moss still grew on the decently-sized log in the back of Link's truck. It looked to be about 15 feet in length and no less than five feet across.

"So here's the deal," Frankie said, after they ordered Americano pour-overs and sat down in a booth. "I get into the office on Friday, and I've really got nothing going on, and I had the story in the paper the day before on the credit card scam, OK? So I call the acting U.S. Attorney and I just throw it out there that we've got all this Russia stuff going on in Washington about hacking the election, and now we've got a hacker here stealing credit card numbers and high school kids' report cards and Social Security numbers, and I'd like to know if maybe, just maybe, if ever the two did meet. The guy is a decent enough fellow – non-partisan, career prosecutor, knows he's going to get replaced, wants to stay in the office, wants to keep working, wants to keep living in Sacramento, wants to do some serious white-collar crime. He tells me he can't talk about anything. Period. I get it. So I do the next worst thing. I call the FBI flak at the regional office. I ask her if she saw the thing we had in the paper yesterday. I tell her I'd really like to talk to the agents on the case. She asks if she can get back to me in about 15 minutes. Sure, I say, and the next thing I know I've got an invite to go hang out with these guys. I meet with them yesterday – a Saturday, their off day – and the first thing they say to me is, 'We wondered when one of you guys was going to call us.' "

Link cupped his chin in his hand, intent on this new intelligence from Frankie.

"They tell me they're deep into an investigation into something called *vor v zakone*," Frankie continued.

"I don't believe I've ever heard of the fellow," Link said.

"It's not a person, my man. It's a Russian organized crime thing, and it's very big around here."

"I don't believe I've heard of them, either," Link said, though he was thinking of his long, rambling phone conversation with Rubiks the other day, which included quite a bit about Russian organized crime.

"Nobody has."

Frankie gave Link a quick rundown on "the *vor*," as he called them. His incomplete understanding was based on the one related to him by the FBI agents, who didn't have the greatest hold on what they were talking about, either.

According to Frankie's primer, the name means "thieves in law," with origins going back as far as theft and corruption did in Russia. The *vor* did not become notorious until after the 1917 revolution, when everybody in the organization got rounded up and thrown in jail. Inside the prison system, the *vor* grew. It became more notorious. It became the only organized force in the Soviet system that had any success at all in taking on the Communist regime. It became powerful as well as notorious. Its people in effect ran the inside of the prisons. Its people reached agreements with the regime. Its people in effect became part of the regime, as far as governance of the prisons was concerned.

Like everything else in the Soviet system, the *vor* was

disrupted by Gorbachev-era restructuring. The *vor* leadership, for the first time, began to see a role for itself outside of the prison walls. Amid the restructuring of *perestroika*, the *vor's* crooks and killers restructured themselves, making contacts in the worlds of business and politics. They went international when the Soviet Union broke up and spun off the old socialist republics, expanding into the new republics at the same time that they partnered with the old-line Communist leadership. They helped the old-line Communist leadership smuggle an estimated $600 billion in Russian wealth out of the country for the old party faithful, according to some reports. They did business in Europe. They popped up in Paris. They popped up in Madrid. They popped up in Rome. They popped up in the United States of America. They popped up in New York City. They popped up in Miami. They popped up in Atlantic City. They popped up in Trump Plaza on the Boardwalk.

They popped up in Sacramento.

"Everybody in Russia knows who they are," Frankie said. "They are accepted as a way of life, a nuisance to be accommodated. They're also a big job-provider, for the poorly educated, or the unemployable, or displaced military veterans, or just your average every-day lazy schmuck."

All over the world, wherever Russian communities sprang up, *vory* types ran the same rackets they did back home – extortion, drug dealing, and some new ones that came into play in places like Sacramento, like stealing cars. They chopped them up and sold them off part by part, from Northern California all the way east of the Mississippi River.

"The smarter ones, they expanded out of chop shops about 10, 12 years ago, when real estate started blowing through the roof," Frankie said. "They studied it, and they saw another opportunity, especially with all the easy money floating around during the subprime days. They'd buy a house with like no money down, then flip it when the prices went up. Mortgage brokers virtually gave money away, and.... Why am I telling you all this? Everybody knows how the scam worked."

Link nodded to confirm his understanding of the financial stupidity that had brought the nation to its knees a decade before.

"These guys, the Russians, the *vors*, they added their own twist to it. They found home owners who would sell for even higher than their inflated values, which wasn't very hard. They found mortgage brokers who didn't give a rat's ass if you had a job or not – they'd still write you up for a loan. They found bankers who didn't check the mortgage brokers who wrote up the paperwork on fraudulent loans, and they found home owners/sellers who would kick back the float for a price. Hundreds of them worked the scam, and they all knew each other, and it was all directed by this thing called *vor v zakone*. At least that's what the FBI thinks was going on."

Link nodded his basic understanding of the scheme. He read the *Beacon*. He remembered reading the little stories that trickled into the Metro section during the Great Recession, about the latest ring the feds broke up.

He also remembered that most of the perps had Russian or Slavic-sounding surnames.

Link wanted to know: why now? How was it that the FBI only now had begun to stitch the thing together, see the connections, talk to reporters like Frankie about what was going on? The outlines of the scam, of the organization, had to be evident to them 10 years ago when the mortgage crisis ate up block after block of the working-class suburbs, leaving entire neighborhoods rotting from foreclosure, overgrown weeds and forests of "For Sale" signs taking them over by the block. Why, all of a sudden, did the FBI call Frankie on a Saturday to fill him in on what really was an old story?

"I'm just getting to the good stuff," Frankie replied.

He took a sip of his coffee, affecting a pause to make sure he had Link's attention, as if there was any doubt about that.

Frankie told Link: "It looks like your gal was in on the scam."

"Angelina?"

"*Si.*"

"Details, please."

"OK, you remember this guy in my first story on the credit card scam, the guy who jumped bail before trial, this Anton Karuliyak?"

"I do not."

"Well, for a short time – at least I think it was a short time, it could have been longer – he came to Sacramento to oversee the *vor v zakone* operation. Or to ramp it up, into action – the feds are not entirely sure. There's a lot of Russians here, you know. More than 100,000. He set the show in motion here on the mortgage fraud, on the credit card thing. Might have even had a hand in the chop-shop thing."

"Like the Russian Don Corleone of Sacramento," Link said.

"More like the Avon lady, and he did it across the country, every place outside of Brighton Beach, Miami, and L.A. He had the entire outback. Set up different teams for each individual scam," Frankie said. "In Sac, your gal was in on one of them, a lower-level lever that he pulled. Worked her through some woman she met in Folsom, somebody named Alana Cosmenko. This Cosmenko woman, she ran a place out there called Folsom Financial Services. We did a couple stories on it – smallish, individualized operation, one of dozens going on at the time. We do have clips on Cosmenko, and on your gal – what's her name? Portanova?"

"Puchkova."

"That's right. She pops up in a story, too, when her little group first got indicted. Only thing we ever ran on her. I looked her up yesterday on PACER."

"PACER?"

"The federal electronic court files. Turns out that her case is still open. Very weird. They run the Cosmenko scam in 2007, they don't get busted until 2011, and then in 2014, Cosmenko and some doofus named Sergei and the mortgage brokers cut a deal. She gets three years, the brokers get two, Sergei gets time served and is deported. Karuliyak, nobody knows who the hell he is until they find out about this credit card shit I just wrote about."

"What about Angelina?"

"Your gal," Frankie replied. "I'm reading some of the transcripts from her court appearance from when the feds first made the case on Cosmenko and Folsom Financial. She gave her occupation as a waitress, at the Denny's on Sunrise Boulevard, in Rancho Cordova. She goes into the case denying she has anything to do with anything. The feds said she got recruited into the scheme to work for this Cosmenko woman. Probably the most interesting thing about her is that she hasn't even been to court yet."

Link took a sip of his coffee. He closed his eyes. He let the information sink in.

"'My gal', as you call her," he asked Frankie. "What was her role in this?"

Frankie explained that according to the court files, it appeared as if Angelina acted as what they called a "straw buyer."

"Karuliyak and Cosmenko hooked her up with some guy named Sergei – I can't remember his last name," Frankie said. "He had just moved to the United States from Russia. Worked as a janitor in Kansas City, of all places. Went to junior college for a while, dropped out – going nowhere. He meets Karuliyak in a chat room, an old friend from the old country. Karuliyak asks him if wants to make some easy money. Sergei says sure. Karuliyak sends him money to go to Sacramento with an address and phone number for Alana Cosmenko. She finds him a place to live and puts him to work in the office in Folsom, doing nothing. This is right around the time Cosmenko offers Angelina a job. Wouldn't you know it – Angelina soon enough heads downtown with this Sergei to take out a marriage certificate. They get a traffic court judge to make it official. She wore her white Denny's outfit. He wore dirty blue jeans with holes in the knees. Alana Cosmenko served as witness. I think your gal's Uncle Nikita and his wife also attended. A few years later, after the feds blew the thing up and people are going to jail left and right, and after about 20 banks got scammed for a hundred million dollars or so, Mr. Sergei files for an annulment."

"You know what that means," Link said.

"Right. No nooky for Sergei."

Frankie did not know for sure if the couple ever consummated their relationship. He did know that Angelina and Sergei made a believable cutout for Folsom Financial Services. Their pose: a young couple looking to buy a starter home.

"Cosmenko took them to a mortgage broker she had on the hook," Frankie said.

Link figured that sex may have played into whatever compromised the money man.

"You'd think," Frankie assented. "Cosmenko had a lot of good-looking Russian immigrant women at her disposal, thanks to Karuliyak, who had his mitts in every racket from here to Brighton

Beach. You know they buttered up their fair share of mortgage brokers. Your gal and Sergei, Cosmenko has them fill out paperwork saying they each had incomes of more than $100,000. Sergei lists his occupation as vice president of Folsom Financial. Angelina put herself down as a financial consultant. The mortgage crook qualifies them for a loan. Cosmenko writes down an address and tells Sergei and Angelina to go make an offer. The owner is waiting for them. He names a price – $800,000, for a four-bedroom job in West Sacramento. They accept it. They go back to Cosmenko who writes out a check for $1,050,000. The owner remits the overage to Cosmenko – your basic quarter-million-dollar kickback. She cuts checks to the mortgage broker, the home owner, Angelina and Sergei, and one very big one – I think it was $175,000 – to a phony business with an account in a Cayman Islands bank. That's got to be the one that fed Cosmenko and Karuliyak. I don't think Sergei and Angelina ever lived in the house, but they did make a couple of payments, until – poof, no more payments. They walk away from the house, the value plummets, and the house goes into foreclosure. The bank eats the $250,000."

"I have to say," Link said. "I am not crying much for the banks."

"Of course not," Frankie said. "They are despicable institutions, and the people who made these loans had to know they were rotten. But they all got their fees, and it was legal, except for the wire fraud."

"And they did this, how many times?"

"Had to be at least 40 or 50 in Sacramento, each with about six or eight Russians and a dirty mortgage broker – usually American – and banks that played dumb. And these are just the ones that we know of, in Sacramento. The FBI guys told me they think they did even more in Stockton, and Phoenix, and Florida. And that's just one Russian operation."

Frankie took a sip of his coffee, his story finished.

"Now," Link said, "Angelina is missing."

9. DEATH OF INSPIRATION

For two days, Link laid low. He took a long bike ride up the American River. He searched for inspiration all the way to Folsom Dam. He looked amid the vacant oak trees and green river banks that rolled next to the water. He couldn't find it.

What a joke, he thought to himself. You can't be looking for the thing. When it was gone, it was gone, and it would come back on its terms, when you least expected it. It wasn't like just pulling a tap to pour out frothy foam with a tint of citrus.

He stopped into his studio midweek and looked at the log he'd brought back from the visit to the Witch Doctor. Frankie had helped him lug it out of the truck and mount it on the pedestal in the middle of his studio. He still had the pictures he had taken of Scrounger's tee shirt. He still had the sketches. What he didn't have was a snifter of inspiration. The spirit of Che remained embedded in the log.

He inspected the log. He circled it. He inspected it from all angles covering 360 degrees. He pried into its soul. He waited for the energy from the center of the universe to punch him in the gut. He gave it until 5 o'clock in the afternoon. He couldn't muster a peep. He got nothing. He didn't even get a tingle. He called it a day. It was the torture of nothingness. He felt worse than being taken over by the spirit of dead animals. He felt like he deserved to be sewn into the belly of an ass.

Was it Trump's fault?

The failure of the creative spirit to fire forced Link to contemplate his presence in advancing late-middle age.

He'd certainly spent way too much time thinking about Agent Orange.

Each day spun faster. He couldn't slow them down. The clock was running. He had no timeouts left. He felt weary in his hips and head. His gait stiffened and his thinking clouded. He grew into an aloneness.

The mendacity of the moment could not last.

He sat with his log. He dug deep. He searched for passion. He rolled snake eyes.

He'd always had days like this, here and there. Now it's all he had. Everywhere, every day, with a president he had allowed to get under his skin.

The president to whom he had unwittingly become attached. The president who had destroyed his beloved detachment.

He thought about going blind. He thought about going deaf. He thought about not being able to walk. He grew sad when he thought about all the music he'd seen and all that he wouldn't be able to hear once he went deaf. He wondered how long it would be until the sound went off – 10, 20 years? He wasn't as worried about his vision. He'd seen enough to get him to the finish line. He could always watch movies on the inside his eyelids. He'd seen "On the Waterfront" enough times to run the picture across the screen of his memory on demand. He could live with that. He wondered if he could live without sound.

He also needed to use the bathroom more. A few more years and he'd have to be planning his day around a strategic plan that would take him from toilet to toilet. Beer took a toll. He would never quit. A good IPA made him think he had something to say. He reached the height of his brilliance at 22 ounces. Returns diminished at 23 ounces and more.

He hung the do not disturb sign outside his studio door. There was no need. Nobody stopped by. He shut off his phone. He shut it off for a couple days at a time, and discovered when he turned it back on that nobody called.

Better for nobody to call or visit than to receive a letter from Blake Shelton. He opened it to read a message from a representative of the country music star: Shelton was offering him $100,000 to carve a log that looked like Gwen Stefani.

"That's not the way it works, Blake," Link said aloud as he flipped through his mail.

Link punched the clock at sundown.

He headed home by way of the food co-op about 15 blocks up R Street from the studio.

He could go for a salad.

Approaching 19th Street, the bells and whistles created a racket at the railroad crossing. Link made no effort to hustle across before the locomotive rolled through. He saw the three engines at the front. They told him it could be a long wait. He considered doubling back to the R-15, a bar located at R and 15th. He could get his body chemistry right. He was now in the fifth day of a planned dryout. He'd already achieved his goal of three days without a drink. He took a reverse step. He stopped himself. He thought, "You're going to pass up a train for a Sierra Nevada?" He stuck around for the train.

He fell into another train trance. His mental clutter cleared away. His troubled mind shook loose from anxiety. He realized he had no idea where he was going, except to get a salad. He did know where he'd been. He tried to connect his trajectory, project a linear path forward, to see a spatial realm beyond the salad. The train speeding past him at 65 miles per hour, he saw 20 years down the tracks. His bones would ache. He'd barely be able to walk. He would have an even tougher time staving off the void of afternoons such as this one, where he accomplished nothing and understood less. The train told him to just follow the path. The train's path had been predetermined by the evil genius of Collis P. Huntington. But Link had nobody to tell him what to do, or how to do it.

The Witch Doctor tried. The Witch Doctor's advice: trust yourself. Trust your gut. He didn't know if that was such a good idea when he was in the midst of a psychological crisis. Link had once observed a mentally disturbed homeless person standing on a street corner and screaming and attempted to calm him. He stood and watched as the mentally disturbed homeless person reached over a sidewalk café barrier and grabbed a chair and threw it through a picture window.

He could not imagine advising that young man to trust himself. He would have advised him to take anti-psychotic medications.

10. SEDUCTION AT THE TORCH

Weeks went by before Frankie Cameron's Russian-mob mortgage fraud story found its way into the ethereal world of search engine optimization. The story earned him a few thousand clicks. The number was not terrible for a court story. It filled his quota for the month.

Frankie's story laid out the existence of *vor v zakone* in Sacramento. It established the connection from the local operation to the international crime boss, the mysterious Mr. Karuliyak. The story did not answer every question. In fact, it left a lot of information hanging, such as, who was this Mr. Karuliyak, the one who appeared to be running the show? The story did not say who ran him. The story did not say how Mr. Karuliyak managed to slip away before trial. The story didn't have the dirt on how a judge let a guy who'd been the recipient of a Hefty bag filled with $249,000 cash go free on an unsecured $25,000 bond.

By St. Patrick's Day, the buzz around Frankie's story had died. Frankie thought it had legs, but Frankie's editor wanted him to move on to other subjects. The editors would probably prefer if he could somehow get cute puppy dogs into federal courts stories, especially if there were pictures.

Link, meanwhile, couldn't break through on his log. Che put up a huge fight. Che would not come out. Che had an easier time with Bautista than Link did trying to get Che to unlock himself from the wood. Che needed a boost. Che needed Link to liberate him. Che was being held hostage by Link's lack of inspiration. Link's lack of inspiration was holding himself hostage. Link was spiritually exhausted.

Maybe a basketball game would help.

The NCAA tournament came to town, and Link scored a pair of seats for him and Frankie, about 15 rows up behind the basket. He wanted to check out this Lonzo Ball guy from UCLA. He and Frankie agreed afterwards – pretty damn good – as they walked out of the arena and up K Street to the Coin-Op for a night cap, when

Link's cell phone beeped.

Linked looked at his phone. The caller went by the name of "Unknown."

Link clicked the green button and plugged his off-ear with an index finger. He could barely hear above the din of the exiting crowd.

"I must see you, as soon as possible," said the voice on the other end.

The voice sounded very much as if it belonged to a tall, lean Russian woman with long arms and blonde hair and who liked black leather jackets and skinny jeans. One who liked to play mortgage fraud.

The call surprised Link. He did not think he'd ever hear from Angelina again, not with Frankie having outed her as a participant in a Russian organized crime ring.

"You have the voice," he said, "of a straw buyer."

"More American newspaper lies," she said. She did not sound taken aback. "When I can see you?"

"Why would you want to see me?"

Angelina's voice softened when she said:

"I need to know American people, and I see you are artist."

"But your people think I am a kidnapper."

"They make big mistake. I like to make up to you."

Though he shuffled off away from Frankie, Link did not immediately respond. Angelina broke the silence:

"When you can meet?"

Link looked at his left wrist for where his watch would be if he was wearing one.

"Fifteen minutes."

"That is good. Where?"

"How about Jack's?"

"Jack's? What is this Jack's?"

"The place we met last time."

"I am not hungry."

"OK, how about the Torch Club, on 15th Street?"

"I know Torch Club. I make many pick-up of drunken American."

"OK," Link said. "I'll see you there."

Link clicked off the call. He looked at Frankie who apparently had not learned the fine art of eavesdropping.

"You'll never guess who that was," Link said.

"I'm not good at guessing."

Link told Frankie: it was Angelina on the phone.

"You are shitting me," Frankie said.

"No, I am not. But I've got to go now. I'll be meeting her at an undisclosed location."

"I'm coming."

"No, you are not. I will report back."

"She's the last one standing," Frankie persisted, almost sputtering. "She can take me right to the top. Karuliyak. Putin. Khrushchev. Stalin."

"Sharapova. She kind of looks like Sharapova."

"Her, too."

Frankie wasn't much up on women's tennis. But he needed to know why Angelina's case still had not been fully adjudicated. All the others pled out, except for Alana Cosmenko, who'd been sentenced to two years. She appealed. The conviction assured her deportation. Her lawyer told the court she'd leave immediately if they didn't put her in prison. The government objected. Cosmenko had been sent off to a federal prison, pending her appeal.

Sergei pleaded guilty and had since been kicked out of the country. The American mortgage broker took a deal and paid a fine. Prosecutors did not charge the bankers. They knew who ran the country. They didn't charge the homeowner, either, probably because he was innocent – just a dumb Russian who didn't know he was being used for a kickback. Karuliyak was never charged.

For some reason, the judge separated Angelina's case from the others. Additional hearings had been scheduled: status conferences, pending change of plea.

Still, Frankie demurred. He ducked into the Coin-Op and wished Link luck.

"Tell her to call me," Frankie said.

"I will forward your request."

Link walked up K Street up and over to 15th Street, past the 168-year-old granite-encased St. Paul's Episcopal Church. It was famous for its stained-glass windows. They were salvation plays by Charles Crocker and Leland Stanford. The Robber Barons thought the windows would get them off the hook. It worked during their lifetimes. Who knows how it played with God.

These days, the church fed the homeless and let them sleep in the courtyard facing 15th Street, in front of a trailer that served as an office. Dozens of homeless lay around there all day, dozens more at night. They waited for hot meals. They needed a safe place to sleep.

When Link walked by on his way to the Torch, he heard a familiar voice.

"Hey, man," the Scrounger greeted.

Link strode intently when he was thinking deeply. Scrounger had to call again to get Link's attention. The two hadn't seen each other since the night the Scrounger showed Link his tent in the bushes outside the Sterling Hotel.

"Oh," Link said, his thoughts interrupted. "Hi, Scrounger."

"Man, you seem a bit, preoccupied?"

"I am something," Link said. "I do not think it is good."

"You must still be thinking about that log," the Scrounger said. "You still want me as your model?"

Link did not want to explain how the brief moment of inspiration had slipped away from him.

"Yeah, yeah. We'll make that happen."

"Make it happen?" the Scrounger asked. "What the fuck does that mean."

"No, yeah. I'll give you a ring. I have been preoccupied lately."

"With what."

"Nothingness."

"That'll get you nowhere."

Link stopped cold, stuck by the simple profundity of Scrounger's observation. Scrounger seemed surprised by the effect of his own insight. "Fuck," the Scrounger said. "I just sounded just like my dad."

Link shook himself out of his head. He told Scrounger he was going to the Torch. He asked if the Scrounger would like to come along.

"Was just headed over there myself," he said.

Link pulled five $20 bills out of his pocket and slapped them into Scrounger's hand.

"Down payment on the modeling gig," Link said.

"Hey, thanks man."

"Spend it wisely."

"You know I will – first round's on me."

"I was thinking maybe you could use it for a down payment for a month's stay on West Capitol Avenue."

The three-mile stretch of road on the other side of the Tower Bridge was infamous for the dozens of motels that catered to drug dealers and prostitutes as well as the homeless like the Scrounger who were down on their luck.

"No, I'm set up pretty good right now," the Scrounger said.

"Outside the Sterling, still?"

"Yeah, man. It's great. Weather's turning nice, too. Best spot in town. Security's good, too. Very important in my line of work."

"Or non-work."

"That, too."

Scrounger joined Link for the one-block walk to the Torch. A minute later, they stood in the gloaming outside the Torch front door where the Happy Hour crowd filtered outside to smoke Marlboro lights and something else with a higher THC content.

The two caught up with some other Torch regulars before Link excused himself and went inside. He ducked around the far corner of the bar and past the ordering stand. He took one seat and saved a second, in the dark, where nobody could see him.

He waited for his guest.

Angelina made her entrance a few minutes later. Link first saw her standing in the doorway, outlined against a blue-gray March sky, the soggy winter weather still hanging around. Her height cast a striking silhouette. Her blonde hair fell straight inside her thin shoulders covered by the constant black-leather jacket cut to the waist to highlight an athletic upper torso.

You can practice all the balanced detachment you want. But this woman, damn. She was *striking*.

The musicians in the jam band, with a floor full of pot heads twirling in front of them, gulped when she walked past them in her tight black jeans.

Link did not stand when Angelina approached. She did not mind. She sat down. She ordered a Grey Goose and tonic. He kept his cool. He made his a Panic, the hop-laced signature IPA of the local Track 7 brewery, the beer that Sacramento beer lovers say put Sacramento on the map. As if the Gold Rush had nothing to do with it.

In the darkness of the bar, he detected a hint of makeup and a sheen of pink lipstick.

They exchanged brief pleasantries.

"I have learned you are a log-maker," she said.

She looked down at her drink, then sideways towards Link.

She must have Googled him.

"Not a maker," he said. "I try to carve sense into them. Or out of them."

Angelina smiled. Sinister.

"Creative. I like creative," she said. "World need more creative, less political. No?"

"I think we need good measures of both," Link said.

Angelina smiled and laughed, lightly. She swerved her bar stool toward Link and gave him a longer look, unmistakable, her eyes locked into his. He could not look away. So he looked back at her, with a deepening gaze that she acknowledged with a little movement on her lips. Anyone would have known: something was happening here.

"I read in magazine *People* you are famous."

Link's smallish circle of friends knew better than to bring this up. He would cut off conversation. He wouldn't finish his drink. He'd look for the first excuse to leave the room. It was the best way to disrupt his balanced attachment. But here, on this night, he couldn't walk out on his discomfort.

Angelina picked up on his unease. She still had to ask:

"How much for log?"

"Excuse me?"

"Cost. For your work?"

Could that be what this was all about?

"I'm not really following," he said.

"I am interested in you making a sculpture, for me. Maybe, a sculpture of me. Where you can see maybe all of me."

Her eyes bore into his, and this time he looked into his Panic for relief. He soothed the quiver inside him with a long, aromatic draw. The 7 percent wattage calmed him down some.

"I have been winding down my operation," he told her. "I'm kind of, shall we say, spent. I need a long vacation."

"Where are you going?"

"No place in particular. Just away from sculpture for a while."

"When you get back, do you think you maybe spend time with me? There is much I can show you."

Link felt he needed to break this off right now.

"A better question would be, where have you been?"

Angelina looked at him quizzically.

"I understand," he said, "that you are missing."

She looked at him mendaciously.

"I don't know what you say," she said. "As you see, I am not missing. I am right here."

Link could not argue that fact. Nor could he mistake the way she looked at him. She wanted something. His intuition told him it was him. And maybe she could have him. First, he had to clear up a backlogged order of business – two cops waiting on his doorstep and dragging him to the station to answer questions about her family filing a missing person's report and suggesting that he had something to do with it.

"Yeah," he said. "The police thought I kidnapped you."

Angelina recoiled.

"I do not know that," she said.

"No, really. The cops asked me if I kidnapped you. They said your family gave them my name. I don't recall having ever met your family."

She swizzled her drink with a suggestive look. Her narrow eyes narrowed some more. She leaned in to whisper:

"Maybe they find your card you give me at end of Uber ride. Maybe I tell them about dark, tall, handsome American man I meet."

Angelina stirred her drink again and took a sip. She kept her eye on Link as the booze went down her gullet. She wasn't sure he was buying it.

"Maybe I leave town for few days," Angelina continued. "Maybe I no tell anybody. Maybe I need get away from family and job."

"Tell me some more about Nikita Maslov," Link asked, about her simpleton uncle who was mentally unfit to stand trial in the credit card case.

"Uncle Nikita," she said, dismissively. "He is not very interesting man."

"He was interesting enough for you to call me one night about a story in the newspaper that mentioned him," Link responded.

She rolled her eyes in feigned exasperation. She momentarily lost her mesmerizing look.

If Link insisted on knowing about Uncle Nikita, she would tell him, and she told how Uncle Nikita and his wife owned a tract house in Rancho Cordova, a shaky suburb still not recovered from the closing of a nearby Air Force base 25 years ago. She said they'd been living there since the early 1990s, a time in which Link now knew there'd been a mass emigration of Russians into Sacramento, by the tens of thousands after the collapse of the Soviet system. She said she moved in with them 10 years ago. She said they were all from Siberia.

"They come to this country for American dream," Angelina told Link.

Angelina took a sip of her vodka tonic and shot Link another look, this time different. This one flashed danger, much like the tone of her voice the first time they met.

"I no call you for all these questions."

Link stone-faced her. He was not bothered by her anger. He wasn't sure it was any more genuine than the come-on she laid on him a few minutes earlier.

He decided to bring up Frankie.

"The reporter who wrote those stories in the paper is my best friend," he told Angelina. "I was with him when you called me today. He asked if you'd be willing to talk to him.

"Are you kidding?" she said. "No."

"I see you are now divorced," Link said, her marital status having been revealed in the Beacon.

"Annul," Angelina curtly countered. "Another wrong thing in American newspaper by your 'best friend'."

Link let silence ring, in a bar where the St. Patrick's Day drunkery had reached a cacophony.

Within the noise, Angelina broke the quiet tension they shared.

"Can't we just make nice talk? About your logs? You are very good. How you get to be such? Tell me on that. You make log for me? Of me? I see you make one for Kardashians."

She referenced a small item that appeared recently in the celebrity news columns of the Los Angeles papers. The stories said one of the famous celebrity sisters bought an authentic Lincoln Adams. The eldest apparently picked it up at an estate sale in Eagle Rock. Link sold it 15 years earlier to an Occidental College professor. Original purchase price: $500. The professor had recently died. Khloe's purchase price: $125,000.

"I didn't make it for reality TV types," Link said, hunching his shoulders in discomfort.

He searched the sharp angles of Angelina's thin face for motivation. It revealed none. Link looked deeper. Nothing there, either.

He told Angelina he had been giving serious thought to shutting down the art operation, entirely and indefinitely.

"I need rest," he said.

"But you start up again sometime, no?"

"Maybe. Probably. Right now, I'm not seeing any shapes jumping out of the wood. That means I need time off."

"I see now. Maybe, when you work again, I call you?"

"It depends."

"Depend on what?"

"On whether I can trust you."

The statement provided Angelina with a new opening.

"Trust me? It would be hard to trust before you know me. So, you should come to know me?"

She was back with the look.

"That's the problem around here," Link said, "the main thing I know is, you and I speak two times and I get dragged down to the police station in the middle of the night."

He paused for a second and asserted:

"From now on, no logs for anybody I don't know."

Angelina saw this as another opening. She leaned in to whisper in his ear, barely touching it with the tingle of her lips:

"Then you must get to know me."

Link maintained his resistance, but it was not easy.

"Let's start by you telling me why you all of a sudden are so interested in me," he said.

Angelina swiveled around on her stool so that she was facing away from Link. She drew her elbows back and rested them on the bar. She let her jacket relax down and off her shoulders. It was obvious. She flashed her exquisitely-developed trapezius muscles, through a silky, cream-colored top. Link enjoyed the view. He'd never seen a set like them.

She scooched down in her seat. She looked relaxed, like she might have been interested in the band.

She swerved back toward Link.

"You are very tall," she said. "You are honest. You are handsome."

Her smile softened Link's inquisition.

"OK," Angelina said. "I tell you my story. I think I need second drink."

Link ordered her another vodka and tonic.

She sipped. She unwound the tale of a young immigrant woman from Siberia who came to California to help care for her uncle. He was a veteran of the Soviet war in Afghanistan. The mujahedeen shell-shocked him. They made him dumber than he was before he'd been forced to defend the Khost-Gardez Pass. He needed in-home care. His wife asked Angelina for help. Angelina had been attending college in Siberia. Maybe she could transfer to Sacramento State. She supplemented her income with the part-time job as a waitress at Denny's. She met Alana Cosmenko. She went to work as a crook for Folsom Financial. She saw the Cosmenko operation as easy money. Cosmenko ran the scam with a half-dozen different mortgage brokers. They all knew each other. They were all dirty. They all saw a chance to get rich. They shared information, details, contacts.

This confirmed an element of organization, but she denied that she'd ever heard of the *vor v zakone*. He asked again if she'd be willing to tell that story to Frankie.

She again refused.

When the feds broke up the ring, six years ago, Angelina said she spent one night in jail. She said Uncle Nikita's wife posted her unsecured bond. She claimed indigence at her arraignment. The judge appointed her a federal public defender. Her case and those of the rest of the Cosmenko group languished for years while the government worked through the dozens just like it that had flooded the system toward the end of the Great Recession.

She told how all the cases played out, except for her own.

Now, in the Torch, she sought to explain:

"My lawyer, he come to me. He say government prosecutors

want make offer on me, but I must testify against Alana Cosmenko, and not only Alana Cosmenko, but Mr. Karuliyak, too. But I cannot testify against Mr. Karuliyak! Mr. Karuliyak not even in this country! Why they want for me testify? I know nothing about Mr. Karuliyak. I never meet Mr. Karuliyak!"

She took a sip of her vodka tonic.

"So, I leave Uncle Nikita house."

"I see," Link replied. "Where did you go?"

"I know nice people in San Francisco. They have big nice house. They invite me to stay for while if I like. I go there for a while. I drive Uber in San Francisco. I make very much money. Nobody know where I am."

Sitting at the bar, Link drank his beer and felt it continue to relax his body. He looked Angelina over in the dim bar light. Flickering Christmas bulbs that illuminated the room year-round reflected this night off the sheen of Angelina's lips. She looked him over, too, again with intent.

Link caught her assessment of him. It was hard to take it as anything other than confirmation that for the third time in a matter of minutes, she was coming on to him.

It boggled his mind.

She smiled again, holding her drink in her left hand. She reached over with her right to run the back of her fingers across the top of his left thigh.

This was exciting. The excitement made his whole body tighten up.

Angelina sensed she had stirred something.

"I like honest man," she said, in a reassuring sort of way. "I like see you more."

She wrote her phone number on a cocktail napkin. She handed it to Link. She finished her drink and stood up, all six feet of her.

Then she leaned over and kissed Link softly on the lips, before she got up and left, without another word.

11. A BRIEF AFFAIR

They were 14 days that shook the world.

First, FBI director James Comey testified before Congress that he was investigating Russian attempts to throw the U.S. election to Trump. Comey and the feds wanted to know whether any "U.S. persons" in the Trump campaign participated in the subversion of American democracy.

Then, Trump fired Comey.

The next day, Trump yukked it up in the Oval Office with a gaggle of Russians that included their U.S. ambassador and foreign minister. The American press was not invited to the love-in. The Russian press was. Trump told the Russians that Comey was crazy. The Russian press took pictures.

Trump assigned Deputy Attorney General Rod Rosenstein the task of establishing a pretext for firing Comey. Rosenstein wrote a memo saying it was because of the way Comey handled Hillary Clinton's emails. Trump came clean a couple days later on national TV. Trump told Lester Holt it was all about Russia. The *New York Times* reported that Trump wanted Comey to lay off his deposed National Security Advisor, Michael Flynn. The Times' story hit hard. The next day, Rosenstein appointed Robert Mueller as special counsel.

Lincoln Adams caught up on the news in the breakfast nook of a house in the Inner Sunset neighborhood of San Francisco. He'd just spent the night there with a relatively new friend. She was a long, lean, Uber-driving Russian woman named Angelina Puchkova.

It didn't happen overnight.

Link never did call the number she wrote down on the cocktail napkin. He left it up to her to make the next contact. Angelina must have read his mind. She called him back a week after St. Paddy's-at-the-Torch. She invited him to the city, took him out to lunch, and arranged a visit to the art museum in Golden Gate Park. Van Gogh was the featured attraction. She could not pull herself away from "Starry Night." She walked out of the museum inspired. She was lit. She pried him for everything he knew about art. She grilled him on how he became an artist, the same way he questioned the homeless on how they wound up on the streets. They walked through the meadows, past the buffalo grove, all the way to the ocean. He told her what little he knew about hall of famers like Van Gogh and, his favorite, Michelangelo, the only one he had ever taken any time to read up on.

"He loved Medici girl but never make love to her, and his patron woman marries powerful other man, and he spend whole life as single man," she recounted, based on his recitation of what he remembered from *The Agony and the Ecstasy*. "Life of artist must be miserable, no?"

Crossing the polo fields on a typically crisp, windy, and cold spring day in San Francisco, Angelina slipped her arm through Link's and snuggled up to him.

"You need woman," she told him. "You need woman who understand artistic impulse of kind, handsome man."

He knew he really didn't. He knew he really didn't need anybody, man or woman. And he was the type who was not terribly huge on public displays, so he wondered what was going on when he turned toward her and locked her in a supercharged embrace.

To hell with balanced detachment.

At dinner, at a Greek restaurant in Noe Valley, she opened up some more.

"My husband – my ex-husband – Sergei, he know a lot, and accusing prosecutors think he can tell them more than about free house money deal."

"You mean the mortgage fraud," Link said.

"Yes, mortgage fraud. Sergei, he know Mr. Karuliyak, years ago, from Moscow. He tell me things about Mr. Karuliyak, about Soviet army. Government prosecutors try talk to Sergei, but he no talk to them, so they want me to talk about Sergei and how he know the Mr. Karuliyak operation. My lawyer hold me out in court case while everybody else, go for trial. Mr. Karuliyak get angry when he find I am not in case any more. After your friend publish story in paper, Mr. Karuliyak call me. He say I no should talk to government lawyers about Sergei. He say government lawyers will ask questions about *vor v zakone*."

"So, you have heard of them."

"I cannot admit that," Angelina said. "Nobody in *vory* can admit it is there. Mr. Karuliyak very afraid when I am arrested that I will admit the *vory*. Mr. Karuliyak say I should make guilty plea and go back to Siberia so I can no talk to your government, about *vory*, about anything else. I do not want to go Siberia, or Russia, and I become very scared. Your government say I can go to prison for five years if I do not testify against Mr. Karuliyak. So I leave Uncle Nikita house. I need to get away from whole mess."

"Why did you get involved in the mortgage scam in the first place?"

"Everybody do it," Angelina said, waving a hand. "Many of our people, from the church. Alana Cosmenko tell them that nobody get hurt. She say it is free money, from bank deals. She explain these, what you call them, unprimed loans?"

"Subprime mortgages."

"That," said Angelina, with a nod of satisfaction. "Subprime mortgages. She tell us banks are giving money away and nobody is getting hurt, that price of houses keep going up and up and that you only need way into system and that her business from Folsom only make it easy for Russians in America to become part of America."

Link found her story believably interesting. The true selling point was her tacit admission about her participation in *vor v zakone*. He felt she was beginning to tell him some truth. That would be a start for them.

Her vulnerability made an impression on him. He did not exactly know why. He knew, intellectually, that it can be in some men's nature to want to protect women from danger. He didn't know how. He hadn't had a father, or uncles, or a grandfather, or any father figures, until he started playing high school basketball, and the head coach of that outfit was a complete asshole, he thought. He never had a mentor until he had the Witch Doctor, who was a genius on the things he was a genius about, but otherwise a nut. The nature of women happened to be one of the things the Witch Doctor was clueless about.

When it came to women, Link too was a lifelong rookie. He'd never made it past the 90-day electrical attraction phase of a relationship. Maybe he wasn't anybody's type, he thought, even if he was good looking, rich, and tried to be a good listener.

The women he never tried to hustle, women who were usually happily married, told him he was wonderful. They could not understand why he wasn't married or at least in a long-term relationship. Or any relationship. They all knew single women who told them they'd be good for a go with him. Sometimes he took them up on it, and things went along pretty good, with a chance of becoming great, and then, 90 days in – pfft.

With the healthy ones, he could never figure out what went wrong, or even if it was wrong that the relationships came to an end. The only thing he knew was that it was over.

The sick ones, they were all too sick, and they usually didn't last a week.

Angelina asked for the dinner check in the Greek restaurant. Link said no way. He picked it up, and she rolled her fingers across his thigh again.

Link fell, and he fell hard.

She took him back to the house where she'd been staying in the Inner Sunset. It belonged to a nice married couple, Gordon and Leia Kahananui, who she met years earlier on vacation in Hawaii.

Gordon was a burly, muscular, soft-spoken, and exceedingly kind, hang-loose native from the islands who looked to be a few years younger than Leia, who appeared to be in her mid-50s but still retained her thin frame and natural blonde hair. Like Gordon, Leia was extremely welcoming, happy to share their comfortable home with strange, interesting people. Exceedingly content in their existences, it seemed to Link that they became invigorated by their guests. Maybe they should open up a bed and breakfast. They did not have any children. They did not mind that Angelina had a house guest.

They didn't even mind Link spending the better part of seven weeks there, going home here and there only to pack a suitcase. They liked Link – who didn't?

They liked him so much that Leia had breakfast and the *Times* waiting for him when he went downstairs the day after Mueller got his new job.

Leia poured Link another cup of coffee while they waited for Angelina to make her appearance. "Aren't you the guy who carves the logs for celebrities?" she said abruptly, with an almost apologetic smile as she leaned over his mug.

Maybe he didn't like publicity, but Link was not an asshole. He tried to be polite in all circumstances. He tried to be especially polite when he was staying in somebody else's house, and more so when he spent his time there sliding under the covers with a gorgeous woman he barely knew.

"I've been very fortunate to have my work recognized," he lied.

Link and Leia chit-chatted about her house and how it had been in her family for more than a hundred years. Leia's mother's people landed in San Francisco more than a hundred years earlier. They came from old money New England. They spread roots in Northern California way back in the 19th Century, before the Gold Rush. They made a fortune as fur trappers along the Russian River, north of San Francisco. Link knew fur trappers as the people who wiped out anything that moved. He knew them as the same people who nearly eliminated the native Kashaya Pomo native peoples, to whom he was ancestrally linked. They also chased and trapped and cut and killed the sea otter to the brink of extinction.

"It was the Delta smelt of its day," Leia told Link. She was referring to mankind's modern-day indifference to the finger-sized species of fish that was being sacrificed to the transfer of Northern California water to the corporate farmers and urban sprawlers to the south.

"I am glad to see that the otter made a recovery," Link said.

"Speaking of otters," Leia said, "do you think there is any chance that you could carve me one?"

Link laughed. He valued politeness.

"Sure," he said. "But it may be awhile. I think I am in need of a long break from sculpture. But a celebration of the otter's survival would be a worthy comeback piece."

"I can't pay as much as some of these other people I'm reading about, but..."

"Don't even mention money," Link said, cutting her off. "Your kindness is more than enough for me in terms of payment."

"But Mr. Adams..."

"Please, call me Link."

"Link, I would insist. I see how much these people are paying you."

He could only mumble a response. The vortex of the insanity of success put him at a loss for words.

Link and Leia had been talking for about a half-hour by the time Angelina emerged. She wasn't wearing a black leather jacket, or skinny jeans.

She wore, instead, a lot of money. Her sleek black designer business suit must have cost a fistful of dollars. The high heels went for a few scoots, too. They brought her almost up to Link's height.

This new look struck him dumb.

"Wow," he and Leia said, almost simultaneously.

Angelina shrugged, and said, "I have big day today."

Very big.

The U.S. District Court in Sacramento called for her appearance that afternoon, to resolve all charges against her in the matter of the Alana Cosmenko mortgage fraud ring.

Her lawyer worked out a deal: like everybody else in the Cosmenko group except for its namesake, Angelina would get no jail time. Even better, unlike her co-defendants, the government would take no steps to deport her. They told her the price: she had to testify in front of a federal grand jury that had been empaneled to investigate Anton Karuliyak. She would swear under oath that on or about Feb. 2, 2017, a man who identified himself as Anton Karuliyak contacted her on her cell phone and instructed her to not to answer questions the FBI wanted to ask about her conversations with Sergei Andropov. They wanted to know what Sergei had to say about the activities of Anton Karuliyak. She'd claimed a marital privilege, which flew out the window when she filed papers in court to annul her marriage to Sergei. Federal prosecutors leveraged her dumb move in negotiations with her lawyer. The prosecutors upped the pressure. They played hard ball. They told her lawyer that if she didn't cooperate, she'd go to prison. She was looking at five years. She agreed to testify. Her statement would represent the best evidence in what federal prosecutors were confident would be an obstruction of justice indictment against Karuliyak, to go on top of the one that was already pending for the hacking of the school kids' social Security numbers and the American Express accounts.

Link and Angelina finished their breakfast at a leisurely pace.

Leia kept their coffee cups full ahead of their drive to Sacramento.

On the road, Angelina's serenity in the face of her court appearance struck Link as a bit unusual.

"Why I nervous?" she said. "This make end of case for me. No more problem for me, no more worry."

"What about Mr. Karuliyak? Won't he be upset?"

Angelina wasn't so worried anymore about Mr. Karuliyak. "Why he become upset? I no tell police more than what they know. Mr. Karuliyak gone from country. He no can hurt anybody here."

"But the FBI didn't know he was even a part of the mortgage fraud until just a few weeks ago," Link said. "Now you'll be confirming his role in the operation. You might have to testify in public."

"Testify when? When they catch Mr. Karuliyak? How they catch him? In Moscow? And he already have one case on him here. What is so bad to have a second one? Especially when he never want to come back?"

A silence filled the car for a few minutes.

"I guess somebody else will just take his place, right?" he asked Angelina. Link didn't know a whole lot about how organized crime organizations operated, but he'd seen enough movies to know that the creation of a power vacuum usually creates a competition to fill it.

"Take what place?"

"As the boss of the rackets."

Angelina cut off the discussion.

"We no talk about that," she told Link.

Traffic was light and conversation nonexistent the rest of the way into Sacramento. Talk about flipping the switch. He was reminded how little he actually knew this woman. It felt to Link like the honeymoon was over. He could barely remember the walk through Golden Gate Park. Maybe it was his Russian mob crack. Maybe it was the fact that, Link was continuing to discover, she really didn't have a funny bone in her body.

Angelina parked on the street a few blocks from the Robert T. Matsui United States Courthouse. Inside, she and Link were stopped by an abstract, four-story high architectural rendition of the Scales of Justice, in an atrium attached to the courthouse. Link led Angelina by the wrist for a better look. Each of the golden scales must have been 30 feet across, cabled to a riveted, two-ply golden balance beam that extended halfway across the atrium where light poured in from the glass ceiling and from horizontal windows a half-story each in height. The top plank of the two beams served as arms that connected a pair of hands with palms held outward, flat, and down, in the manner of a child mimicking an airplane in a banking maneuver. The beams hung about a story-and-a-half down from the top of the atrium from nearly invisible steel cables that gave the piece the appearance of being suspended in mid-air. Four shining silver strands dropped down another story and connected the beams to the scales. Each of the scales featured crystal pyramids rising from their gold-and-steel circular center. They reflected a rainbow of color and light through the picketed spaces infused outward from the middle of each scale.

"This is the best piece of public art in the city," Link said. "Too bad nobody can see it."

"This is best? It looks like pile of junk," Angelina said. So much for the park and Michelangelo. She'd reverted to Uber Angelina from the first night of their acquaintance.

"All criticism is valid," Link replied, beaten.

He walked beneath the scales and circled them from the ground below.

"It's the size and by the light," he tried again. "The light is truly amazing. The removal of Iustitia…"

"Justy, who?

"The goddess of justice. The Lady Justice, in the robes, with the sword and the blindfold, holding the scales. She is completely missing from this equation. It is fascinating, the removal of the human form, leaving only the purity of the concept."

Angelina looked at Link as if he were crazy and said something about not wanting to be late. They made their way out of the atrium to the bank of elevators where they saw a *Sacramento Beacon* reporter, who had just finished up a conversation on college football with the courthouse security guards after passing through the metal detectors. Link saw Frankie Cameron first and clasped the much smaller man softly around the shoulder.

"Frankie Cameron," Link said. "I'd like you to meet Angelina Puchkova."

Link had told no one about the time he spent with Angelina in

San Francisco. For his part, Frankie went along with the introduction as if it were not much of anything. He acted as if it was no big deal that he was meeting the woman he'd been writing about, a cog in a local Russian organized crime conspiracy. So what if she was more than six feet tall and striking in high heels. Who cared that she wore about a few thousand dollars' worth of clothes (not counting her underwear). Big deal that Link also was dressed like you'd never find him at Benny's, with a black cloth sports coat over a white dress shirt fastened with a bolo tie containing a chunk of turquoise in its silver clasp.

"Nice to meet you, Ms. Puchkova," Frankie said. He craned his neck to see her, just as Link and Angelina had craned theirs to see the justice scales dangling over their heads a few moments earlier.

"Call me Angelina," she replied.

The two had reason to be wary of one another, but they shook hands easily enough. She had no huge problem with anything he'd written, except for putting Uncle Nikita into the first story. She felt he did not deserve to be portrayed as a mentally incompetent Russian criminal, even if it was true. Otherwise she maintained her calm demeanor about her impending court appearance.

Frankie's antennae quivered more at Link's presence in the courthouse with this woman, than to the presence of the woman herself.

He locked eyes with Link momentarily on the ride upstairs in the elevator. An element of the quizzical was included in his look. Link caught it. He deflected it with a contrived stone-faced stoicism. He tried for the inaccurate, statuesque stereotype of natives from the North American plains depicted in photographs going back 150 years.

The elevator was quiet to the 15th floor, where they walked down a hallway with the courtrooms on one side and a full-story high window on the other. This gave them a spectacular view of downtown and the southward flow of the Sacramento River. They could see all the way to the bypass on the horizon, where the river spread out to the size of a lake and sparkled beneath a sunny spring sky.

"We'll catch up," Link said, as they headed into court, single file.

Frankie turned left and sat in the first row of the gallery, up against the rail and behind a team of federal prosecutors.

Link followed Angelina, and noticed that she jolted as she scanned the room. In the back row on Frankie's side of the courtroom, Angelina had spotted a Babushka-looking woman, maybe in her mid-fifties, sitting by herself. The woman's presence noticeably perturbed Angelina, who turned in the opposite direction, to the seats on the right, as if she wanted to avoid her. She took a spot in the second row and Link filled in next to her on the aisle. Directly across from him, right behind Frankie, he saw a familiar face.

He nodded hello to Detective Andrew Wiggins of the Sacramento Police Department. Detective Wiggins nodded back. Link wondered why the officer would still be interested in Angelina Puchkova, seeing as she was no longer a missing person. Wiggins found it curious, on the other hand, that Link, who had before professed limited knowledge of this formerly missing Russian expat, was now in her company. You could almost hear the wheels spinning in both of their heads.

The spinning came to a halt when U.S. District Judge Roy Hanley emerged from his chambers and his clerk called Angelina's case.

Her lawyer, United States Assistant Federal Defender Jason Dillon, crooked his finger to direct her inside the bar and up to a podium in front of the judge. As Angelina came forward, Frankie and Link noticed that one of the federal prosecutors – a woman – whispered something to one of her male colleagues at the U.S. Attorney's table.

It took the judge nearly a half-hour to run through all the formalities leading up to Angelina's purpose in court that day: her ultimate admission to what she did.

"Guilty, Your Honor," she said, under coaching from Dillon, when it came time to admit to the federal crime of conspiracy to commit wire fraud.

"Is there a factual basis for the plea?" the judge inquired.

"Yes, Your Honor," replied Michael George, the assistant U.S. attorney, who laid out the details: "From the time approximately in June 2008 through January 2009, a conspiracy existed in the Eastern District of California whereby several parties worked in unison to defraud the Bank of America through the use of wire

transfers of several hundred thousands of dollars in U.S. currency.
Ms. Puchkova was a willing participant in this scheme, acting as a
would-be purchaser of a home in the city of West Sacramento,
Calif., at an inflated value. The excess amount of cash used for the
purchase was remitted back to the conspirators. A portion of these
funds was paid to Ms. Puchkova."

The judge nodded. He'd taken dozens and dozens of such pleas
in the dozens and dozens of cookie-cutter mortgage fraud cases
that had come before him in the previous six years, as the *vor v
zakone* scheme wound down. This one was no different than any of
the others.

"I will make a restitution order of $350,000, the estimate of
what was lost to the victims in this case, for which the defendant is
joint and severally liable with all the previously sentenced
defendants in this case," the judge said from the bench. Like all the
other cases, there was no expectation this money would be
recovered. "Do we have any estimates on Ms. Puchkova's ability
to pay?"

Angelina's lawyer informed him that she was destitute.

At this moment, the prosecutor broke in. "Your Honor, may we
have a moment?"

"By all means."

The female government attorney scurried to the prosecutors'
podium to confer with George.

"Your Honor," George said, after the brief consultation with
his team member, "the government has reason to believe that Ms.
Puchkova has assets at her disposal far beyond what she has
represented to the court. Our office has not been able to ascertain
them completely, and we ask that the issue of restitution be held
open, until such a time that the government is able to complete its
additional investigation into Ms. Puchkova's financial status."

George asked for another moment to talk to his colleague, after
which she made her way back to her seat.

"Your Honor," the assistant U.S. attorney went on, "the
government also is asking for a remand on Ms. Puchkova. Given
her status as a foreign national who has now admitted her guilt to a
very serious federal felony, we are also asking that she be held
without bail."

The request stunned the courtroom, most of all Angelina's

lawyer. Angelina's face revealed nothing at all.

"Counsel?" the judge said, looking at the federal defender.

Dillon's face reddened with blood, which came pouring out of his mouth in what was almost a scream.

"Your Honor," he choked, "this is an outrageous, egregious effort on the part of the government. It may be worthy of a censure, given that the government gave no indication to counsel prior to court today that it intended to pursue a remand of this nature. It is completely distinct from how the court has handled every other matter of this nature in this jurisdiction over the past years, and had the government indicated or suggested it intended to travel down this road, Ms. Puchkova would never have agreed to enter the guilty plea that she put forward today. A remand by the court would represent an outright abrogation of the agreement that Ms. Puchkova had entered into with the government."

Judge Hanley took a moment to digest Dillon's diatribe, as the lawyer gained his composure and his breath. Judge Hanley glanced at Assistant USA George standing at his podium. Judge Hanley thought he detected a smirk or a shrug from the prosecutor.

"As Your Honor knows," Dillon added, before the judge asked George for a response, "some of the details of this agreement cannot be discussed in open court."

Judge Hanley nodded his assent.

"And, Your Honor, Ms. Puchkova would ask that if the government intends to proceed with its request for a remand, that these proceedings be delayed in order that she may reconsider her plea."

"Sounds reasonable to me. Mr. George?"

"Your Honor, we bring this request to you based on information and belief, and on new evidence that the government obtained just today in court."

"Information and belief?" the judge said. "Mr. George, this is not a law and motion court to resolve petty squabbles between petty interests that cannot reasonably work out their differences. A woman's freedom is at stake here. So, what is the 'new' evidence?"

George cleared his throat.

"Your Honor," he said, "the new information we have obtained is the attire that Ms. Puchkova is wearing into the courtroom today.

It is our belief that her suit is a Yves Saint Laurent and that it is worth more than $1,000. Her shoes, we believe, are from Salvatore Ferragamo, and it is our further belief that they are worth in the neighborhood of $700."

"I see," Hanley said. "And Ms. Puchkova previously represented to the court that she qualified for the services of the federal defender?"

"Yes, Your Honor," George said.

Angelina's leaned down to whisper in her lawyer's ear.

"Your Honor," Dillon said to the court. "Ms. Puchkova has represented to me that in the period since she retained the services of the federal defender, her earning capacity has substantially increased, and that she has been able to generate far greater income in recent weeks."

"And what does she do for a living?"

"She is an Uber driver, Your Honor?"

"And she dresses in designer labels?"

"She does very well, Your Honor."

Judge Hanley laughed to himself. Then he made his ruling on the remand.

"I am going to continue proceedings on the government's motion for remand," he said. "But I am going to order for the preparation of an additional pre-sentencing report to examine her finances, and I am going to delay the imposition of sentence until that is completed."

"Your Honor," the prosecutor asked, still standing at the podium in the well of the courtroom. "Do we need to ask for the defendant's passport?"

Before her lawyer could respond, the judge said there would be no need for such a confiscation.

George protested, citing the previous disappearance of Anton Karuliyak.

Hanley cut him off:

"I've made my ruling, counsel."

The action did little to console Angelina. Her Siberian cool melted. She muttered angrily as she walked out of the courthouse, ahead of Link, unsmiling, and in a hurry.

12. TEAM NOVOSIBIRSK

Link walked with Angelina to her car parked around the corner on H Street. He retrieved his suitcase from the trunk and she slammed it shut behind him.

"I do not understand your justice," she said.

He didn't understand her.

Angelina rolled her eyes and snorted. She did not appear to be pleased with the lack of disposition in her case. She'd have to return to court. She faced the possibility of jail time.

He faced the reality of going back to his life before her.

"Why they need to know my money?" she asked. "They want I pay my lawyer, I pay my lawyer. It is no big deal."

She slid into her car for the drive back to San Francisco.

"I call you," she said, just before she took off. "And think more about what I ask."

Link looked at her like he didn't know what she was talking about, which he didn't.

"Log," she said, just before she rolled her window up and drove off. "Of me."

It sounded more like a demand than a request. He did not wave as she departed. Nobody could turn off the emotion as well as Link. He had lots of practice at it.

As soon as she pulled away in the Corolla, Link pulled out his cell phone and called Frankie, who did the talking.

"You want to tell me what's going on?" the reporter asked.

"Going on?"

Frankie laughed.

"You walk into the courthouse with a woman I've been writing about, who appears to be part of the Russian mob, at a time when the Russians are trying to take over the country, and you play dumb with me?"

"Oh, Angelina. I told you about her."

"You told me that you met her at the Torch, and you said it was no big deal, then I don't hear from you for two months, and the next time I see you, you're walking into the courthouse with her."

"Well, I guess you could say that I have been seduced."

"Seduced."

"I gave into it, Frankie."

"Seduced."

"By all means."

"So, what does she want from you?"

"What makes you assume she wants anything?"

"You're old and ugly. She's young and beautiful."

"That is a very superficial assessment."

"I'm a very superficial guy."

"She has made mention of a sculpture. Kind of alluded to it the night at the Torch. Then today, when she was leaving, it was almost like she was ordering me to do it."

"What does she want, a naked Putin on a stick?"

"No. Just something of herself."

Frankie laughed.

"Very presumptuous of her, to think anybody is all that enthralled with her."

"I deflected her at the Torch Club. We've been together almost the entire past two months, and the subject did not come up again until today."

"Get over here," Frankie ordered. "I've got to finish this story. Then we'll find out what's wrong with you."

Link walked back to the courthouse. He took the elevator up to Frankie's office on the fourth floor. The room was a little larger than a prison cell, windowless, next to nothing on the walls. He poked his head in the door to see Frankie at his computer. Frankie was on the phone with an editor back at the *Beacon*. Subject: the story on Angelina's court appearance that Frankie had just filed. Frankie did not sound pleased. Frankie motioned Link inside without missing a beat with the bosses.

"No," Link heard him say, "we don't have pictures. You may have heard, they don't allow cameras in federal court."

Frankie covered the phone and whispered to Link, "If they wanted pictures, maybe they could have assigned a photographer to wait outside the courthouse, instead taking pictures of the new duck pond at McKinley Park."

The reporter looked at Link and held his index finger to his own temple with his thumb raised as if he were about to pull the trigger.

"I know it probably cost us clicks," Frankie went on with the editor. "A thousand at least. Maybe two thousand. Maybe a link to Drudge. I'm sorry, OK? I will shoot myself. And then I'll quit the business."

He clicked off the phone and looked at Link.

"Seduced," he said.

"And loving it," Link replied.

Now Link didn't need to use his imagination to see Frankie roll his eyes. He sighed and looked around the tiny room.

"My time around here is short," Frankie said.

Link laughed and pulled up another broken-down plastic-cushioned office chair. At one time it must have been ergonomically correct. Now it creaked and moaned, and the adjustor knob didn't work.

"It's the same for all of us," Link replied.

Frankie hit the send button on his story. He swerved his seat around, from the computer, to point himself, with his arms folded, at Link.

"OK," Frankie said, leaning back in his chair, his arms folded across his chest. "Come clean."

Link filled him in on everything that had happened, once more, from the beginning: the Uber ride home from DQU, the Groundhog Night's phone call, the night in the police station, St. Paddy's at the Torch, San Francisco.

"I'm still not getting it," Frankie said.

"Not getting what?"

"Why she's going after you. You're at least 30 years older than she is. And, she's hot."

"I told you. I think she wants me to do a statue, of her." He rubbed his eyes, a little embarrassed. "I thought for a little while it was more than that, but..."

"There's got to be more to it," Frankie interrupted. "She's tied into all this Russian shit, and I'm betting you a million dollars it's got something to do with her going after you."

"That is crazy talk, Frankie. I think it was all about the log to start out with, but now I think she might genuinely like me."

"You are delusional, my friend. She wants something, and believe me, it's not you."

Link was well aware of the dangers of having illusions. Yet he had convinced himself that it made sense for her to reach out to someone. "And why not me?" Link said aloud.

"How many times do I have to tell you? You're old."

It was time to practice some balanced detachment.

"That is an undeniable fact," Link said.

They both laughed, before getting down to the more important business of parsing through the events they had just witnessed in the courtroom. Link told Frankie about Angelina's apparent irritation that the case had not been resolved to her satisfaction.

Frankie stood up from his chair and adjusted one of his kid's scraggly cartoon drawings pinned to the wall.

"So here's what I know," Frankie said. "Back in 2014, I'm still working at the county courthouse, when the feds made the bust on the Mazmonyan case. I get a call from the city desk and they tell me they need some help on this breaking story, that somebody had hacked the San Juan Unified School District and stole the Social Security numbers of all these high school kids. They ask me if I can help out on the story. I'm pissed, of course. For once, I had a quiet day – no daily going, and I'm thinking about taking an early out and slipping up to Track 7 for a pop. Fuck, I say. But what the hell – I do it. We've got addresses on all the defendants, and I get sent out to Rancho Cordova to see if I can get anything out of the village idiot, Nikita Maslov. I knock on his door, and the meanest, toughest guy you ever saw – she answered."

Frankie saw Link's confusion at his mishmash of pronouns, but held up a hand and shrugged as if to say he'd been just as confused and continued the story.

"He, she, whoever she/he was, they answer the door and looked at me as if I was the person that they had been searching for their entire life, the person who had killed their mother and father and all their brothers and sisters, and upon whom they wanted to exact revenge," Frankie went on. "Now, you think I might be a little bit scared. But I explain that I'm working on a newspaper story about this case in federal court and how the feds listed this as the address of one of the defendants, and how I'm just looking for relatives of the guy who lived at this address, to tell me his side of the story, maybe fill me in a little on who the guy is and all that stuff. Well, this . . . person – she, he, whomever – they come out onto the front porch and they tell me to get out of there before they call somebody to come out and hurt me. I look inside the front door, and I see the outline of this guy inside, through the screen door. I see him get up out of a chair. He was watching TV, and he gets up and he's walking to the door and he's as wide as he is high, which is about five-foot-six, but you can tell he is somebody not to be fucked with, and he comes out, and he's looking mean, and he says something in Russian that really got me to thinking that he wasn't very happy with my presence, so I leave my card with the first person, the woman/man, and I say thank you very much and call me if there's anything I can do for you."

Link said he found the story very interesting, but thought it was possible that he might have missed the point.

"Well," Frankie said. "Today, the person, the man/woman person – she was standing at the elevator right next to me when I was pushing the button, and this time she really was a she, without doubt. At least she was wearing a dress and all, and she looked like she'd just stepped off the steppes."

"And?"

"And I recognized her. You don't forget a face like that."

Frankie and Link stopped to think for a second, and at the exact same time they said to each other:

"Uncle Nikita's wife."

They smiled at this mutual realization. Link announced:

"I shall call her Mrs. Uncle Nikita."

Now Link had an idea why Angelina braced herself when she saw Mrs. Uncle Nikita, why she took a seat on the other side of the courtroom as far away from this person's presence as possible.

That had been her roommate for the past 10 years.

This also was the person who, in all likelihood, called the cops on Link.

"What do you think she was doing in the courtroom?" Frankie asked.

"I try not to dabble in speculation," Link answered.

"How about she's in there keeping an eye on things, making sure your gal doesn't go off script?"

"Who am I to say," Link said. "I just wonder if she is the person who called the police on me. I can't think of who else it would be. Why would she have done that? There's a lot of things I just don't get."

"We're going to have to get into that one later, pal. I've got work to do."

Link understood. He said goodbye and he headed home.

Thoughts cluttered his head as he headed up H Street. He pulled his suitcase behind him. He looked forward to spending a little time to himself.

When he got to 12th Street, a light rail train had stopped on the tracks and blocked traffic. It wasn't a four-engine Burlington Northern-Santa Fe. But it got the job done. It was enough to kick off a train trance.

A sense of calm settled his mind. He saw the clarity in a landscape of confusion. He realized he couldn't figure everything out. Maybe not anything.

Why overthink the entrance of a gorgeous woman into his life?

He'd never had a long-lasting relationship with a woman in his entire life. Nothing more than physical attractions, flings, all of which turned into dust. He had no family alive that he knew of. His mother had been dead for years. He never had any aunts or uncles, brothers or sisters, distant cousins. Science told him he had to have a father. His mother never spoke of one. He never thought to look one up.

He'd lived his life alone, with a select few friends, and so far, that had been OK.

Solitude gave him more time focus on the logs. Solitude gave him time to allow the figures inside the logs to reveal themselves. His appreciation of solitude inhibited the idea of relationship. Solitude enabled his journeys into the depths of mystification. Solitude led to the discovery of the truth. Solitude kept him from having children. Solitude got in the way of coaching a Little League team or driving kids to recitals or dance classes. Solitude didn't jive with him helping anybody out with the homework. Solitude directed him to the forms locked into the dead trees. Solitude liberated him to liberate them.

He is the only person who could possibly discover them, release them, in a way that reflected the world the way he knew it.

He had to give these reflections life, and he had to do it or face a fall into insanity. If he didn't have a chance to unleash the inspiration inside him, he'd have been one of those babblers on the streets. He'd be the one with his hand out. He'd be the one living on the river bank polluting the river with his human waste.

He had only one enduring relationship in his life, and it was the one he established with his craft. It was the only one he had time for. It left him with nothing left over, except maybe for light conversation with casual friends at Benny's about sports and politics.

When he was going good, he spent every waking hour in the pursuit of artistic perfection. Even the ones he spent drinking or in other forms of diversion were aimed at opening up avenues for whatever it was inside him that needed to get out. He wasn't so mad that he thought he could achieve perfection. He also knew that the ends were contained in the means. Compulsive gamblers never really cared if they won or lost. Money was only the gas that fueled the drive. What gamblers wanted, what gamblers needed, was the action. They needed the rush of the horses coming down the wire or the fourth-down play from the 3-yard line with the point spread on the line.

Same for him. A piece could turn out failed or it could approximate an ideal of beauty. Neither mattered. What lit Link was the process, of finding out what stirred inside himself and how he could fuse it with the inanimate object.

He was good at it, too. He lived his life exactly as he wanted. He never had to report to a boss or punch a clock. Yet he was just as much beholden to a controlling force as any wage slave. He couldn't escape his art.

He knew he was lucky to be on this path, luckier still that he didn't have to rely on patrons or government support.

Standing in front of the stalled train, he thanked his mother. He thanked her for seeing what was inside him before he saw it himself. He thanked her for her sacrifice. He thanked her for being Nisenan. He thanked her for living in the rancheria instead of some ghetto in L.A. or Oakland. He thanked her for pushing him to apply for grants. He thanked her for taking him to Mendocino and introducing him to the Witch Doctor.

He thanked the Witch Doctor for beating creativity into his soul.

The bell on the light rail clanged. The light rail moved and got out of his way.

Soon as the train passed, his cell phone beeped.

"Sorry I didn't say hello," said the voice on the other end.

It belonged to the Sacramento police detective, Andrew Wiggins.

"No need to apologize," Link said. "I caught the head nod."

Ten minutes later, Link and the cop sat together at a little black two-seat table underneath a billowing elm tree outside the front door to The Mill, another coffee joint in midtown.

Bearded hipsters with asymmetrical haircuts and tattooed young women with nose rings hid behind their laptops. They played computer games. They did their homework. They paid no attention to the tall Native American who took a meeting with the city cop.

Wiggins got right to the point. He told Link that a couple days after their meeting on Groundhog's Night, he got reassigned to a federally-supervised organized crime task force to investigate local Russian operations.

"I'm still on Crimes Against Persons, but business has gotten so bad in there that they figured they could get a better and higher use out of me."

"OK," Link said.

"And I've got a little information you might want to slip to your friend at the newspaper," the detective said.

This confused Link. Wiggins was just at the courthouse. He sat one seat behind Frankie. Wiggins could have left Frankie a note, asked him for his phone number.

"He's not too hard to get a hold of," Link said.

Wiggins looked at Link as if he were stupid.

"I realize that, but then if somebody asked me if I ever leaked anything to a reporter, I'd have to say yes," Wiggins said. "If I said no, and if they had a lie detector hooked up to me, I'd be in trouble. So I use intermediaries. Trusted intermediaries. Can I trust you?"

Link got it.

"Of course."

"Besides," Wiggins said. "I really don't like reporters. I don't trust them."

Link looked around and nodded toward a young man seated with a book and latte not five feet from him and Wiggins, to remind him that the two of them were not exactly alone. Wiggins seemed unbothered by anybody else's presence.

"Here's what I know," Wiggins said. "And here's what your reporter friend needs to know. And he can't know that it's coming from me."

"Before you get started," Link said, "I've got to know one thing. Were you aware of the presence of that Russian-looking woman in the back of the courtroom today?"

"That's exactly where I was going to start."

"Does she have a name? I only know her as 'Mrs. Uncle Nikita.'"

"Her name's a good place to start with her," Wiggins said. "It's Alexa, and it sounds like you already know she's romantically involved with Nikita Maslov. But her maiden name is what I find most intriguing."

"And that is?"

"Would you believe 'Karuliyak'?"

Link let the information sink in. It took a few moments for it to penetrate. "Sister? Mother? Ex-wife?"

"It appears as if she is his sister," Wiggins said. "The information I'm receiving from my FBI sources is that she and Karuliyak and Maslov, as well as that Mazmonyan fellow, the stooge who took the fall in the credit card case, are all from Novosibirsk."

"Of course."

"It's the capital of Siberia. You've been there?"

"Not lately."

"Me neither, but it sounds like they all wound up in the Soviet army together. Mazmonyan, Maslov, that Sergei guy, they were all part of the same unit. Karuliyak was their captain and the rest were grunts. Then the Soviets realized the impossibility of Afghanistan and they got the hell out. Next thing you know it's Glasnost time and the whole country goes to hell. Everybody wants out, and you've got a zillion of them who wind up over here, including about a hundred thousand in Sacramento. Just about everybody in the mortgage fraud cases made the move right then, including all of our guys. Except for this Angelina woman. She came later. And now that we're talking about her, what's up with you escorting her into court today? People are talking."

"She is seducing me. Or she was, anyway. Until today."

"Looks like she was doing a pretty good job. Did you ever close the deal?"

"What do you think?"

Wiggins covered a little snicker with a sip of his dark roast.

"Pretty good," he said. "I like this place. Where were we before real coffee came to town?"

"I think we were in Nosibirsk."

"That's Novosibirsk."

"Whatever."

"Right. Anyway, so Alexa Maslov and her brother, Anton Karuliyak – you got them straight?"

"Yep."

"They come over right about the same time as Mikhail, and Nikita made his move not long after that. I think Uncle Nikita and Alexa had already been married, but he had some health problems related to the war. The Russkies were cleaning out a mountain pass near Khost at the end of the deal and he got the worst of it. Got shot, got an eardrum blown out, nasty shit. I guess he was never a Rhodes Scholar to begin with, but the war left him pretty much unemployable."

"I'm sorry to hear that."

"Well, they took care of him pretty good, and used him pretty good, too, in all the shit they were up to."

"Such as?"

"You know about the credit cards, but the real deal was his bank account. The feds are still tracking back all of his transactions, going back 27 years, but the most interesting stuff didn't happen until about three years ago."

Wiggins paused for more caffeination.

"Thousands and thousands of dollars, and I mean tens of thousands of dollars, start flowing through it. This starts up in mid-to-late 2014, or right about the time that the sanctions kicked in."

"Sanctions?"

"Soon as Russia racked up Crimea, we popped the sanctions on them, right? Basically shut off financial transactions between us and their biggest banks. Putin's pals really didn't like it. Fuck, Putin didn't like it. And, like, they had a little bit of business going on over here, political as well as financial, and all of a sudden they can't move their money around? So what did they do?"

"I've got no idea."

"Well, I can't talk about the entirety of everything they did. I don't even know. But I do know what happened with Nikita Maslov. This money starts pouring into his account, and it is reported in through his bank here as his pension. For a hundred years, he'd been getting maybe a thousand, fifteen hundred a month. All of a sudden, it's $20,000, $25,000 a hit."

"You think he'd move out of Rancho Cordova."

"His lifestyle didn't change a stitch, and neither did his wife's."

"He could have made the rent in midtown."

"He could have bought in the Fabulous Forties. But nothing changes, with him, or his wife. You saw how she was dressed today."

"Right off the tundra."

"And it's June."

"So what are they doing with the money?"

"That, my friend, is the $25,000 question."

13. COMEY DAY

An unusually cool spring persisted into the second week of June, and it created the best of days in the town.

Link sprang down the steps of his high-water Victorian to soak it in. He quickened his pace down D Street, beneath a brilliant blue sky, through the nearby Alkali Flat neighborhood where new, three-story houses rose from what used to be a creamery. They sold in the $700,000s. Sleepy and seedy gave way to industrial moderne.

The homeless trail still ran up and down the 12th Street corridor that separated his Mansion Flats neighborhood from Alkali and connected downtown to the shelters and food lines and tent cities. Over to I Street and west, Link strolled through the great room of the refurbished train station – the seventh-busiest in America – to check out the restored mural of the launching of the Transcontinental Railroad in Sacramento. It spread from wall to wall. Crocker, Huntington, Stanford, Hopkins – the Big Four, the Robber Barons – they were all in it.

Out of the Sacramento Valley station, he skulked under the roaring Interstate 5 and into Old Town, around the back side of the Railroad Museum, and then into the eight-square block zone that had once been a jazz district, and probably still would be, if the freeway hadn't cut the neighborhood off from the rest of the city. With a little forethought the place could have been fashioned into a Sacramento version of the French Quarter.

Link walked along the sidewalks above the river and over to the Tower Bridge that provided a golden, arch-like entrance into the city, or out of it, depending on your direction. The Sacramento River rolled easily beneath it, shimmering and rippling on the perfect 75-degree morning. Link soaked it in from above, before the hour hit him –he'd better hurry if he was going to make it to Benny's on time to meet Mike Rubiks and Frankie Cameron to watch the fired FBI director stick it to the President of the United States.

Mike Rubiks had arranged for Om to open early so they could

watch the greatest show on earth. Rubiks took the day off so that he wouldn't miss a peep. Link walked into Benny's just as Comey stood to his full 6-foot-8. He raised his right hand and swore to tell the truth.

Om served tea to Link and Frankie. Rubiks ordered a boilermaker, Early Times over a Budweiser longneck.

Comey had barely begun his opening statement – "I first met then-President-Elect Trump on Friday, January 6, in a conference room at Trump Tower in New York" – when it became apparent that Mike Rubiks was about to put on a special show of his own for the small crew at Benny's.

Rubiks' first shot went down fast, with an expletive right behind it.

"Motherfucking asshole," Rubiks muttered. "Comey should have come in with handcuffs and arrested the son of a bitch."

Frankie took a sip of his tea. He mistakenly responded to Rubiks as if he was conversing with a normal human being.

"I don't think he had probable cause," Frankie said.

"Oh, fuck me," Rubiks shot back. "The fucker had already laundered money in Atlantic City, cheated on his taxes, broke in on naked underage girls, winked off the Russian computer hacking, refused to rent to black people, and stole paydays from the Polish who built his goddam building. He was then and he is now the most arrestable motherfucker in America. Anytime, any cop, anywhere in the country – they could throw him over the hood of the car and shove his fucking orange head into the back seat. The fact he isn't in prison right now is the biggest mockery of justice in the history of the United States."

Frankie and Link exchanged looks like Bert and Ernie did the Christmas Eve that George Bailey saw what the world would be like without him in it. Yep, Frankie and Link agreed: we've got a live one this morning.

Comey went on to tell the committee that he'd been there to brief Trump on some "personally sensitive" information in the Steele dossier. Everyone in the room, not just Rubiks, tingled with excitement about the impending unmasking of the president of the United States of America as an international laughingstock.

"This is beautiful," Rubiks said, downing his second shot when he heard Comey say "salacious and unverified."

Comey told the committee how he and the leaders of the major intelligence agencies of America held a pre-briefing briefing on how they would brief the president-to-be about how he had allegedly been caught on tape in with a couple of hookers who pissed the bed in a Moscow hotel room. Comey told the committee that he drew the short straw.

As of Comey's January meeting in Trump tower, the only people who knew about the alleged pee tapes were federal intelligence agents, Christopher Steele, Christopher Steele's sources, the prostitutes, the employees of the Ritz-Carlton Moscow, top level security officials in Russia, Vladimir Putin, and the online news agency, Buzzfeed, which meant that within a matter of weeks, the entire world know about it.

The FBI felt that it would probably be better if they told Trump first that Buzzfeed had the dossier and was going to post the news about the pissing prostitutes. The FBI worried that if somebody didn't tell Trump about the dossier, and soon, that the Russians would, and that they would blackmail him.

"This part of the story I don't understand," Link said. "I mean, did these women actually urinate on Trump?"

"I don't think we know for sure that they did," Frankie said.

"And we don't know for sure that they didn't, either," Rubiks shot back, as he took a pull on his Budweiser longneck. "It makes you wonder. What exactly is the protocol for an FBI director to ask a president-elect if a couple of Russian whores peed on him?"

Comey revealed some of the secrets of FBIs counter-intelligence work. He outlined how the FBI deals with targets of foreign spies. He insinuated that he had never before come across a situation where somehow maybe the president of the Unites States had skulked into office as a compromised person, as a result of his "personal conduct." Comey figured he better write it down, and fast, on his laptop, in his car, in the White House parking lot.

"Creating written records immediately after one-on-one conversations with Mr. Trump was my practice from that point forward," Comey told the panel. "This had not been my practice in the past."

The booze had begun to hit Mike Rubiks. He took a turn for the mean.

"Tell me, you asshole," the reporter said, addressing Comey.

"What was your 'practice in the past' when it came to dirtying up some presidential candidate 11 days before an election?"

Rubiks referred to Comey's decision, less than two weeks before the 2016 presidential election, to go public with information that Hillary Clinton emails showed up in the laptop of the pornographic former congressman, Anthony Weiner, whose wife, Huma Abedin, had been Hillary Clinton's top aide for the past several years. Rubiks raged about how a week later, the FBI determined there was really nothing to the October surprise. Rubiks charged that the bad news on top of fake news on top of the Russian computer hack-and-meddle was more than Hillary Clinton's campaign could bear. Rubiks blamed Comey for the election of Donald Trump as president of the United States.

"Comey's going to have to wear this for the rest of his life," Rubiks said.

Frankie Cameron didn't quite get his colleague's logic, and was also trying to watch James Comey's testimony. Frankie Cameron asked Rubiks to quiet down, please.

"Can't we just watch this?" he said, as Comey moved from the January 6 meeting to his dinner with the president a week after Trump's inauguration.

Comey characterized his January 27 one-on-one with Trump as "strange." The president began "by asking me if I wanted to stay on as FBI director," Comey said. The president was trying to "create some sort of patronage relationship" between the two of them, Comey said. The president's imprecation "concerned me greatly, given the FBI's traditionally independent status in the executive branch," Comey said.

"Stop it right there!" Rubiks screamed.

Om, who was watching the hearing along with the two reporters and Link in the otherwise empty bar, picked up the clicker and hit the same pause button that came in handy for football replays at the bar.

Comey's face froze on the screen.

"He should have been wearing a wire to this meeting," Rubiks said. "Why wasn't he? He knew Trump was dirty. They knew Trump was dirty. They had probable cause to believe that a crime had been committed and that he could have been a participant in a conspiracy. They had shit on this guy going back to when he first went public in the 1970s."

Om set up Rubiks up with another Early Times, his third, and Budweiser back, his second.

"I mean, how fucking many shots do you get at a guy?" Rubiks went on. "You're the fucking director of the FBI. You think Trump's going to pat you down? They goddam should have gone to a judge and gotten the wire before this meeting ever took place. It is fucking dereliction of duty that they didn't."

Comey picked up the story:

"A few moments later, the President said, 'I need loyalty. I expect loyalty'," Comey was saying. Comey had been flabbergasted. Comey tried to stay cool, tried not to "change my facial expression in any way." Comey sat there in face of the president's remark "in awkward silence" while the president apparently sought his complicity in the politicization of the FBI.

Rubiks went nuts.

"I got my face shot off in Iraq!" Rubiks screamed at the television, after politely asking Om once again to hit the pause button. "They damn near blew my leg off. I saw some of my best friends in the world blown up right in front of me. And for what? So we can let a fucking fascist steal the election? Let this bastard think he can take over the FBI? And then have the FBI director say he's too much of a pussy to do anything about it? Or say anything about it? 'Awkward silence,' my ass. How about you say, 'We got some rules around here, and one of them is to tell the fucking president to shove it up his ass anytime he comes to us and says, 'I expect loyalty.''

Rubiks downed his shot and followed it with a swallow of Budweiser.

"What the fuck has happened to this country?" Rubiks said.

Frankie and Link sat in awkward silence of their own. Unlike Comey with Trump, Frankie and Link could not disagree with a word Mike Rubiks said.

Rubiks collapsed in a heap into his bar stool, straightened and took a sip off his longneck, and nodded toward Om to resume the show.

Comey stepped sideways into some gobbledygook about the FBI's "independence."

"Independence," Rubiks mumbled, his head now sandwiched

sideways against the bar like an open-faced tuna melt laid on its side. "If he was independent, he would have slapped the cuffs on him right there."

Comey rolled back to Trump's "I need loyalty" rap. Comey promised "honesty." Trump heard "honesty" as meaning "honest loyalty." Comey, adoptively, gave his loyalty to the president. Comey told Trump, "You will get that from me."

Hurricane Rubiks blew again. Hurricane Rubiks flew into another tirade. Hurrican Rubiks drowned out Comey. Hurricane Rubiks contributed to the irritability of everybody in the bar.

"You rat bastard!" he yelled at Comey's image on the television. "You rotten, no-good motherfucker!"

Comey calmed Rubiks down when he returned to Rubiks' favorite word of the morning: "salacious." The context: Trump's obsession with the prostitutes.

"He said he was considering ordering me to investigate the alleged incident to prove it didn't happen," Comey said.

"What a dumb fuck," Rubiks said of the president. "Doesn't the fucker know you can't 'investigate' something that didn't happen? That's called a cover-up."

Comey moved into his account of his scheduled February 14 counter-terrorism briefing with the president in the Oval Office. Trump shooed out a room full of muckety mucks that had been in attendance, saying he wanted to speak with Comey alone, again.

"Why the fuck would he stay in the room alone with the guy?" Rubiks wondered. "After the loyalty oath shit? I'd want a witness for anything Trump ever said to me. Wouldn't you?"

Nobody had a good answer for Mike Rubiks, least of all, Comey. "When the door by the grandfather clock closed, and we were alone, the President began by saying, 'I want to talk about Mike Flynn,' " he said.

"Pause!" screamed Rubiks.

Link, Frankie and Om cringed at the outburst.

"Play that back."

Om complied.

"Mike Fucking Flynn," Rubiks bellowed, repeating the name of the former national security advisor, with an air of drunken authority, as if he were to reveal a piece of information that only he could disclose. "The motherfucker has just been fired, and Trump wants to talk about him, and Comey puts up with this shit? Jesus Christ. Comey is a complete fucking incompetent. No wonder Trump fired him."

Rubiks looked straight down at the bar. He shot his head up in revelation:

"More whiskey!" he demanded.

Om provided him with another Early Times-to-Anheuser Busch exacta box. Boom went the shot, with a long swig of Bud right behind it, to cool the gullet.

Comey recounted Trump's mealy-mouthed excuse for firing Flynn – lying to the vice president, Mike Pence.

"As if that lie was any worse than the 10,000 other lies that propped up this presidency," Rubiks said. "Propped up his entire fucking career. He fires Flynn over this?"

Comey on Trump: "He added that he had other concerns about Flynn which he did not specify."

Rubiks: "Stop the fucking tape!"

Om clicked it to a stop.

"So, he just said that Trump had 'concerns' quote unquote, about Flynn?" Rubiks said. Like, maybe the fact that Flynn was on the take with Russia? And now Comey's got him admitting it? And he does nothing about it? If it's me, and I'm the FBI director, I'm taking the fucker to the ground, throw him in jail for treason. Knee in the back, cuff him the fuck up, and call for back-up on the walkie-talkie. You don't know what he's carrying – knife, .22 on his ankle, AK down his pants. This could be a dangerous fucking situation."

"Can we just watch the guy fucking testify?" Frankie asked. Om pressed play.

About Mike Flynn, Comey reported Trump as saying " 'He is a good guy and has been through a lot. I hope you can see your way clear to letting this go.' "

Rubiks hunched over his longneck. He mumbled incoherently, about storming into Iraq in pursuit of Saddam Hussein, only to have to come home and see what he perceived to be treason and cover-up and complicity everywhere he looked.

"I can't believe this shit," he said.

Comey understood Trump "to be requesting that we drop any investigation of Flynn in connection with false statements about his conversations with the Russian ambassador in December." Comey found Trump's ham-handed effort to be "very concerning."

Rubiks: " 'Very concerning.' Not just concerning, or a little concerning, but 'very' concerning. Lawman of the year."

Rubiks appeared to be circling the drain.

Comey advanced to a March 30 telephone conversation with Trump in which the president "described the Russia investigation as 'a cloud' that was impairing his ability to act on behalf of the country."

"I've got a cloud impairing my ability to watch any more of this shit," Rubiks said. "Get me the fuck out of here."

"Do you want me to call you a cab?" Om said.

"I've got it," said Link, who pulled out his cell phone to arrange an Uber ride home for his friend.

Rubiks stumbled toward the door.

"Whoa, Mike," Frankie said.

"We'll get you home, Mike," Link said.

Rubiks retreated unevenly to one of the high-tables along the front wall of the bar. He boosted himself up into a stool despite his serious wobble. The observers thought he might take a fall.

Comey continued on about the "cloud" that Trump complained hovered above his presidency.

"Ain't ever going away," Rubiks mumbled.

Rubiks made it to his feet, drool running down from his mouth, before collapsing again into a table, as Comey's testimony rolled back to Trump's concern about the hookers. Comey: "I responded that we were investigating the matter as quickly as we could..."

"Om, could you please stop the tape?" Rubiks slurred.

Om complied.

"I mean, like, what's the rush?" Rubiks asked. "Why would you want to investigate anything quickly as possible? You need to take your time, son. Om, I would like another beer."

The bartender popped another beer.

With the bottle in hand, Rubiks stood relatively stable in the middle of the barroom, swerving only so slightly, back and forth, side to side. He watched and listened. He folded his muscular arms across his burly chest, the beer bottle extended outward from his right hand.

"You've already got him for obstruction of justice," Rubiks told everybody at the bar with drunken authority. "He tried to get you to swear a loyalty oath. You know you can't talk to the attorney general, Jefferson Beauregard Secessions, because he is a Confederate sympathizer. You know Trump let the prostitutes piss on him and that the Russians have it on tape direct from the presidential suite of the Ritz Carlton Hotel in Moscow, USSR. And now you tell the son of a bitch that you're going to investigate the matter 'as quickly as possible?'"

Om hit the play button.

Comey described how he and Trump spoke for the last time on April 11. Trump wanted the FBI leader to tell the world the president of the United States was not under federal investigation. Comey said he took the president's request up the ladder in the Department of Justice hierarchy. Nobody ever got back to him. Comey suggested that Trump might have had better luck if he had his lawyer call the Department of Justice.

"That's how you do it when you want to fucking kill an investigation," Rubiks said. "You don't go whining to the cops and say you've got a cloud over your head because you let a couple of Russian whores piss on you in Moscow."

"That was the last time I spoke with President Trump," Comey told the committee.

"Lucky you," Rubiks said. "The rest of us are still stuck with the fucker."

14. QUEEN FOR A DAY

Link hadn't seen Angelina in more than a month, since her day in court. He called her a couple times. She didn't answer. He didn't leave a message.

It looked like another two-month stand, about his 800th.

In the meantime, Link waited for Frankie's second big takeout on Russian organized crime.

He told his pal everything Detective Wiggins told him the other day at The Mill. Now all he had to do was wait for Frankie to do his thing.

Frankie dug through court records. Frankie called the cops and the FBI (on background only). The prosecutors talked to Frankie off the record; he couldn't print a word of it. They pointed him to public records in the court files. He'd already gone through them. He went through them again, on all of the 50-plus cases. He went through them three times. He worked the lawyers. He interviewed a couple of the crooks and worked them. Speaking to him in the courtroom hallways, they portrayed themselves as total dumbfucks. They said they were just a bunch of stupid immigrants who got taken for a ride by the likes of Alana Cosmenko, bumpkins who never fully integrated into the American system. They were just folk in search of welfare handouts, suffering from the opioid crisis just like all Americans. They just didn't have the music to pull off the Appalachia story.

Most of them said they'd never even heard of Anton Karuliyak. The few that said they had said he directed them to Sacramento from wherever they had landed in the United States – Fargo, Detroit, Wapakoneta Falls, Louisville, Brighton Beach, North Beach, East Carolina, South Dakota, West Sacramento. They said Karuliyak directed them to other managers, other Alana Cosmenkos who had incorporated their own little crooked mortgage fraud enterprises.

Frankie tried to talk to the crooked mortgage fraud entrepreneurs. They told him to go to hell.

He went to Rancho Cordova instead. He went back to Uncle

Nikita's house. Mrs. Uncle Nikita slammed the door in his face. He went to the houses of dozens of other Uncle Nikitas. Not a one of them sounded like they knew how to conjugate a verb in English. He thought they were smarter than they looked. He didn't trust a single one of them.

He called Moscow. He told them he was trying to track down Mr. Karuliyak. Moscow didn't know what the hell he was talking about. Moscow told him to go to hell.

Nobody knew anything.

None of the lawyers for the crooks attempted to dig beneath their clients' stories. Why should they? The system only required them to assess the facts and determine how the law applied to their clients. Their clients all agreed to plead out early, to get the best government deal, as if they were buying a used car. A couple of the crooks did minimal jail time. Most of them agreed to deportations and small fines, which they failed to pay before they were deported. The lawyers banked easy, pro forma money.

All of the cases played out the same way, off the same script, except Angelina's.

Frankie couldn't figure out why her case was still open, and neither could her lawyer. Off the record, Jacob Dillon described his conversation with the government after her arrest as "perfunctory". Dillon told Frankie that he touched bases with the prosecutors to see if they could work out a plea, the same way he did whenever he knew his clients were guilty. The same way he did when he knew they lied to him. Or withheld information from him. Dillon told Frankie he thought Angelina hit the trifecta – guilty, liar, withholder of information. He didn't know what the prosecutors had on Angelina, other than that they had a lot of it. Dillon knew, the prosecutors knew – everybody knew – that mortgage fraud suffocated Sacramento like the spring pollen.

Filed in 2011, the cases didn't get moving in court until late 2014. Jacob Dillon had found it odd when the government, right out of the chute, had asked if he was still interested in a deal. Of course he was. Would Dillon mind if the government put Angelina's case off a while? Dillon agreed, no problem.

Junior U.S. attorneys handled most of the cases. Most of the junior attorneys looked like they just got out of diapers. Dillon's junior prosecutor told him that circumstances complicated the matter of USA vs. Angelina Puchkova. Dillon's junior prosecutor – the one before Michael George – told him her case was different from the others, the mules, the Alana Cosmenkos, the know-nothings, the straw buyers, the fodder, the easily expendable. The Puchkova case might take a little more time. But Dillon's junior prosecutor did not tell him what was so unique, and Dillon did not ask her to elaborate.

In a short time, Dillon's junior prosecutor was replaced by a team of senior prosecutors led by Michael George.

That's when the government prosecutors told Dillon circumstances had changed.

"They didn't say why," Dillon told Frankie. "The next thing I know, three years have gone by. They call me in for a Queen for a Day. I bring Angelina in to hear what they've got and what they want and she gives them a bland statement that says nothing. Sure, she'd testify to the grand jury, but she said she'd have a real problem testifying in a public trial. This is like late last year, when they've got a trial date coming up on the credit card case. I stay in touch with them in the meantime, and everything's copacetic. Then, in the courtroom, all that business about restitution comes up, and the deal flies out the window."

Frankie and Link tried to piece the whole thing together. They got together at Benny's, not long after the Comey testimony, during a mid-week Happy Hour. They sat down at the end of the bar, away from the dice slammers.

"Where's Mike?" Link asked.

"Couldn't make it," Frankie said. "Checked into an insane asylum."

"No, really."

"Actually, he's still on vacation. He needed to get away from it all. I think he went to Yemen."

Link nodded, knowingly, as if it made perfect sense.

"Actually, Lake Tahoe," Frankie said. "Took off the day of the Comey testimony. His wife's family gets a beach pad every year around that little bar in Camp Richardson."

"He sounded like he could use a few days off."

"Looked it, too."

"His accounts ring of truth," Link said. "When you strip away the emotion, there is not one thing he said the other day that I have the evidence to refute."

"Me neither. His problem is nobody listens to him except me and you."

"History has had a way of casting out the truth tellers. It is my sense that they would not make good politicians."

Frankie laughed. The bar perked up with the crackle of the blue collars mixed with what Link noticed to be an uptick in Millennials, the young people with more cash driving up the rents and pressuring the working stiffs to look elsewhere for affordable housing. Like Stockton.

"So how's your story going?" Link asked, after Om brought him his Sierra Nevada Pale Ale with the pretty green label on the bottle and Frankie Cameron his pint of Racer 5 from the tap.

"It's coming together," Frankie said. "Slowly. Lots I still can't figure out. Like, why all of a sudden this intense law enforcement interest in a bunch of white collar cases that have been hanging around for years? The FBI's been busting Russians for mortgage fraud since 2007, 2008. Nobody in the Justice Department's made a damn bit of noise about any of them. Nobody gave a single shit. Who were the losers here? The banks. Who didn't do their due diligence on the loans? The banks. What American institution became the most reviled in the country? The banks."

Link nodded assent.

"People back east have been writing about Russian organized crime for 25 years," Frankie continued. "But it was all Brighton Beach. Miami. A little bit of L.A. Nothing about the fact that this kind of mortgage fraud shit popped up anywhere you could find established Russian communities. They'd been doing shit here going all the way back to the chop shops, and we'd been writing about them in our paper since 1990. The cops, the feds, they all had to know what was happening. I remember seeing the little stories in the paper. Then September 11 happens and the last thing anybody around here cared about was the Russians. It was all Islamic terrorism. The feds admit it. It's like they said, we've got other problems to worry about, like Islamic terrorists in Lodi."

"I remember them well," Link responded.

"Yeah, I remember, too. They arrested a dingbat high school kid who had an IQ in the low 70s. I think he visited an uncle in Karachi and came back with some crazy Cliff-note distortions of the Koran. Dominated the news for two years."

"While Putin was taking over America."

"Exactly."

"The public didn't care."

"That's because the public lost its shirt in the crash."

Frankie said his newly-found sources told him that about mid-to-late 2014, they started seeing mortgage fraud links to Russia.

"The cases were getting processed," Frankie said. "We wrote about the bigger ones. But we never looked at them as anything more than a series of one-offs. We never linked them to each other or to rings that worked Stockton and Reno and Phoenix and Fresno and Florida. We got into Alana Cosmenko a little bit. Jesus Christ, she had eight different teams doing the same thing as the one that had your gal on it."

"Make that, my former gal. She stopped returning my calls," Link fact-checked with a dismissive wave of the hand. "Go on with your story."

Frankie's speculation was this: in 2016, the United States elected a new president. The deep state thought the Russians played a role. The deep state instructed its agents in every judicial district, especially ones with high Russian populations, like Sacramento's, to look back on all these mortgage fraud cases for new angles.

But he wasn't going to let Link off so easily about Angelina. Link told Frankie that, in the time between St. Patrick's Day and Angelina's court appearance, beyond her physical beauty, he was taken in and bemused by her suspicious view of America. She also came along at the perfect time of his creative lapse. A fling, he thought, just might be the thing to re-charge his mojo, he told Frankie. He knew that he was old enough to be her father, that there was nothing in his life's background to suggest a match with hers, and that age and culture gaps precluded any chance of a long-term thing. He confessed to giving into to the emotion of the moment.

Then came her abrupt attitude shift when she left the courthouse, and then she did not return his phone calls, and then he knew that whatever it was that existed between the two of them had and gone kaput.

"You seem to be OK with it," Frankie said

"No other way to be, really," Link said. "Looking backwards, detached from my feelings, you can see it was really kind of interesting. She's been in the United States for 10 years, and you would figure that she had a better sense of American customs. Yet she displayed the cultural knowledge of somebody who had been chained in a basement for the entire decade. She never made an effort to break away from Mrs. Uncle Nikita's psychological grip. The way she talked, her accent, it would make you think she just made it across the Bering Sea. She'd never heard of the Grateful Dead. She'd never been to a baseball game. She'd never seen *The Godfather*. She never rafted drunk down the lower American River. She never ate a hamburger at Jim Denny's. She'd never been to Lake Tahoe, or heard of Burning Man. She never played nine holes at William Land Park. I guess the only thing she ever read was the Russian-language papers. She only hung out with people she met at the Russian Orthodox church and a few others who converted to Slavic evangelicalism. She only had one idea on a place for us to go in Sacramento, and it was Neroe's Russian bakery in Carmichael."

"I've been there," Frankie said. "For the *plombir*."

Link nodded. He recounted their weeks at Gordon and Leia's, now unreal, again. "Spent almost all of it in San Francisco, going to restaurants – she really liked the Tadich Grill. Going to the art museum, walking along the wharf, all the way from Pier 39 to the ballpark. Took her to a couple games at AT&T. Showed her the Haight. Baker Beach. Got rip-roaring drunk at the Cliff House. Brought her back to my pad a couple times. She was unimpressed. I'd say the main thing I got out of it was probably the most intoxicating sex I've ever had in my life."

"That's usually the bottom line, isn't it?"

"It is a fairly important component," Link said.

"Sometimes," Frankie said. "It can even lead to – what do you call it? Conversation?"

"We did some of that, too, although she was less than forthcoming. She seemed to enjoy herself with me, but I found her... guarded. She held something back."

"Like the truth?"

"Isn't that the case with so many of us when it comes to revealing ourselves? I cut her a break. I was having a good time."

Link told Frankie that Angelina's ostensible apprehension about Mr. Karuliyak, parlayed to her declaration that she did not want to return to Siberia, convinced Link that she was sane. He always found rationality to be a good starting point for a getting to know someone, so this belief in her balanced state of mind opened him up to her physicality. He liked the way she walked, the color of her hair, the way she talked. He liked the accent. He loved the way she mangled the English language with a coquettish flick of the head.

More intriguing, Link said, was the obvious and rapid transformation in her political outlook. In their weeks in San Francisco, she appeared to shed her reflexive defense of her homeland and all but sign on with the spirit of the Resistance.

"Every morning, first thing she did was pick up the *Times* and go straight to the back of the front section," Link said. "By noon, she was quoting the lead editorial. Then, Krugman and Kristof."

"So, she was not stupid," Frankie said.

"Hardly. In fact, I'd say she was super smart."

"Now I'm becoming suspicious," Frankie said.

Link laid out more details of Angelina's political transformation. She expressed an interest in the Indivisible movement, the national alliance of anti-Trumpers who took to the streets in protest against every Trumpian initiative. She thought Devin Nunes should be impeached from his congressional seat in California for undermining the work of the House Intelligence Committee. She wanted to sit in on the Senate's interrogation of Jared Kushner. She though Mike Flynn should spend the rest of his life in prison. She found out more about Carter Page than Carter Page's mother ever knew about him. Sally Yates was her girl.

"Normally, I would not care too much about these matters of government," Link said. "I almost never have based friendships on politics. But in these times, things have changed. I don't know whether or not it was intentional on my part, but it wasn't until I got a sense that she had arrived at a realistic view of the world that I could even think about going to bed with her, as crazy as that sounds. I don't mean to sound so self-important, but I accepted her based on her unacceptability of Trump."

"Politics are weird," Frankie agreed.

"Worst thing in the world to build a relationship on," Link

agreed.

"As if you'd know."

The two of them laughed.

"I have to admit," Link told Frankie. "I did feel something for her."

Then, poof. No call backs.

Frankie pursed his lips to his pint, narrowed his eyes, and took a sip. This was the most Link had ever opened up to him about his feelings. Link's obvious discomfort told Frankie to change the subject, for both of their sakes.

"So," Frankie asked. "How's work?"

Link hadn't been in the studio since before the Comey hearing. For weeks and weeks, nothing was clicking inside. He told him about his abject lack of inspiration.

"I think I'm going to do that Che thing," Link said, in an attempted to brighten the mood.

"Does anybody remember who he is?"

"I do. Scrounger does."

It was still light and pleasantly warm when Link and Frankie finished their beers and said goodbye and headed home.

15. FISA TIME

Link picked up the paper the next morning and walked two blocks to Shine. In a town where you could get a locally-brewed cup of coffee on nearly every street corner, Shine was his favorite. Decisive factor: proximity. It was the closest to his house. He also found the friendly tattooed baristas to be a plus.

They fixed him up black.

Link sank into a deep-leather sofa chair to read the paper and get high on caffeine.

His phone beeped. The telephone number moderately surprised him.

"I would like to see you," Angelina said, flat-toned, before she said hello, as if it was completely normal to call somebody out of nowhere after you'd blown them off for weeks.

Link knew she had an upcoming court date. Subject: restitution. He hadn't planned on attending.

He had taken a purposefully mindful walk the night before, after his beer with Frankie, to take a dispassionate look at what he had said and felt about Angelina. By the time he passed the Stanford Mansion and circled Capitol Park and made it back home to D Street, he was done with her. He stopped thinking about her. He stopped caring about her. Now she's calling him? Now she wants to see him?

The tone of her voice reminded him why it had been so easy for him to forget her: it was cold. In response to this cold voice, it was easy not to betray any pain or anguish or longing. He no longer felt any.

"Today," she continued.

Link accessed the blank recesses of his mind for his schedule. He didn't have a job. He had nothing he really had to do. He had way more money than he'd ever need. He had more fame than he liked. He had no family. He had no responsibilities. His artwork was on hold. He had total freedom. What good did that do him? It didn't answer any ultimate questions. It didn't solve the riddle about who he was and where he was going, if anywhere, or if those questions even mattered. All he knew, he was running out of time with each passing day. People died around him almost every day. Eventually, he'd be the one in the obituary box.

Right now, he had to deal with Angelina.

"Can't make it today," he told her.

He made sure she heard the ruffling of his newspaper.

During his walk the previous evening, Link concluded that Angelina was an inconsistent human being. The category placed her in the predominance of the species. Inconsistency bothered him. Inconsistency was why he never had a girlfriend longer than three months. His own he could deal with. Theirs he could not.

Angelina persisted.

"I have meeting with lawyer today," she told him. "He wants know about my money. Maybe he no longer can have my case."

"I'm sure the two of you can work that out," Link said.

He got up from his chair and folded the newspaper under his arm, holding his cup of coffee with the other hand. He stood up with the paper under his arm, the coffee in his hand and the phone in his ear. He stepped outside to the corner of 14th and E. He saw that a yoga class was just letting out two doors down. Women in yoga pants and athletic bras and men with their hair bunned up on top of their heads said their goodbyes to each other before they headed off to whatever sort of work it was that supported people who could afford to take an hour out of the middle of a workday morning for a yoga break.

He strolled past the yoga studio. He strolled past a used record store. He saw a box full of used albums for sale. He thumbed through while Angelina yammered away. He tuned her out. He came across a used Hank Williams. He saw it had "Your Cheatin' Heart" and "Hey, Good Lookin'" on it. He went into the store and bought the album. He pulled a twenty out of his wallet. He got five dollars in change. Used albums cost a lot these days.

"Why money of my they want?" Angelina went on.

It sounded to Link like she hadn't spoken English since the day she pleaded guilty in court.

"I live nice San Francisco people with, in while, buy nice dress and money save," she stumbled on. "That is crime? That make me bad person? Why you no want see me? What is it with you American peoples?"

Link couldn't speak for the non-natives., but he did have a couple of questions of his own.

Mainly, he wanted to know why she never returned his calls.

"I call you now back," she said.

Link understood that a month or two didn't register as a blip in the expanse of time. Unfortunately, he dealt in the realm of the earthly human condition. A man in his early 60s valued a month twice as much as a man in his early 30s. He didn't want to waste many more of them.

If that's how she wanted to play it – one month on, one off, as if she worked a deep-water oil rig in the Gulf of Mexico – fine. Just leave him out of it.

Angelina said she had taken a little vacation, to her favorite port of call, Lahaina.

"This news, this – events on my case – it make need me get away," she said.

Link retreated from the record store to Shine and the overstuffed chair where he again dropped his lanky frame.

"I got there and I go to relax my mind, and I how I want to do with this case," Angelina continued.

"So, what are you going to do with it?"

"Well, first, I must find out if I still have this lawyer," she said, of Jacob Dillon. "This government think I have money for pay my own lawyer now. He supposed to know today. I think he might should still be my lawyer. I want him for my lawyer. I cannot want my own lawyer to pay."

"You mean pay for your own lawyer?"

"Yes, that. I cannot pay for your own lawyer. My own lawyer. I need this government, to pay for this lawyer."

"I thought it was no big deal for you to pay for your own lawyer."

"It is, as you say, principle. They make case on me, they should pay for lawyer."

"That is an interesting concept. It probably won't help your case that you just spent a month in Hawaii."

"How should they know? How should that matter? Why should for I tell that? Why they find out?"

Link couldn't answer those questions intelligently, largely because he couldn't understand exactly what she was saying.

"When you can see me?" she asked.

Angelina's persistence started to make an impression. He asked her what time she was supposed to be in court. He entertained a vague hope that she might be available in the afternoon. He'd get a suite at the Sheraton.

"I think right now," she said. "I am in your city."

She did not sound at all frisky.

He gave her the Shine's coordinates.

A few minutes later, she pulled into an angled parking space on 14th Street, in a late-model black BMW 320i. The car didn't go with the neighborhood, where most everybody walked. He looked out the 14th Street picture window from Shine and saw her step out in the same sort of black jeans she wore in winter, cut a few inches higher at the ankle, and with a beige cotton pullover sleeveless top, cut enticingly low. Her outfit exposed a few square feet of milky white skin along the arms and shoulders. You saw it all over town in the early months of the Sacramento summer, when the women first shed their layers and had not yet gathered tan. Sacramento wasn't like L.A. where white people stayed brown all year. Or San Francisco, where they wore black year round, cover to cover.

He sat up straight when she walked in and spotted him. She took a chair on the other side of the end table between them.

In her hand, she held an 8 1/2-by-11-inch manila envelope.

"I don't see how you are going to convince the government that you still qualify for a public defender," Link told straight-faced Angelina, nodding toward her ride. Not much of a greeting on his part.

She made no attempt to put her seductive charms on display, either. This was a business meeting.

"I only lease car," she said. "They not know how I drive."

Link said nothing. Angelina made her case.

"Your government must pay for this lawyer. I am not the one who did make this case. This government make this case, so your government must provide my lawyer."

Link smiled and shrugged. The last thing he wanted to do was argue with her, or anybody else, over who should finance her legal representation.

"Maybe the Russian mob should pay for it," he said.

He looked her straight in the eye.

Angelina dirty-looked him hard. She could be abrupt. She looked like she could commit murder and not think twice.

She changed the direction of the conversation. This was a business meeting.

"I have something for you," she said.

She handed Link the envelope. He took his time opening it. He fumbled with the metal thingamajig with one hand while holding his newspaper with the other. He finally got it open.

He nearly broke out laughing when he looked at the contents: four glossy photographs, of her, in the nude.

He knew on sight that these pictures were legitimate, having seen her naked in person.

They could have been worth millions, except nobody picked up the terrific story coming out of the Sacramento federal courts about the knockout Russian Uber driver who got caught up in a Russian organized crime ring that slopped over into the Trump-Russia scandal.

Angelina appeared maybe 10 years younger in the photos, cellulite free, more muscular, maybe five pounds lighter, but the same long blonde hair parted down the middle, the same thin and angular face, the angry eyes slicing sharp off the glossy page – very similar to the pair she wore into Shine. The pictures all appeared to have been taken in the same shoot, in a studio, with grey umbrellas reflecting light off a green backdrop that came out grey in the pictures.

The studio gave the pictures a sheen of professionalism. The quality of the shots reflected the work of an amateur.

The first picture was a simple straight-on, of her standing straight up with her legs maybe a foot apart. Her unusually long arms and hands hung freely at her sides, her palms flush against her thighs. Her face contained no expression. Neither she nor the photographer did anything to enhance her natural beauty. They did nothing with her homicidal eyes.

The other shots were just as lousy – Link had been around enough to know good work from bad. Another frontal shot angled her slender hips slightly left to right, as if in a belated attempt to chastely avoid full-frontal nudity – which had been the featured attraction of the first photo, if only by default. This time, it looked like the photographer did try to bring something out in Angelina's face, but it was clear that she wasn't into being anything other than what she was: slightly perturbed. The third picture was a mirror of the second, although this time she feebly sought to portray an element of the flirtatious. The photograph looked phony and contrived, an embarrassment, Link thought, to whoever took it. In the final shabby effort, the shooter turned Angelina around with her hands on her hips, her shoulders veered around looking backward – again, with a completely unconvincing expression of sexuality. This picture accentuated a skinny bottom – probably her least compelling physical feature; it distracted from the best thing about her, which were her rippling triceps linked across a leanly-muscled back that exhibited strength and power, even in this horrible photo.

Link studied each of the pictures. He nodded. He told her: "Congratulations."

He handed the pictures back to her, or at least tried to. She refused to accept them. She got up from her chair to leave.

"You are to study these," she commanded. "And then you carve log, in my likeness."

Link couldn't hold back a laugh this time.

"You will be paid one million dollars."

Link did not spit up his coffee, but he stopped laughing. Angelina was not kidding. Angelina didn't kid about much of anything.

Angelina departed the Shine with a lengthy stride. He tried to process the brief encounter. He held the envelope in his hand and thought about throwing it in the trash. He would not sculpt her naked likeness. He would not sculpt her clothed. This would not be art. This would be an abomination.

She should have known Link would react in this fashion. He told her how uncomfortable he became after the *People* magazine publicity. Why would she even approach him with such a ridiculous proposal?

Link watched Angelina duck into her car, the two of them barely 20 feet away from each other, their eyes meeting through the window.

The look on Angelina's face reminded him of the one Mike Tyson wore in the seconds before he knocked out Larry Holmes.

All he could do was shake his head. She drove off, and after taking about five seconds to process the entire interaction, Link went back to reading his newspaper.

He got a kick out of the story about the attorney general, Jeff Sessions, who was lying again to Congress when he said it was a "detestable lie" that he had already lied to them – twice. His phone rang. Frankie Cameron had some news for him.

"Guess who just walked into the grand jury room," the reporter said.

"Angelina Puchkova?"

"Your prescience amazes me."

Link informed Frankie about his brief meeting with Angelina. He told him about the pictures. He told him about her demand and the big money she promised to deliver.

"Well, I've got another little piece of news, too," Frankie said.

"And that is?"

"There's a FISA warrant out on this case."

Link nodded to himself.

"As there should be," he responded. "As there should have been."

Frankie laid out for Link what his FBI sources laid out for him:

"Financial transaction records on everybody – Uncle Nikita, the old lady, your gal. Wire taps. Phone records. Phone surveillance. The works."

Link knew that Foreign Intelligence Surveillance Act investigations often swept in previously-uninvolved "U.S. persons." He qualified for that category.

He thought back to his second conversation with Angelina, at Jack's. From that point on, he surmised, they had his phone number. He figured that everything he'd ever said on the phone to her since then had been downloaded into some FBI agent's iPhone. Maybe everything he said, period.

If only he lived a more interesting life. It would have made their listening hours so much more entertaining.

All they'd get would be his increasingly preposterous conversations with art brokers.

Earlier in the day, he spoke with a representative for an actress he'd never heard of. He asked around the neighborhood and learned she was the female lead in "Curb Your Enthusiasm," which he'd watched for about a season before deciding the lead actor was not a very likable guy. He chose to spend no more time with him.

Link asked Frankie if he thought the FISA warrants had anything to do with the police on his front porch and their delivery of him to Detective Andrew Wiggins after the Kings' game. Link asked Frankie, "Are you going to put this in the paper?"

It sure looked like a story to Link: federal agencies obtaining a warrant to look into these Sacramento Russians, Angelina appearing that day in front of the grand jury, Kremlin money flooding the bank accounts of former Soviet soldiers.

"Not right now," the reporter answered. "The sources tell me the thing is getting way more complicated. In fact, they asked me to hold off on writing anything."

Frankie said the agents had no problem, however, about him reporting that Angelina had been subpoenaed to testify in front of the grand jury.

"They even tipped me off to her arrival, so I could get a picture," he said.

"She give you an envelope, too?"

"No, no. She was fully clothed. But she'll definitely up the click count, the way she looked. The story we did last month on her guilty plea, it didn't do shit online. Barely a thousand. Watch today, with the picture. I'll bet we get at least 10,000."

Frankie already gathered no-comments from the U.S. Attorney's Office, the FBI, and the Federal Public Defender's Office. He pulled everything out of the story he did on Angelina's court appearance in May. He didn't mention a word about FISA. He kept out all the pass-along information that Detective Wiggins gave to Link.

"I am identifying her as 'a Rancho Cordova woman'," Frankie said.

"Be sure to catch her on the way out," Link said. "You're going to need a shot of her car. It does not correspond to her plea of poverty."

"The BMW? I've already got her pulling into the H Street parking lot in it."

Link asked if he could see the pictures. Frankie obliged and sent them over text. Frankie captured Angelina in her full-blown petulance. She pouted. She looked put off by this rumpled little fellow who wore cargo pants and frayed ties and no sports coat, even in open court, who pestered her with his cell-phone camera.

Angelina never acculturated to American ways, but she knew enough about certain forms of expression, such raising a middle finger to signify displeasure with another's actions. Frankie of course got the picture of her flipping him off. It gave him and Link a nice laugh.

Frankie even shot a video of Angelina walking away from him, an action shot of her turning the corner onto I Street, just when a homeless Asian woman with a shopping cart who spent her days screaming at people coming in and out of the downtown jail across the street from the federal courthouse broke into the frame. Short and skinny, the homeless Asian woman hopped the curb and jammed the shopping cart right into Angelina's path. The Asian homeless woman screamed in the witness's face. The Asian homeless woman cut Angelina off on the sidewalk and slashed at the air with karate chops as if she was a Samurai warrior trying to take Angelina's head off.

"I need to see it," Link said.

"You're going to have to come over here then," Frankie told him. "I've got all this shit loaded into my computer and I don't have time to be sending shit to you. I'm on deadline. I'm always on deadline."

"Another side benefit of the new digital journalistic world." Eighteen blocks later, Link had pulled a chair up to Frankie's computer and the two were laughing their heads off over Angelina's confrontation with the homeless Asian woman.

They played it over and over again. "This is the one for the sculpture," Link said. "I've got to figure out how to get Shopping Cart Lady in there."

"That could be a challenge," Frankie said.

"For a million bucks, I think I could do it." Frankie showed Link the rest of his shots, all the way back to the top deck of the parking garage when Angelina was just stepping out of her car.

"Let me see that one up close," Link asked.

The picture showed what appeared to be a marking on the inside of Angelina's right ankle.

"I never noticed that before," Link said. "Can you blow it up?"

Frankie widened the shot with his thumb and index finger to

where the marking on her ankle took up the entire screen.

It appeared to be a tattoo, of a circle, half of it filled in with pure black ink, the other half left white.

16. OFF TO THE CONSULATE

"Don't ask me how I got it. All you need to know is, I got it."

Frankie Cameron threw down a transcript of Angelina Puchkova' grand jury testimony on Lincoln Adams' coffee table. They sat in the living room of Link's high-water Victorian on D Street.

The transcript was marked confidential. Frankie and Link were committing a federal crime just by possessing it. Neither Frankie nor Link were too concerned. Link was enhancing his appreciation of the transcript with a 22-ounce bottle of Bike Dog Mosaic Pale Ale. Frankie favored Knee Deep's Breaking Bud.

The transcript showed that Angelina had answered nothing. To every question put to her by Assistant United States Attorney Michael George, she responded:

"I refuse to answer on the grounds that it may incriminate me."

She wouldn't even admit that her true name was Angelina Ludmila Puchkova.

Probably because it was not. Apparently it was Olga Malvina Puchkova Leonova, or at least this was what George implied in his second question.

"A liar from the beginning," Frankie said.

The government grilled Angelina under this other name for more than an hour. The questioning revealed much about what it knew and what it didn't know, about her, and about her role in Sacramento's Russian underworld.

They got her birthdate down – July the 4th, 1986. They knew where she came from – a hospital on the outskirts of Novosibirsk. They knew where she went to college – Novosibirsk State University. They asked how it would incriminate her if she merely confirmed it.

"I refuse to answer," she said, "on grounds that it may incriminate me."

"I see," George said. "So, I take it you will not answer whether you majored in Rural Studies, on grounds that it would violate your Fifth Amendment rights against self-incrimination?"

Angelina confirmed nothing. She answered, "I refuse to answer on grounds that it may incriminate me."

She again asserted her Constitutional privilege when the prosecutor asked if she had ever entered the competition for Miss Novosibirsk State University in 2005, when she was in her sophomore year. She stayed quiet when asked if she won the contest, and whether she advanced to other pageants in other Russian cities, including Moscow. She took the Fifth when George asked her about her presence at the Moscow pageant with many national celebrities in attendance, including a war hero from the Afghanistan campaign, a Siberian homeboy named Capt. Anton Karuliyak. She refused to answer on grounds that it might incriminate her when George asked if she knew whether Karuliyak was from the same neighborhood in Novosibirsk, where they both grew up.

Angelina didn't answer anything. She declined to elaborate about immigration documents she signed. George showed her the papers, in which she identified herself in her immigration application as the maternal niece of Rancho Cordova resident Nikita Maslov. George asked about Mrs. Uncle Nikita. To answer that question, Angelina said, would violate her constitutional right against self-incrimination.

Frankie and Link wowed and whistled when George asked Angelina if it was true that Mrs. Uncle Nikita's maiden name was... Karuliyak, and if it was true that Mrs. Uncle Nikita was in fact the older sister of the former Soviet Army captain.

"I refuse to answer that question, on the grounds that it may incriminate me." Angelina dodged confirming information Frankie and Link already knew to be true.

The prosecutor pounded Angelina on her early history in America: a quick stop in Brighton Beach, a couple weeks in Omaha to break up the bus ride from New York City to Sacramento, her employment at Denny's, her job at Folsom Financial. He asked her if she came into the country on a student visa. He wondered if she'd been accepted into an agricultural studies program at the University of California at Davis. He wanted to know why she never enrolled when she made it into America.

"I refuse to answer that question on grounds that it may incriminate me," Angelina replied.

Why wasn't her visa revoked? How did she qualify for a green card? Why didn't she apply for American citizenship?

Same answer.

George implied in his questioning that she applied for and received unemployment benefits. He accused her of accepting Medicaid and food stamps. He suggested she got on Sacramento County general relief while she lived with Mr. and Mrs. Uncle Nikita.

"Isn't it true," the prosecutor asked, "that you applied for health benefits, under the Affordable Care Act?"

Angelina ducked the question: "I refuse to answer that question on the grounds that it may incriminate me."

Michael George jumped ahead to the night of January 6, 2017 – the night she picked up Link at the Indian college.

Last question:

"How did you know to pick up a Mr. Lincoln Adams on that particular evening?"

The question was pregnant with implication.

Angelina answered, "I refuse to answer, on the grounds that it may incriminate me."

Link and Frankie finished reading the transcript and drinking their 22-ouncers, and Frankie had Link's front doorknob in one hand and his car keys in the other on his way out when his cell phone interrupted him.

All Link heard on his end before the hang-up was "Yeah… yeah… yeah…" and finally, "Oh, really?"

All of a sudden the afternoon wasn't over.

"Get ready for a ride," Frankie told Link.

"OK. Where are we going?"

"Twenty-Seven Ninety Green Street," Link answered. "San Francisco."

Around 7 p.m., they crossed the Bay Bridge. The sun dropping between the 45-story Google apartment towers south of Market Street blinded them. Frankie swung north on what was left of the Central Freeway. He hung a left on Fell Street and turned right on Divisadero into Pacific Heights.

Frankie's sources had come across the Green Street address in an interesting context: while searching through California Department of Motor Vehicles computer records. They were backgrounding Angelina Puchkova and learned that she renewed her driver's license online. They traced the transaction from the DMV main frame to a computer located at 2790 Green Street in San Francisco.

Frankie knew the neighborhood a little bit. He wrote about a murder there once, years ago when he worked cops for the San Francisco Examiner. The unfortunate dead was some guy who sued everybody in town until he sued the wrong somebody and wound up getting shot and killed outside the house of a lawyer who helped him formulate his crackpot legal theories.

"The case of the vexatious litigant," Frankie called it.

Up to Green and left, and there it was, an eight-story brick building with a polished granite base and a sixty-million-dollar view that looked out over the Golden Gate Bridge, the Marin Headlands, and the expanse of the northern Pacific Ocean.

"Weird place to have your car registered to," Frankie said.

"Especially if it's a Toyota Corolla," added Link.

"And you're an Uber driver."

They drove past the building, to Lyon Street, and parked a couple blocks down. As they walked back to Green Street, it dawned on Frankie's faulty memory that he had been to this building once before – 27 years before, when he was at the *Ex*. It had been the site of a reunion of a couple of old Cold War buddies who got a lot of credit in the history books for ending it. Their names were Ronald Reagan and Mikhail Gorbachev, and only one of them was still in office when Frankie showed up on the sunny morning in June of 1990 with a thousand other reporters at the Russian consulate.

"Only time I ever saw a president live and in color," Frankie said, "even if he'd been out of office a couple years."

They walked up the steps to the front door and let themselves in. For a country that had succeeded in overthrowing the American government by installing its own agent into the White House, security seemed lax, though Frankie and Link didn't know they were being photographed by surveillance cameras.

Inside the front door, the consulate looked no different than the waiting room of a doctor's office. One thing made it different: the wall of bullet-proof glass that separated the visitors from the inside of Mother Russia's listening post in the western United States. They rang a bell for service. A few moments later, a tall, young man who looked to be in his mid-twenties, in a brown suit and short brown hair, greeted them. It looked like he hadn't been in the sun since the Gorbachev-Reagan meeting.

"Can I help you?" the young man asked, in perfect, unaccented English.

He stepped around the security glass, through a wood-paneled door, to greet his visitors with a polite handshake.

Link and Frankie didn't have an answer. They didn't know what they were doing there. They didn't know where they were even going until they arrived. They should have Googled it first. They would have learned that everybody in the building, including the polite young boy in front of them, had been declared persona non grata by the United States government. It would have been useful information. The reclassification was the official U.S. government response to the Russian invasion of the American presidential electoral process. It came straight from the deep state; Trump had no control over it.

Frankie and Link looked at each other. Link shrugged in deference to Frankie, as if to say, you figure it out. You're the one who dragged me over here. I'm just along for the ride.

Frankie did the only thing he knew how to do in circumstances such as these, when he was working a story. He knew not to bullshit anybody. He knew he was a terrible bullshitter. He knew his inability to bullshit properly was probably why he still worked a courthouse in his mid-50s instead of pontificating in academic settings or on television about the great value he had added to the journalistic profession.

"Uh, yeah," he started out, to the baby-faced inquisitor.

He gave the kid his name and affiliation. He told him he'd been working on a story out of Sacramento. He said the story related to the eruption of mortgage fraud cases from Bakersfield to Yuba City over the past decade. He called the story a byproduct of the Great Recession of 2008.

The Russian greeter looked at Frankie with an expression that suggested he had no idea what Frankie was talking about. The greeter exhibited a tic of fake curiosity. The tic told Frankie that the Russian greeter was lying when he said:

"I haven't heard about that, but go on."

Frankie picked up the story with a dissertation about Angelina's role in the fraud. The Russian greeter nodded. The greeter acted as if he was just taking it all in. He pulled out a notepad and asked: "And her name, again, is what?" Frankie told him both of her names, Angelina Puchkova and Olga Malvina Puchkova Leonova. The brown-suited Russian greeter wrote them both down in his notebook. The greeter then asked: "Your name again is what? And you work where? And can I get a phone number and your other additional personal information."

No problem with the name, *Beacon*, and phone numbers. Frankie did not provide his Social Security, bank account, or credit card numbers. He assumed they already had them all, as well as any other item of his personal identification and any scrap of public record recorded on him in any public or private computer database. What they didn't have, Frankie knew they were now in the process of retrieving, through Spokeo, as they spoke. Or even deeper data banks.

"This Angelina of whom you speak," the young man said, "why are you coming here to ask us about her?"

"Well," Frankie said. He stalled for time. He tried to make sure he wasn't about to burn any sources. "We've got reason to believe that she may have been doing some work out of here."

"In what capacity?"

"I don't know – chauffeur? Maid?"

"Art broker," Link chimed in, his first words since he and Frankie walked in the door.

The Russian greeter smiled, as if he knew what Link was talking about. The knowing smile unnerved the sculptor, who prided himself on almost always keeping himself nerved.

"Personally," the greeter said, "I do not know the name, but I will make some inquiries, and I assure you, I will have somebody get back to you."

The Russian greeter walked to the front door of the consulate as if to show his visitors out. They got the cue.

"Oh, and Mr. Adams," the man said as Frankie and Link were leaving, "I am a great admirer of your work."

Link rolled his eyes. Link thanked the lad. He had never given the greeter his name.

Frankie and Link walked down the front steps of the consulate. They stepped off the porch where Reagan and Gorbachev stood more than a quarter-century ago, where Reagan had waved to the reporters wedged into a media pen across the street.

"That was a little scary, him knowing who you are, don't you think?" Frankie asked.

Link was used to it. He never should have consented to the *People* magazine piece.

Frankie and Link turned up Baker Street, towards Union, on the west side of the consulate, when Link saw a man working on a little construction project. It looked like the man was framing an awning over a side door.

Link knew he had seen this carpenter before. He stepped up his pace. Frankie followed suit. Link did not want to been seen by the woodworker, whom he recognized as Gordon Kahananui. He, along with his wife, Leia, had been kind enough to put up him and Angelina in their gingerbread-like Inner Sunset home while Link and Angelina gave the bed in the upstairs guest room a workout.

"What's the hurry?" Frankie asked.

As soon as they got back in their car, Link filled him in on the carpenter they had just seen at the consulate, how he owned the house where Link had spent a couple weeks sleeping with Angelina.

Granted, Gordon was laboring only as a common craftsman and not as a techno-operative. He was not an intelligence agent. He did not establish GPS coordinates on fiber-optic cable nodes and flash them up to spy planes that received their overflight direction from the consulate. He wasn't out to steal Silicon Valley's trade secrets. Maybe his carpentry work for the Russians was completely innocent. Maybe it was coincidental, inconsequential. Maybe Link was being a dick when he didn't stop to say hi to the guy that helped arrange his sleepovers with Angelina.

"I think we need to look into this further," Link said.

He punched an Tenth Avenue address into Frankie's navigation system.

"Go there," he instructed Frankie.

About 20 minutes later, they parked a half-block down from Gordon and Leia's house in the Inner Sunset.

"And, we are here – why?" asked Frankie.

Link explained that this was the house where Angelina stayed when she split from Sacramento a few months earlier. This was the house where the carpenter from the consulate lived.

"I'm not so sure I want to be here," Frankie said.

Link told him it was no problem, that Gordon was as cool as they come.

"Then why did you damn near run out of there without saying hi to him?"

"It wasn't the time or the place to say hello to anybody," Link responded. "Let's see what happens here."

"Let's see if what happens here? If this guy's a problem at all, I'm not so sure this is a good idea."

"Maybe you'll get a story out of it."

"I've already got a story."

Frankie set his reluctance aside and accompanied Link on the half-block walk back to the golden house with the Hawaiian greeting signs. They walked up the steps to the front door where they could see Leia sitting in a chair watching the Giants game that had just come on TV. She got up to answer the door and broke into a big smile when she saw Link.

Leia hugged him warmly. They'd only known each other for a few weeks but it felt like longer. Same with Gordon, whose shared status as indigenous peoples gave them an intuitive bond.

"Where have you been? Where has Angelina been? Gordon and I became very fond of you two, and then you're both gone."

"I'm so very sorry I have not kept in touch," Link said.

"Oh, don't worry about it," said Leia, with a wave of her hand. "But I'm sure you didn't come here to see me. I take it you're here for Angelina?"

"Not exactly," Link said. "But kind of."

Leia invited Link and Frankie inside and offered them a beer or to make some tea or to throw a frozen pizza in the oven. She told them she hadn't seen Angelina since the day she took off for court with Link in those expensive clothes.

"She came back that night to get her stuff, and she left Gordon a contact number at the office where she worked," Leia said. "She seemed a bit beside herself, for the first time. She'd always been so nice. It's not like she was mean. Just – it was as if something bad had happened and she had to leave."

"Office where she worked?" Link asked.

"Yes. It's over on Green Street. I'm not exactly sure what she did, or even where she normally lived – it was in Sacramento, wasn't it?" Leia said. "I know she drove some for Uber, but I think she had another job at this office. I'm not exactly sure what it was, or what she did, but I know that a couple times when Gordon was between jobs, looking for carpentry work, she arranged some projects for him at the Green Street office. The money was really good."

"Cool," Link said. "You know, though, that the office is the Russian consulate?"

"We never really asked. All we know is she was always very nice to us from the time we met her in Lahaina. She dropped by regularly, gave us presents, always had a case of Bud Light for Gordon and a nice sauvignon blanc for me. We were a little surprised when she asked us if she could stay in our guest room for a while, but we were happy to put her up, and she was always very nice, and she was never nicer than during the time when you stayed here, Link." She paused, as though wondering more for the first time why exactly Link and this stranger were there. "Is everything OK?"

Link introduced Leia to his reporter friend Frankie and filled her in on the status of his relationship, such as it was, with Angelina.

Sitting on the couch in Leia's living room, she got up from her chair in front of the TV and turned off the Giants game.

"I'm sorry it didn't work out between you two," Leia said. "I'm not an expert or anything, but I had a sense that you two seemed to be good for each other." She seemed to sense Link's discomfort so she turned her warm smile toward the reporter. "So, Frankie, tell me more about this story you're working on."

Frankie came off sheepish when approaching people who were not regularly part of the news, people who really were not part of the story and who were not public figures, even though they were the public. He could never just brace them like he was a cop. He had to hold back his intensity. He didn't want to overwhelm anybody.

Frankie explained his federal court reporter beat and how he had come onto the stories about the hackers and the mortgage crookery, about the existence of the Russian organized crime operation, how recent political events had made it all more interesting, and how Leia's house guest was right in the fucking middle of all of it.

"Wow," was all Leia could say.

He pulled out his cell phone and called up his story from a few days earlier, about Angelina showing up at the courthouse for her grand jury testimony.

He handed the phone to Leia, and her brightness continued to dampen as she read the story.

"Oh, my God," she said. "I had no idea." She put a hand to her mouth. "Am I in trouble?"

Frankie looked at Link, who looked back at him, before they both looked at Leia, who looked to be a little bit scared.

"I'm not a cop, but I can't see how you would be," Frankie said. "You're just an unbelievably nice person who was very nice and kind to a woman who happens to be a Russian spy, an international criminal, or a gangster, or whatever the hell she is."

The three of them laughed hollowly.

Leia's mind jumped ahead. "What about Gordon?" she asked. "Is he safe working over there?"

Frankie told her that in his limited understanding as a federal court reporter, he had no reason to think Gordon was in any danger.

"So, anyway," he said. "I'm just working this story, and I guess I'd just like to get your sense of her."

"Angelina? You're not going to quote me, are you? Or use my name?"

"Of course not," Frankie said. "There's really no need to quote you, I don't think. I'm not sure how this information will fit into the coverage we've done, or that we're planning. In fact, we weren't planning on coming here at all until Link recognized Gordon at the consulate."

"Well," Leia went on. "It was actually quite funny how we first met her. She was alone in the bar at Lahaina, sitting at the table next to us – we go there all the time, to visit Gordon's family. That's where we met, actually, me and Gordon, at the Pioneer Inn. We had smiled and said hello to her, and then during a break in the music, the ukulele player starts hitting on her, and she was not comfortable with it. She said she was with us, and we acted the part, and the fellow backed off, easy enough, and we got to talking to her and she said she was from Sacramento, and so of course we said, 'Oh, we live in San Francisco,' and she said she actually had a lot of business in San Francisco and that she would like to keep in touch, and so we did. We've never gone to see her in Sacramento, though, and she never invited us. We were fine with her dropping in and seeing us every once in a while. We told her as long as she was in the city, if she had business here, she would be welcome to spend the night, too, and she began to take us up on the offer. She always offered to pay, and of course that was stupid – we liked having her around. She was always very pleasant and interesting."

"Did she have any, habits?" Frankie asked. "Did she ever, like, say, 'Excuse me, Mrs., Mrs....' "

"Kahananui. But Please, call me Leia."

"Did she ever say anything like, 'Excuse me, Mrs. Kahananui, but I'm helping the Russians hack the Democratic National Committee headquarters, and is it OK if I use your WiFi?' "

"No!" Leia laughed. "Only sometimes she'd show up late at night and work upstairs on her computer. Clicking away, 2, 3, 4 o'clock in the morning. I'd hear her when I went to bed after the late-night TV talk shows, or Gordon would hear her when he got up early in the morning to go to work. She never told us what she was working on, and it really wasn't any of our business. Then she brings you around, Link. That was kind of a surprise. But we enjoyed your company very much and we thought that you softened her up a little bit – she was always so serious, though always pleasant. We thought you were good for her, and we were happy to have you."

Leia stopped to take a sip of her white wine and looked at Link again.

"It's really too bad that didn't work out," she said pointedly.

"We had our fun," Link said. "It was time to move on."

Frankie and Link thought it was time to get going too.

"You're sure we're OK?" Leia asked as she walked them back to the door. "You're sure it's OK for Gordon to be working over there? The FBI's not going to be knocking on our door, are they?"

"Probably not," Frankie said. "But your info sure is interesting. I could pass it along to my sources. Somebody's got to do their work for them."

This time only Frankie laughed.

"If you think it would be good for the country..." Leia said hesitantly.

"You know, it just might be. But I don't want it to look like I'm working for the FBI, because I'm not. What I do is write stories, and these details you gave us are pretty interesting. Maybe I can use them?"

"Mmmm," Leia said. "I'll think about it."

"Thank you, Ms. Kana...Kaha..."

"Leia," Leia said.

"Leia. It was great meeting you, Leia," Frankie said.

She hugged them both as they walked out the door.

"How's my otter coming?" she asked Link.

"Almost done with it," he lied. "Tell Gordon I said hello."

They were all laughing when Leia closed the door.

Link and Frankie got back in their car and headed down Tenth Avenue to Irving, and then left to Stanyan across the lower Haight and right on Oak Street through the Panhandle.

Right about when they were getting back on to the Central Freeway, they realized that they were being followed.

17. SLOW SPEED CHASE

Frankie knew a little bit about deceptive driving. Back when he reported in L.A., he staked out a Colombian drug dealer's money house with a team of undercover narcs. They sat every day for a week. They sat until the garage door finally opened. A seven-car chase team followed the car all over Bell and Bell Gardens, Monterey Park, Alhambra and Temple City, back to Bell, and then onto the Long Beach Freeway to the San Bernardino Freeway, to the I-15 split to Victorville, towards Las Vegas. They followed the car past Apple Valley. They said to hell with it when it passed Barstow. They turned around and drove home.

Now Frankie and Link were the chased.

Just to make sure he was being followed, Frankie exited the freeway at Van Ness and scooted down Market to the Castro and down Castro to 24th Street and through Noe Valley to Mission and north again to 5th Street. A white, late-model Impala stayed with them.

"Might as well head back to Sacramento," Link said, balanced detachment and everything else that had happened the past few weeks keeping him apathetic. "If we're going to get killed, I'd rather it be closer to home."

Frankie nodded. His job had put him in more than a few tight spots like this one.

About the time they hit Berkeley on Interstate 80, Frankie's cell phone rang. Violating the California Vehicle Code, he dug into his left front pants pocket for his phone. When he saw the number, he groaned:

"Holy shitfuck."

Link had been fiddling with the ESPN app on his phone, to get an update on the Dodgers. They were beating the Mets, 12-0, for their sixth straight win and their 12th in the last 13 games.

"It's the damnedest thing," Link said.

"Being followed by a couple of people who probably want us dead?"

"I was talking about the Dodgers' winning streak."

"Fuck off," Frankie said. "How the hell did you ever become a Dodger fan, anyway?

"I've always had a great appreciation for Jackie Robinson," Link said, "since I saw 'The Jackie Robinson Story' when I was young. I also liked Walter Alston. He reminds me of the Dalai Lama."

"Give me a fucking break."

Link switched the conversation back to the matter at hand.

"Who called?"

"That was my FBI source. They might have gotten around to reading the story we had in the paper the other day on the grand jury."

"I assume this is the source who leaked you the transcript?"

"I didn't say that."

"Why else would he be upset?"

"Who said he's upset?"

"I believe your exact words when you saw the telephone number on your screen were 'Holy shitfuck.' That made me think that you think his calling you is a problem."

"It is."

"It's not my position to tell anybody what to do, but I would recommend that you call him back."

"Why would you assume it's a 'him'?"

"I would recommend, then, that you call him or her back."

Frankie and Link's back and forth persisted all the way to Vacaville. Frankie looked in the rear-view mirror. The late-model sedan remained on their tail.

"What the fuck," Frankie said. "I'll call her."

He held the wheel with one hand and dialed his phone with the other. He did his dialing with his right thumb.

Link listened in on half the conversation.

"Hey . . . Yeah . . . Oh really? . . . That is good to know . . . You know, I think they found us . . . In fact, they are on our ass as we speak . . . Cannot tell what they look like, and we don't recognize the car . . . Hold on, I'll see what we can do."

Frankie held the phone away from his ear and turned to Link to ask a favor.

"Hey, Link," he said. "Could you possibly get the license plate number on the car behind us?"

"I'll try," Link said.

He unbuckled his seat belt. It wasn't easy, but he climbed over the seat and poked his head up as best as he could over the rear dash to get the best view possible under the difficult circumstances. These kinds of maneuvers weren't so easy for him anymore.

"Can't make it out," Link said. "Too dark."

Frankie told the voice on the other end that he could not get the license number on the car.

"Oh. OK," he said. "We'll be careful . . . If they're still on us as we get closer, we'll give you a call . . . OK, that would be great, too. Sure. Thank you so much. And . . . Oh. Yikes. I am sorry to hear that . . . Yes. We will be careful. And thanks again for the warning. Er, I mean, the warnings . . . Right, right, this call never took place."

Link looked up from his phone and said "My God," in a tone that suggested the president had been shot.

"What?"

"Corey Seager just hit his third home run, and it's only the fifth inning. He may break Ruth's record tonight."

"Fuck you," Frankie said again. "And it's not Ruth's record anymore. It's Barry's."

"Didn't he take steroids?"

"By the way, Brilliant, you might want to know. That's the Russian spy team that's following us."

"Interesting. How do you know?"

"I guess the FBI picked up some intercepts off their FISA phone taps, after we left. They had us at that woman's house, coming out of it."

"Who had us?"

"The Russian spies."

"Are they planning on killing us?"

"I don't really know what their intentions are, but I think we'll be OK."

Right about then, Frankie noticed the red and blue flashers in his rear-view mirror. They looked to be about two car lengths back. The late-model Impala was now sandwiched between Frankie and Link, and what they made out to be a California Highway Patrol cruiser.

The First Year

By the time they reached the landmark Milk Farm road sign near Dixon, the cops had pulled the spies over. Link and Frankie laughed their heads off, all the way to Benny's.

The boys had pre-ordered their beers and made another call on the way to the bar. Jimmy Reilly, the night man in Benny's, popped a Sierra and poured a Racer by the time Frankie and Link hit the rail.

It was getting close to 11 o'clock. Benny's was changing on the fly. The blue collars from happy hour gave way to the first wave of hipsters and cranksters, part-time burglars, smokers, shooters and sniffers who filtered into the bar after most of America had gone to bed.

Link kept peeking at the door. Eventually, the person he was waiting for arrived.

"Nice joint you guys hang at," Detective Andrew Wiggins said, as he slid into the stool on the other side of Link. "Good thing I'm carrying."

He patted the revolver holstered on his hip.

Wiggins didn't need the gun. He had the wrong take on Benny's. He perceived it to be a dangerous joint, based on a homicide he worked outside Benny's a couple years earlier. A drunken gang banger argued with everybody in the place one night until somebody knocked him on his ass. Om and Jimmy Reilly conducted a thorough investigation and kicked the gang banger out. The gang banger didn't like the verdict. He stuck around outside. He waited for the guy who put him on the ground. Out came the KO artist. The gang banger lunged at him with a knife. The KO artist had a knife of his own and knew what to do with it.

"Best part about the case," Wiggins told Link and Frankie, "is when I'm going through the night's receipts, I come across your names."

Wiggins laughed to himself.

"I could have had you all on the stand, but the DA didn't file anything," Wiggins said. "Justifiable homicide."

Link turned to the matter at hand. He asked Wiggins:

"So, what do we know?"

Link had called Wiggins from the road, after the Russians got pulled over back around Dixon. He thought Wiggins might have some more information, which he did. Frankie's sources didn't drink. Wiggins did. He agreed to meet them at Benny's.

He greeted Link warmly. He said nothing to Frankie.

"Him being here is a problem," Wiggins told Link. "It blows my plausible deniability if I get braced about talking to reporters."

"I'll move down a seat," Frankie said.

He moved down two.

As Link and Frankie had suspected, their visit to the consulate set off some alarms – from San Francisco to the Kremlin to Novosibirsk. The heightened electronic activity detected from inside 2790 Green Street woke up the FBI monitors. They alerted the counter-espionage unit, which picked up the spies coming out of the consulate. The CEU reported this to the main office in San Francisco, who had no idea who the two dumbshits following Link and Frankie were. The main office in San Francisco had no idea who Link and Frankie were. But they caught up quickly.

It worked out well for them. Link and Frankie brought the spies into the open.

Word of Frankie's feeble counter-surveillance driving maneuver provided agents with some decent evening entertainment. His inexpert driving ability made things easy for the spies, the feds, the California Highway Patrol. It made it easy for everybody.

It took the feds about a minute to catch up to the two-car caravan. They could have made the stop themselves, anytime, but didn't want to blow their cover. They turned the whole thing over to the Chippies.

"What was their probable cause for the stop?" Frankie asked.

The question irked Detective Wiggins.

"I told you he was a problem," Wiggins said to Link. "First of all, it's a dumbshit question. Who gives a fuck what their probable cause was? Second of all, I can't respond to anything he says. I probably shouldn't even be in the same room as him. So if you want anything answered, you're going to have to do the asking."

Frankie remembered the rules and shut his mouth.

"What was their probable cause?" Link asked.

"Asshole," Wiggins answered. "But since you asked, I'll tell you. They were going 66 in a 65."

The detective said the CHP couldn't find a reason to arrest the pair. Besides, the two men had diplomatic immunity.

"But they did find them with all this electronic spy crap that the cops confiscated," Wiggins said. "Stuff where they could download all your phone contacts from a car-length away. Listening devices, bugs of every stripe. Cameras that could take pictures through walls. Shit, they could read your mind with this shit."

"Lucky for me, I have no mind," Link said.

"It's your strongest quality," Frankie interjected.

"You're going to have to shut him up, or I'm out of here," the detective said.

"Tell you what," Frankie said – to Link. "I'm beat. I'm going to leave you two alone. I'm the one who is out of here."

Frankie said goodbye to Link and flashed a dirty look at Wiggins.

"Once again, my instincts were right – reporters are assholes," Wiggins said.

Jimmy Reilly brought Wiggins a scotch and soda. The drink seemed to mellow him out some.

"I don't want to seem rude, but I've got to protect myself here," Detective Wiggins said. "If my department finds out I'm giving stuff to you, I'm finished."

He sipped his drink. He told Link without prompting:

"I'm talking to you as a favor for a friend of mine in the bureau who wants all this shit out but doesn't want it to come back on him," he said. "Besides, I got a little piece of the case myself, thanks to that phony missing person's call."

"Phony?"

"As the day is long," Wiggins said. "Your girl…"

"Why does everybody call her 'my girl'? "

"Angelina was never missing. Her family stiffed in the call. Which, from our standpoint, turned out to be terrific. Once we got done rubber-hosing you, we launched an investigation into them. How do you think I'm still on the case? It actually worked out pretty well. The feds eventually put me on their federal task force. I get information, I give it to you, and then you give it to that Cameron guy. My hands are clean. I didn't leak a thing, and we still stir things up."

Link told Wiggins he thought Frankie was doing pretty well with his own sources.

"It's not every reporter, I'm told, who can come up with secret grand jury transcripts," Link said.

"That one really pissed them off in fed-land," Wiggins said. "They are going to get to the bottom of it."

Link was still trying to regain his center after the revelation about the missing person's report.

"She was never missing?"

"Nope."

"What could have motivated them to screw with me?"

"Don't know. Don't care. All we know is they phonied up a police report, and now we've got probable cause to tear them to shreds."

"Interesting," Link said.

"What?"

"That she never was missing"

"Why?"

"Because she always acted like she was."

18. THE ANGELINA FILE

Frankie's federal sources invited him into their offices the next day. Purpose of meeting: leaking more information on Angelina Puchkova. They seemed to be getting the hang of this.

A few hours later, Frankie leaked some information of his own. Location: Benny's back porch, the shaded, concrete patio of the once-great newspaper bar.

Summer had scorched into Sacramento on a flamethrower.

Link had one question:

"We couldn't find a place with air conditioning?"

"I thought a secure location was more important," Frankie said.

"The Cathedral of the Blessed Sacrament would have worked."

"Stop your whining."

The deal was this:

"OK, your gal was a beaut – is a beaut," Frankie said. "I think the only thing she told you about herself that is not a lie is that she's Uncle Nikita's niece."

"Which makes her what to Anton Karuliyak?"

"What are you talking about?"

"If she is Uncle Nikita's niece, and Mrs. Uncle Nikita is married to Uncle Nikita, and Mrs. Uncle Nikita's brother is Anton Karuliyak, what does that make 'my girl' to Anton Karuliyak?"

"Would you believe, lover?"

Frankie's suggestion stopped Link like a Sonny Liston jab. Frankie's suggestion left Link speechless. It took a minute for Link to regain his center.

"Go on," Link finally managed to say.

"Let's start with Uncle Nikita's wife. There's more to her than just being Karuliyak's sister. She basically ran his Sacramento operation. My people tell me she may have had authority for the entire western region of the United States, except for Los Angeles. Alana Cosmenko and every other manager of every single mortgage fraud caper – there were dozens and dozens of them. Hundreds maybe. They all reported to her."

"So, what was she doing in the courtroom the day of Angelina's court appearance, if she's such a big shot?"

"Making sure Angelina stayed on the reservation."

"What is that supposed to mean, 'staying on the reservation?' Is that one of your white boy expressions?"

Frankie grimaced as he remembered who he was speaking to and moved on quickly.

"Well, apparently Angelina had been wavering. Apparently, you had more of a hold on her than they expected."

"Me?"

"Yeah, you did. They didn't think that in the midst of her seduction of *usted* that she would actually feel an iota of anything for you. But she did."

Link smiled. He felt a flicker of warmth. "I guess that's good to know," he said.

Frankie popped his bubble: "She got over it soon enough," he said. "You remember that tattoo on her ankle that caught our attention?"

"Yeah," Link answered.

"It's the mark of the Russian organized crime group."

"*Vor v zakone?*"

"She was an associate from way back in her teenage years."

Link nodded, unsurprised.

"Apparently she came from very bad blood," Frankie continued. "Her father was a lifelong criminal, a thief and a murderer who had been sentenced to life in prison, back when the *vor* was still the all-powerful force of the prison system. He was like a captain in the organization, maybe higher. When he was inside, he got a female guard to fall for him. She works it out for them to have some private time, which wasn't hard, in that he damn near controlled the place. Next thing you know, boom – the girl guard is with child, a girl child, and in due time little Olga Malvina Leonova is born in Novosibirsk."

"I recognize that name."

"Mom's brother just happens to be Uncle Nikita, and he is drafted into the Soviet Army and winds up in a unit in Afghanistan in a unit commanded by Capt. Anton Karuliyak, who also has relatives in prison who are hooked up with the *vor*. They know Angelina's sperm donor."

"Mr. Leonovo, I presume."

"Correct. And he has a little problem in prison. Things change after the collapse of the Soviet system. The country falls into chaos. The prisons empty out of *vor* after *vor* after *vor*. These are the old-timers, Angelina's dad's guys."

"Seriously, does he have a name?"

"They didn't tell me, and I didn't ask. I just presume the last name is Leonovo, because that's what the feds have for your gal's true identity. I don't know where she got 'Puchkova.' But her biological dad, whatever his name is, he's too much of a badass to catch any kind of a break, and all the old-timers get let loose, and now he's a general in the gulag without an army. The new Turks, they don't like his attitude, his big-man swag. They show him it's a whole new game. He doesn't want to play, so they stick a fork in him. Literally. In the neck."

"And?"

"He's done. Murdered. Dead. So much for him. Right around this time, not long after the war, Karuliyak transitions into civilian life and jumps whole hog in with the *vor*, right about when the goofballs in the military tried to overthrow Yeltsin. Now Uncle Nikita, he is not exactly a great catch, him being damaged goods from his problems associated with manning the artillery battery. But Karuliyak knows him, and the *vors* think Uncle Nikita, as damaged goods, makes for a perfect candidate to apply for a move to the United States. So Karuliyak has his sister marry him. They make the move to the U.S. and in a matter of days Mrs. Uncle Nikita is running every chop shop from Rancho Cordova to North Highlands to West Sac. Only problem is, Uncle Nikita's sister – Angelina's mother, the ex-prison guard, the lonely widow – is killed in a car crash in Novosibirsk. Angelina's – I mean Olga's – closest living relative is way out yonder in Rancho Cordova, so Karuliyak, being the good *vor* that he is, takes responsibility for the upbringing of a devoted member's daughter. Within a couple years of the end of the Afghan war, he becomes the king of Novosibirsk, and she's like his kid, and she lives very well, and she is exposed to drug dealing, and theft, and political influence, and she finds it all to be pretty exciting, and maybe she works a couple angles for the mob. She gets a little older, she grows up, and she goes to college, and she becomes a beauty queen, and there is plenty of evidence that she and Karuliyak become, shall we say, involved. About the time she turns 20, they arrange her passage to Sacramento, to do whatever she can to help out the family business."

"That is a heart-warming story."

"We're just getting started. So, now they're all over here, running their scams, and they're doing pretty well, when all of a sudden, Russia invades Ukraine and declares eminent domain over Crimea. This creates a political problem for Putin and an economic one for his oligarchic asshole buddies. They can't do shit with their money, and they are really pissed at what's going on with Obama, and they know it's only going to get worse with Hillary, and you know what happens next."

"I do read the papers, but I have to say, this is all getting a little hard to believe."

"Come on, you read the Steele dossier. The Russians throw in with Trump, of course. You know they had him on the hook since 2013, at least, if Christopher Steele is to be believed. Plus, he wants to build his hotel in Moscow, and they want to be helpful and all, so they start making the moves to get him elected president of the United States. They come up with their idea for the voter registration hack, the Cambridge Analytica data mine, the Facebook ad buys. All they need to make it work is a little bit of loose cash. But they can't wire it into the U.S. anymore, so what do they do?"

"You tell me."

"They scan the rolls for selected Soviet Army veterans living in the United States scattered around the country – this country – who are on pensions, and they ramp up their payments from a few hundred dollars a month to a few thousand. And just to make sure they don't get caught short, the Russians work something out with the *vor* network that had already proven its value, on mortgage fraud, and they get creative, and the group in Sacramento come up with the credit card-school kids' thing – which Angelina, we now know, was a part of."

"First I've heard of that. I don't believe I read her name in any of your stories during the Mazmonyan trial."

"You did not, mainly, because I did not know. And I did not know because she was never identified in any court papers as being involved. You'll recall that case got filed right about the time that Alana Cosmenko group hit critical mass while the feds kept Angelina on ice. They were still hopeful then that she would flip on Karuliyak. No way that was ever going to happen. At least not then, and apparently not now."

"So what did she have to do with the credit card case?"

"Well, she got into the United States on a student visa – she hadn't quite graduated from Novosibirsk State. She enrolled at Sacramento State…"

"I thought she enrolled at UC Davis."

"She did, but she blew it off, and didn't go to Sac State until later. She took classes there for years, taking like three units a semester, and she's working at Denny's, and she does her straw buyer thing for Alana Cosmenko, and when they crank up the credit card scam and they steal the Social Security numbers from the high school kids, she takes a few of the identities and opens up the bank accounts in their names, and then she helps Mazmonyan with the first couple of cash withdrawals – basically shows the numbskull how to do it – once they start making charges on the credit cards. She delivers the money to Mazmonyan and Uncle Nikita, who sit on it in safe houses until Karuliyak comes around and makes his collections."

"Amazing that Karuliyak ever came around at all, that he was even in the country at all."

"You could say they were pretty arrogant. But they did get a few million bucks out of it before the feds got onto them. And between that and the pension padding, they made more than enough to pay for the election rigging from this side of the ocean. Them and who knows how many more Anton Karuliyaks and Alana Cosmenkos and Uncle Nikitas and Olga Angelinas they've got running around the country."

"So, the mystery is solved."

"That end of it, anyway."

"What is left?"

"Just a minor matter."

"And that is?"

"You."

"Me?"

"Let me explain."

Frankie told Link that almost from the beginning, which began sometime in the 1980s, Soviet and Russian spies had infiltrated Silicon Valley. They stole secrets from the high-tech elite. They figured out their codes. They copied their patents.

They knew how to find out anything about anybody, thanks to a world wired into the Silicon Valley main frame. You download an app, they download everything in the world that there is to know about you. They loved apps. They loved companies that made apps. They loved people who used apps. Once they stole your identity, their favorite thing was to dig into your apps. They knew to be gentle. They knew not to overdo it. They knew they could have their way with you in so many ways. They used them without you knowing you were being used. They used them to know what you were doing. They used them to know where you were going. They used them to know what you were reading. They used them to know what you were thinking.

They could change your social media message to the world. They could change and unchange your schedule. They could defriend your wife. They could run your parking tab into the millions. They could delete the Rolling Stones from your iTunes. They could replace them with Dino, Desi and Billy. They could alter your opinion of a hotel from five-star into a dump. They could edit your restaurant reviews. They could use your name to set up your account with the local newspaper and write insane things in the comments section at the end of an article. They could make you look like genius. They could make you look like an idiot. And you'd never even know it.

Frankie now told Lincoln Adams how they used his phone to throw him into the middle of a mess.

"They had you wired, man," Frankie told him. "Even before the election, they knew every move you made."

Link laughed at what he perceived to be their waste of time.

"What in the world would they find interesting about me?"

"I don't know, but I do know that every time you withdrew money from the bank, charged a beer on your credit card, every time you went to see the Mavericks at the Crest, every time you went on Facebook..."

"Which was never."

"Every time you did shit, they tracked it. They knew what

176

movies you saw, if you charged the ticket at the theater. What TV shows you liked."

Link nodded.

"I'm sure they knew where I liked to drink," he said.

"Absolutely."

"And whom I chose to drink with."

"As a matter of fact, I did get caught up in the web of your collateral contacts. But I don't carve logs. They didn't give a fuck about me, until I did that story on the Mazmonyan trial. Then they start running all my shit. It didn't take them long to put you and me together."

"How?"

"Bank records. Credit checks. Credit card histories. Same-day charges between you and me at Benny's, mainly. Pretty interesting that you got a phone call from your gal on the same day the Mazmonyan trial story ran."

Link tried his best to remember everything he'd done for the several months that he had been electronically monitored. Nothing jumped out at him. He remembered one thing: his increasing irritability with his increasing fame. How could that be of any interest to anybody?

"The good news here," Frankie said, "is that the FBI took out its FISA warrant three years ago, after the shit hit the fan in the Crimea and Ukraine. They were one step behind everything the Russians took out on you."

Frankie took a moment to let that one sink in.

"For your information," he said, "you came back clean."

"A testament to how boring I am."

"It shouldn't come as a surprise to you why the Russians were interested in you."

"Let me guess."

"The logs, of course. What else is there about you that would cause anybody to give a shit?"

"Good point. So I guess Putin wanted me to carve him riding bare shirted and bareback through the Russian countryside?"

"Good guess. But, no. Putin doesn't give a rat's ass about you."

"Well, we know that Angelina wanted one, of herself, for somebody who was willing to pay an awful lot of money."

"You're getting warmer."

A circus-style big top shaded most of Benny's back porch, and it gave cover to Link and Frankie while they sweltered in the late afternoon heat. Link still favored black jeans and a black tee shirt, with his layered hair flowing from beneath a white straw cowboy hat. Frankie accommodated the heat in shorts, a short-sleeved shirt, and flip flops, his usual evening wear.

Link scooted his chair out of the shade and stretched out his arms and took off his hat to feel the sun on his chest and face.

"You're right," he told Frankie. "I am getting warmer."

"I hope you don't believe in coincidences," Frankie said.

"As a matter of fact, I do not."

"Good. Because you realize, of course, Angelina didn't just begin driving an Uber because she needed the money."

"If she was willing to pay $1 million for a carving of her in the nude, I would infer that she didn't."

"No, she did not."

"And if everything you say about the Russian surveillance of myself is true, I also must infer that it was no accident that she picked me up the night I gave that lecture at DQU."

"Now you've got it."

"They had me on a satellite leash."

"Exactly. That consulate had been tracking you by your cell phone, and the night you were out in Winters, it worked out perfectly for them. They knew you would take the bus – fuck, man, they tapped into your tap card. They knew you had an Uber app. And they dispatched her into the area to make sure that she would be the closest Uber to you when you put in for a ride. Just to make sure, they hacked your app. You put in for the ride, and she put in for you."

"And she kept up the Uber ruse for months afterwards."

"Exactly squared."

"So my whole relationship with Angelina, it was a total set-up?"

"You're on a roll."

Sitting in the sun, Link broke into a sweat that soaked through his shirt. He took off his cowboy hat and scratched the top of his head.

"So who wanted the log?"

"I don't exactly know. The feds don't exactly know," Frankie said. "But they do know that whoever wanted it went to great lengths to dupe you into it. The FBI intercepted an email that contained a fairly substantially developed psychological profile. They knew more about you than you knew about yourself."

19. BARGHANYAN AND CHERNEKOFF

Frankie called Link the next morning and asked if he could meet him at the federal courthouse. Link, who was plopped into the deep sofa chair at Shine, reading the *New York Times*, checked his schedule. It was blank, as usual.

"I'm on my way," Link said.

He finished drinking his coffee and reading the paper.

Thirteen blocks later, he poked his head through the open door looking into Frankie's windowless office, in the fourth-floor interior of the Robert T. Matsui United States Courthouse.

"Take a seat," Frankie said. "You've got to see this."

Link sat in the empty cheap plastic office chair and wheeled it next to Frankie's. The reporter perched in front of his computer. Frankie searched his email and clicked onto a video. It had been sent to him by an unknown source.

The film rolled. It looked to Link and Frankie like it had been shot from the deck of a CHP cruiser. The film, in fact, had been shot from the deck of a CHP cruiser. It captured a traffic stop effected near the Milk Farm landmark on the Vaca Hills side of the Sacramento Valley. The date on the video and the time stamp reflected the night and hour of Link and Frankie's drive home from the Russian consulate in San Francisco.

The grainy depiction looked like something out of "Cops". The black-and-white picture of the black-and-white stop picked up the images of the two brown-and-green uniforms exiting their vehicle. The uniforms approached a late-model Impala they had just detained on the shoulder of eastbound Interstate 80. The uniforms covered their service revolvers with their right hands.

It was the same car that followed Link and Frankie out of San Francisco.

The traffic stop looked completely normal. The uniforms ordered the two men inside the car out of it. The men complied. The uniforms ordered the men to put their hands behind their backs. The uniforms pulled handcuffs off their respective uniform belts and fastened them to the wrists of the two men. The uniforms patted the men down. The uniforms removed cell phones, wallets, car keys, loose change, cigarette lighters, ear buds and, in the case of one of the subjects, a shopping list given to him that morning by his wife. The uniforms placed all the items on the hood of the Impala. They walked the men back towards the CHP cruiser and out of camera shot and apparently into the back seat of the black-and-white.

Frankie and Link saw the officers search the Impala trunk. They retrieved several objects that looked like they came off the shelf of a neighborhood Radio Shack. The officers documented the fruits of their search and deposited the stuff into their own trunk, out of camera view. In front of the cop car, the uniforms conferred briefly, before they released their captives, who came back into the picture in front of the dash cam. The driver's body language communicated a fairly detailed protest. The driver shrugged his shoulders. He over-emphasized his hand gesticulations. He swung his arms like a monkey. One of the officers gave the man a card and pointed out some information on it as if to say, Hey, Mack, I'm the wrong guy for you to be taking this up with. You got a problem, call this number. The passenger stood quietly, with his arms folded. The second CHP officer watched him like a hawk, his hand over his pistol and ready for a quick draw.

The cops returned the wallets to the two men, but kept the cell phones. The cops also retained what turned out to be several thousand dollars' worth of sophisticated spy hardware.

The detainees got back into their car and drove off.

The dash cam followed the car to the first off-ramp. The Impala turned around and headed back towards San Francisco. The cops followed the spies back to the Carquinez Bridge. The cops clocked the Impala at speeds no higher than 64 miles per hour.

FBI monitoring confirmed the Impala's return in due time to 2790 Green Street.

"Interesting," Link said, as the dash-cam video came to an end and he adjusted to a new reality in which Russian spies and car chases figured into the everyday.

"It gets better," Frankie said, clicking on another video on another email.

This one appeared to have been taken from the body camera attached to the breast plate of the officer who approached the

Impala from the passenger side of the vehicle. The film was not terribly remarkable. Except for one thing:

"I recognized that guy right away," Frankie said.

The body cam snatched a nice, clean mug shot of the passenger.

"Remember that I guy I told you about when I went to Uncle Nikita's house after the credit card bust?" Frankie said. "The guy who wanted to rough me up?"

"Vaguely."

"Well, that's him."

Link nodded his head and stroked his chin.

"You're right, Ugarte," Link said. "I'm impressed."

Frankie ran down the rest of the story on the passenger:

"His name is Ishmail Barghanyan, and he is an Azeri-Russian citizen who fought alongside all the other soldier boys under Karuliyak in the Afghan War."

"And you know this how?"

"Those body cams aren't just for city councils to hold cops accountable," Frankie said. He turned to Link to emphasize his point: "The cops have stocked them with the best facial recognition software in the business. They had this guy ID'd the next day."

"Very cool," Link said, "as long as you're not the one getting your picture took."

"I wouldn't worry about it if I were you," Frankie said. "You are a complete bore."

"I take it there's more to Barghanyan."

"Lots. He worked in the intelligence unit back in his army days in Afghanistan, and he reported directly to Karuliyak. He supplied the muscle when the Russians captured a mujahideen and needed to break 'em down. Pow, in the kisser, usually worse – he would knock the Allah Akbar out of them until they told them what they wanted to know. The feds tell me Barghanyan has laid pretty low since he came to America, but that they did pick him up on some phony charge in Brighton Beach and downloaded his DNA and his facial features and everything else. They didn't even know he was in California until they saw this."

The body cam video from the other officer filled in a few details from the traffic stop. The other officer used the device to film all the electronic equipment they lifted from Barghanyan and his chauffeur.

"Who's the other guy?" Link asked.

"Last name is Chernekoff, but he doesn't come back with much more of a profile. I think he's just a driver for the consulate. He's officially listed in their data base as a 'technical engineer'. Which means he's a spy."

20. TAKE THEM OUT TO THE BALLGAME

"Melvin Upton Jr.?"

Link posed the question to Mike Rubiks, in the bottom of the second inning of the Sacramento River Cats' game against the Salt Lake City Bees, right when the home team's clean-up hitter stepped into the batter's box.

"You probably remember him as B.J.," Rubiks said. "He changed his name."

"Now he bats fourth in Sacramento."

Upton had signed a Triple A contract with the Giants that spring. He tore into a fastball from Bees right hander Adam Hofacket. The smash wound up in the mitt of Salt Lake City third baseman Ray Navarro.

Upton trudged back to the dugout.

It was a perfect 95-degree evening at the ballpark, where Link and Rubiks stood along the rail above the left field foul line. They liked the spot for a key reason: it was conveniently located near the beer stand that sold the tasty Hopped Lucidity. The new IPA from Moonraker Brewing in Auburn had taken over the town. About 3,000 people were in the ballpark. An estimated 1,000 of them crowded within a sacrifice bunt of the local brewery offerings. They all wanted Hopped Lucidity.

The 6.4 percent wattage kicked in with Rubiks by the time Salt Lake City came to bat in the second. Rubiks stood in the shade and wore sunglasses to protect his eyes from the blinding sun reflecting off the state Board of Equalization building on the other side of the Sacramento River, beyond the right field wall.

"You saw the lying asshole's lie last week?" Mike said, more of a statement than a question.

Link had not been keeping up on the Trump-Russia investigation. He'd been a little distracted.

It had been more than a month since Frankie Cameron's second big story finally ran, detailing the extent of the Russian surveillance in Northern California and *vor v zakone*'s assistance in financing the election intervention. Frankie had since published

184

a follow-up. It incompletely detailed the role of the spy mistress, Angelina Puchkova, who had failed to appear at her restitution hearing. The feds had a new classification for Angelina: fugitive from justice. Frankie's sources told him Angelina had likely fled the jurisdiction. In this case, that meant the entire United States of America.

What made Frankie's story incomplete was its failure to mention anything about his artist pal, Lincoln Adams. Frankie's sources asked him to withhold reporting on the Russians targeting Link. They thought the publicity would compromise their investigation. Cops thought publicity compromised every investigation. The feds also thought the pub might endanger the life of the dormant wood sculptor who knew a few things about the movements of the fugitive felon Angelina Puchkova over the previous few months. Link gave the feds a statement. They offered him a slot in witness protection. They expressed a preference that he be alive when he delivered his testimony, if and when it became needed. Link thanked the feds for their consideration. He declined the placement in witness protection. He told them he preferred to do his hiding in plain sight.

Like at Raley Field, in the company of fellow travelers such as Mike Rubiks.

"So what's the latest," Link asked.

"Well, I'll tell you," Rubiks said.

He filled Link in on the story poised to be a dagger to the heart of the Trump presidency. Trump, it was now learned, helped shape the administration's rapid response when word got out that his first-born son took a meeting with a squadron of Russians during the previous year's presidential campaign.

"This is going to be the end of the bastard," Mike surmised. "Shutting down Comey, that was nothing – he's the president. He can fire whoever the fuck he wants, whenever he wants, and he doesn't have to give you a reason. This Donald Trump Jr. shit – man, this is way different. Mark my words – this is what's going to bring him down. This is not part of the job. There is no cover for this. There is no explanation other than obstruction of justice."

Steven Okert got the Bees out in order in the third, and the mid-August sun had dropped low enough in the sky so that it wasn't bouncing off the downtown buildings and into Rubiks' eyes anymore.

Rubiks kept his sunglasses on. He got more lit with every swig of the beer and swing of the bat.

Link listened politely as the Rubiks rant gathered intensity:

"Sarah Huckabee, you see her shit the other day? 'The president weighed in, as any father would.' Yeah, just like my father did all the time. I can hear him now – 'So, what happened here, Mike? You took a meeting with a Russian lawyer, a spy and a money launderer? Oh, and you had Jared and Manafort in on it, too? Now, the *New York Times* is all over it? Here, let me help you make up a lie about it, just like any father would'."

Link nodded.

Rubiks gathered momentum:

"This Jay Sekulow, is he the worst or what? Trump admits one day that he's being investigated for firing Comey and Sekulow comes out the next day and says, 'No, he's not under investigation.' Now you've got him going on 'Good Morning America' lying about Trump not being involved in helping Junior lie about the meeting with the Russians. I know that lying is a part of politics, but you've got to be good at it. Anybody ever believes a word this guy says is nuts."

"Yep," Link agreed.

"And you got to love it, Manafort wakes up the other day with the cops pointing a gun at his head. Breaking his door down at 4:30 in the morning so he can't flush the shit down the toilet."

"He had cocaine in the house?"

"No. But he probably had the ledgers of his payoffs from the Ukrainians. Now this is beautiful. Feds get a no-knock warrant on the president's campaign manager. I mean fucking beautiful."

Mike Rubiks cackled at the thought of Robert Mueller's team serving the early-morning search warrant on Paul Manafort. The visual, as described by Rubiks, generated a chuckle out of Link, too.

"I wonder if they threw a flash grenade through the bathroom window," Rubiks daydreamed.

Melvin Upton Jr. drove in a run in the sixth and the River Cats took the lead with a three-run seventh. Raley Field cut off beer sales after the seventh inning. Link and Rubiks saw no reason to stick around. They took off for a nightcap at LowBrau, outside, on the terrace overlooking the corner of 20th and K. They drank up and headed home, Rubiks in his car to his home in suburban Elk Grove, and Link, on foot, to his home on D Street.

Walking down the tracks that separated 19th from 20th streets and one side of the town from the other, he saw in the distance the headlight on a southbound train.

Most people in such a circumstance would have stepped off to the left and continued home.

Link veered right, and waited for the thunder to shake up his thinking. It had been awhile since his last forced retrospection. He figured he could use a dose. Despite the bizarre things happening to him the last few weeks, there had been no real change in his circumstances. Single, indigenous male, could not pull a spirit out of a dead tree.

It turned out he never had a chance with Angelina. Big deal. They weren't each other's type. In Link's case, he wasn't anyone's type: it happens when you're a man of the world. When he was at his best, everything he had to give he gave to the sculpture. Without him, these forms were nothing. They would forever remain locked in the wood. Liberating them was more than enough for any one man in any one lifetime. You give your all to our craft and there's not much left for anything else. He was married to the sculpture. It was his life. He produced for the generations. He produced for the ages. He had already fulfilled his quota for one man's life. He didn't have to pick up another log, didn't have to pound another chisel until he bruised the palm of his hands. He didn't have to damn near lose his life in search of spirits that sought to elude his creative emancipation, his dive into the essence of being.

The Russians made him laugh. They thought they had him on their psychological profile. He wondered: how could they write up a psychological profile on him without ever talking to him? He'd never been to a shrink in his life. He'd never even had a job interview. Or an exit interview. *People* magazine and the *San Francisco Chronicle* interviewed him. He answered their questions. He gave them four-cornered answers and no more. He didn't dig too deeply into his psychology in his talks with the writers. He didn't give them much psychological profile material. He stayed factual. He allowed for the emotional. What did the

Russians have on him? And did it work?

He was just a guy who worked hard at what he did and threw himself into it with everything he had and he came out of the deal with some genuine Native American accomplishment. He never worried about his psychological profile. If he stepped on his dick on the way home and stumbled in front of an 18-wheeler, his friends would know that he was a man who had thrived, who didn't worry so much about who he was, rather than what he was. Before anybody even knew he existed, before he became topical, before he made a nickel, he knew he had created something pleasing. He made a difference. He didn't cheat and he didn't cut corners. He did the work and there was nothing else any man could do in the time any man was given. He produced, but he refused to be enslaved by his production. The world changed around him, just like it changed around every man or woman who ever walked it. Nothing he could do about that, except embrace it. He wanted permanence, in a world where the only thing that was permanent was the cycle of impermanence.

21. HOSTAGE SITUATIONS

Wait a second, Link thought. Is that "Watermelon Man"?

Weaving through the tens of thousands of music lovers, the sculptor stepped lightly with a little lift beneath his feet. He aimed himself toward the sound board 30 yards in front of the Swan Stage. He felt light, probably due to his stopping to take a single puff off a pipe that a friend had thrust in his face. The first weekend of October was one of the few times of the year he so indulged. The occasion was the annual Hardly Strictly Bluegrass Festival in Golden Gate Park. Once he got his head right, he made his way to the other side of Hellman Hollow. He needed to catch Poncho Sanchez's band.

Damn if he didn't walk right into the Herbie Hancock hit, inflected with Poncho's Latin twist.

An hour later, he'd never heard Peter Rowan sound better. The day progressed through an hour of Midnight North, a San Francisco jam band that featured Phil Lesh's kid on rhythm guitar and lead vocals. Walking out of their set, Link saw Phil Lesh in the flesh, hurrying away. He said hello and shook hands with the Grateful Dead bass player. He told him his kid's band sounded terrific.

Gillian Welch took Link back in time. The sun went down over Steve Earle, after which Link said goodbye to his Hardly Strictly friends and made his way down the low highway toward Irving Street, for the first of three train rides home.

"C'mon, Link, spend the night – you've got to be here tomorrow," one of his friends implored. "Dave Alvin. John Prine. Emmylou – on the same stage."

He looked at a Sunday schedule. It also included the Secret Sisters, Lucinda Williams, and Ornette's Prime Time Band.

"Inviting, but I have pressing matters in Sacramento," he lied.

In fact, he had nothing waiting for him, there, or anywhere else. He had a gorgeous log on the pedestal, in repose, in his studio. What he lacked was the inspiration or energy necessary to make sense out of it.

Plus, he couldn't let it go that the Russians' had drawn up a psychological profile on him. It gnawed on his psyche, even in the sunny bluegrassed hollows of Golden Gate Park. He wouldn't admit it, even to himself, but it kind of pissed him off.

He still hung with Frankie, but changes were in the air on that front.

Frankie got a great ride on his Russian organized crime series. Back to the routine of the federal courthouse, Frankie did his best to make the most of the churn of the beat, while looking over his shoulder at the *Beacon* bosses who wanted to yank him out of there and put him on something that generated more clicks, like midtown restaurant openings. Frankie talked about getting out of the business. Link suggested instead that he apply to the *Washington Post*. Frankie took him up on the idea. Damn if he didn't get himself a job interview. He'd be flying to the District in a couple of weeks.

By the time the Capitol Corridor 10:42 out of Richmond pulled into the Sacramento Valley Station, Link had played all of the videos he took on the day with his cell phone. He stepped off the train and trudged up I Street from the train station. He headed home, toward Mansion Flats.

Past City Hall, across from Cesar Chavez Park, a familiar-looking white Impala pulled up alongside him.

The driver rolled down his window. Short and stocky, the passenger leaned over and addressed him by name:

"Lincoln Adams."

Link recognized them both from the CHP tapes. Once again, it was Chernekoff behind the wheel. The short and stocky Ishmail Barghanyan sat shotgun.

"Get in," Barghanyan ordered, in perfectly unaccented English.

Link stopped, looked, and laughed.

He continued on his way.

"Seriously," Barghanyan said.

Barghanyan got out of the car and circled over to the sidewalk. He paced evenly alongside Link, Chernekoff bringing the Impala up from the rear.

Link proceeded five more blocks up I Street, to 13th. He never stopped. He paid no attention.

"We do not want to make a scene," Barghanyan said.

"Then don't," Link advised.

A half block down 13th Street, towards D, Barghanyan said: "You might want to look at this."

Barghanyan pulled out his cell phone. Link kept walking. He refused to stop until he stood next to a hedge that swamped the side of the Sterling Hotel. "Get load of this," Barghanyan said, requesting Link's attention again. It was like he was trying to sound like a crony from a film about Capone, but his accent got in the way.

The phone showed a live, FaceTime interaction. The scene: a man with a gun, in a dark room, sitting casually on a couch, waving to the camera phone. The device roamed slowly to the right, to show a man leaning back, comfortably, in a recliner.

If the Witch Doctor was under duress, he sure didn't show it.

"Hello, my son," the Witch Doctor said, waving to Link on FaceTime, a smile settled easily across his own face.

Link waved in return.

"Looks like you've gotten yourself in a pickle," Link said.

"Oh, not exactly," the Witch Doctor replied. "These men came to me with their guns out, that is true. Yet I see this more as an opportunity, for you to light your fire once more. You have not been producing, my son. Talent is a terrible thing to waste. Besides, I have dealt with the likes of these men before, and believe me, they are amateurs."

"I am not exactly following, Uncle."

"These men have told me that I shall remain captive until you agree to the commission that woman offered you."

It was the first kidnapping of its kind in human history: the abductors would not release the hostage until Link agreed to let their people pay him a $1 million commission for a shitty piece of fake art.

Link looked up from the phone, into Barghanyan's face. Chernekoff pulled the Impala up alongside them. Chernekoff got out of the car. He opened the rear passenger door.

Barghanyan nodded his head, in agreement with the Witch Doctor.

"Better listen to your uncle," the Russian muscle man said.

Link explained it was mostly a term of endearment, as was the Witch Doctor's reference to Link as his son.

"Whatever it is that you call each other," Barghanyan
continued, annoyed. "You need to know that your uncle isn't going
anywhere, not even outside for a breath of fresh air, if you don't
come along with us. There is a good chance he might get hurt."
The kidnappers kept the phone camera trained on the Witch
Doctor. The Witch Doctor, meanwhile, had pulled a mandolin up
from the side of his chair. He began to pluck it lightly.

Sensing he was being watched, the Witch Doctor looked up.
He said:

"I find this to be one of the more interesting of the rhythmic
instruments."

"I didn't know you played, Uncle."

"I don't. This was given to me by an old girlfriend who is now
an old woman. She thinks it will make for a fine pastime in my
second childhood. I know somebody in Ukiah who gives lessons. I
think, son, it would be a fine idea for you, too, to take up an
instrument."

Link nodded his agreement. Barghanyan lowered the phone,
increasingly irked by the calm irrelevance of the conversation.

"Nobody is taking any lessons," Barghanyan said, "unless you
come with us."

"To where?"

"It doesn't matter where. It only matters what. What you need
to do is earn that million dollars our people have very generously
offered you."

"And if I don't?"

Barghanyan held the phone up to make sure Link got a very
good look.

"Boys," he said.

On instruction, the man seated on the couch in the room with
the Witch Doctor stood up with his gun trained on the old guy's
head, from point-blank distance.

The Witch Doctor strummed his mandolin. He looked at his
captors and into the camera. He smiled and shrugged his shoulders,
as if to say "What the hell can you do?" before going back to
working on his stroke, getting into the rhythmic nature of the
instrument.

For an assist, he picked up a vaporizing device from an end
table next to the couch. He took one small puff. Link could see the

business end of the vaporizer light up in blue. The Witch Doctor held the fumes in his lungs for a few seconds before exhaling, while his captors looked . . . confused.

"That should last me about a week," the Witch Doctor said, before focusing again on the mandolin.

The armed abductors exchanged a few words in Russian with Barghanyan who told Link that the gunmen were concerned they could get in legal trouble being around a pot smoker.

"Tell them he's got a medical marijuana certificate," Link said. "It shouldn't be a problem."

"Just get in the car, please," Barghanyan said. "We don't want this to get messy."

With no further prodding, Link led himself into the back seat of the car and closed the door.

Barghanyan got in and the Impala drove off.

After it pulled a U-turn away from Link's neighborhood, a shaggy head of hair and an unkempt body behind it crawled out of the bushes that protected the flanks of the Sterling Hotel.

The Scrounger rolled into action.

22. RESCUE MISSION

Sitting alone in the back seat, Link directed the Russians to his studio on R Street.

"This is your place?" Chernekoff asked.

"My studio, yes," Link said.

"Reminds me of boring building in Moscow."

The studio did sport all the glamor of a 1960s-style state-government stucco office building. Probably because the studio at one time was a 1960s-style state-government stucco office building.

Link assumed his two escorts were armed. Why wouldn't they be, based on all the crap their buddies flashed on FaceTime at the Witch Doctor's? His kidnappers still hadn't shown their weaponry. There was no need. Their captive was a picture of compliance.

Walking up to the front door of the studio, Link inserted the key into the lock and clicked it open. He stood back and motioned Barghanyan and Chernekoff inside.

"Be my guests," he said politely.

Barghanyan pushed the door. It didn't budge.

He looked at Link as if he was a nut. "Sign says push," Barghanyan said. "It does not open."

"Figure it out," Link instructed.

Barghanyan pulled on the door, to let everybody in.

"Why such stupid sign?" Barghanyan asked.

"You really don't know who to believe these days, do you?" Link responded.

"You are odd duck," Barghanyan said. "Get inside."

Inside the studio, Barghanyan and Chernekoff found Link's creative environment cold and uninviting. Link kept his walls blank. He didn't need any pretty pictures to stimulate creativity. They'd only impede it. He curtained off his front picture window with pull drapes that looked like they hadn't been cleaned since forever. The only thing he really liked about the space was the high ceiling. It allowed Link to work big, to think big, on pieces tall as 20 feet. With plenty of room to spare.

Scaffolding pipes and floor boards and ladders of varied heights leaned against the walls. The big log still stood on a pedestal 10 feet in diameter, in the center of the room – waiting patiently to be carved. Hammers, chisels, scalpels and other wood-carving implements scattered across the floor. The room had two folding chairs, the fold-out couch, the drawing table, and a small desk littered with what appeared to be dozens of unopened letters. Several dozen more had fallen to the floor beneath the mail slot in the glass front door.

Link hadn't been in the place for a month. It looked it.

He leaned over and picked up one of the letters that had fallen to the floor. He opened it. He looked at it for about six seconds before ripping it in half and letting it flutter to his feet.

"Billy Idol," he said. "This can't be serious. Did you guys send me this one?"

Barghanhyan and Chernekoff looked at each other as if they didn't know what Link was talking about. Which they didn't.

He kept a couple extra logs stashed behind a blue-tarped off space with plastic sheeting fastened and hung from the ceiling. He never used these logs. They never fired. He might as well burn them. They never sparked the creativity, despite the consecration of the Witch Doctor. Whoever said he was perfect?

Barghanyan and Chernekoff walked over to the tarps and pulled them back. They kicked the tires on these misshapen rejections.

For the first time Link put up some resistance.

He pulled the plastic sheeting away from Barghanyan's grasp.

"Don't touch," he told them "Don't look."

The two of them backed off, laughing.

"The artist!" Chernekoff said to Barghanyan in Russian, in a mocking, false-gentile tone, which generated a higher and longer pitch of laughter.

Continuing to explore the room, they saw the big boy in the pedestal in the center of the room.

"What about this one?" Barghanyan asked

"What about it?"

"I think it would make for a fine nude of a woman from Novosibirsk."

"Fine," Link replied. "Have at it."

"But I am not a carver!"

"And I am not a whore."

Barghanyan clearly did not get Link. Not many did. Especially when it came to him and his work. It was his work.

"OK," Barghanyan said. "I understand you are the artist."

Chernekoff chuckled, but nothing was really funny. Certainly not to Link, and not to Barghanyan. Barghanyan was trying to put in some work for the *vor*. Barghanyan was trying to put in some work for Mother Russia.

"What do you say," Barghanyan said, "that you carve us the piece? You'll get your million. We are good for it. And we'll be on our way, no harm, no foul."

"I haven't decided yet," Link responded.

"I would suggest you decide sooner rather than later. Your 'uncle' might be getting hungry by now."

Link knew by seeing the Witch Doctor's image on Skype that he would be good for several days, at least. Maybe weeks. He didn't eat much.

Link ruminated on that thought. He ran some calculations through his head on how long he could stall.

Then Barghanyan's iPhone buzzed.

It was FaceTime. Barghanyan told Link somebody wanted to talk to him.

It was Angelina Puchkova.

Barghanyan turned the phone around to give Link a look. He saw that Angelina looked the same as always. She appeared to be back in her primary mode – surly. She came off like a January day in Novosibirsk.

"I hope for you make new decision, on offer," she said, unsmiling, as if a cold wind was blowing all around her.

It's the way Link would always remember her.

"You hope?" he said. "As if you don't know my answer."

"What? I no understand your talking."

"You know I'm not going to do the piece for you. Why would you say you hope I'll change my mind, when you already know I won't?"

"It is never too late, Mr. Link, to change mind."

"Mr. Link. It seems like you're reading off a script."

"I don't know what you talk about."

"Your psychological profile."

"My psychologic profile?"

"Your psychological profile of me. You know how I'll react to everything. You knew it from the time you picked me up in the Uber."

"Psychologic profile? I have no profile. I have pictures. I have pictures of me I give to you. I have money I can give to you. I have $1 million I can give to you, for you doing log for me."

"I take it you would not be available to model."

"It is true I cannot return to United States. Maybe you can come to Novosibirsk."

"Under a different set of circumstances, maybe, and if I see you, I see you, Ms. Angelina, although it wouldn't frazzle a pimple on my ass if I don't. Now, tell me about the psychological profile your people prepared on me."

Another, quieter voice sounded from the phone, out of FaceTime's view.

"Maybe I can help Mr. Adams with this question."

Whoever the male voice belonged to was holding the phone. He handed it to her to point at him. She turned it around to give Link the picture of the man with the answer. Now Link saw in Barghanyan's phone a man who looked to be in his early-to-mid-50s. He wore a slim grey suit that fit his slim physique in a stylishly slim fashion. He combed his thin hair over his slim and balding head. His beady eyes seemed tiny, even in proportion to his thin face. His nose was exceptionally long and thin, like a talon.

The ears rivaled Obama's, the cheekbones the former First Lady of the same last name.

"Allow me to introduce myself, Mr. Adams," the man said. "We have never met, but I believe you know my name. I am Anton Karuliyak, and it is I who ordered the report on your behavioral patterns, to assist us in gaining your consent to perform this work of art that I would like to commission for our presidential dacha on the Black Sea."

"It won't help you," Link said.

"We shall see about that, Mr. Adams. As for your profile, our top analysts examined all your public documents, and some private ones that they were able to obtain. Perhaps it will please you to know that they determined you to be unclassifiable – an enigma, some might say. In instances such as yours, they have found that a simple money offer of a large sum usually is enticement enough to elicit the behavior pattern that we prefer. You, sir, have defied this common denominator. Your failure to respond to monetary stimuli left us with no choice but to exert force, the same as we exude over Chechen criminals, journalists, and political dissidents. So here we are, with you under our observation there in Sacramento and your 'uncle', as you call him, being held at an undisclosed location, several hundred kilometers from where you reside."

"I am sure he loves the drama," Link said.

"We do not want drama, Mr. Adams. We only want you to perform your fine craft on a piece of wood for us, for a fair and reasonable fee that is commensurate with your talent."

Karuliyak stood silently for a moment. It was evident he hoped Link would agree to his offer and that they could all be done with this messy hostage-taking business.

His hopes were not realized.

"I would prefer not to," Link said.

Karuliyak smiled, admiring and grim.

"Ah, a Bartleby the Scrivener for the Central Valley of California," Karuliyak said. "For the moment, Mr. Adams, let's not, as you say in America, 'go there'. Nothing productive can result from rejecting our offer. For now, let's approach this as a business decision, wherein we retain you for your artistic vision as determined by us and you will be provided more money than most men make in a lifetime."

Barghanyan and Link stood in front of the glass doorway to the studio, in front of the sacred log that had been fastened to its pedestal. Link walked around the log, toward a couch on the other side of the room. Barghanyan followed, with his phone pointed at Link, who took a seat on his couch and leaned backwards, his fingers locked behind his head.

"I need to know what you know about me," Link said to Karuliyak. His nonchalance was now a bit affected – his stalling was motivated by a serious desire. "I need to know what she knew about me when she picked me up in the Uber at DQU."

"That really is not important anymore, Mr. Adams."

"Maybe not for you."

"Nor should it be for you. You are a man in your 60s. Most men in your age group have gained a fairly full understanding of themselves by then. If they haven't, they usually don't make it that far. Are you an exception, Mr. Adams?"

Link crossed his right leg over his left and cracked his back from a sitting position.

"No, not exceptional. Just curious. Like you say, I am a man in my 60s. I always thought I knew myself pretty well. But the last few months have taught me I seem to have a lot to learn. You are the last people I ever thought would be providing me with these kinds of insights, but no one else has been forthcoming."

Karuliyak seemed to give in, in the hopes of speeding things along. "Mr. Adams," he said, his voice clipped and impatient, "as I said, in your instance, our report did not reach any grand conclusions on how to shake the fruit out of your tree. Like I said, our analysts determined you are unclassifiable. Now, I am no expert on such matters of the mind and soul, but having directed our study of you dating back to the publication of the article in your *People* magazine, and having once directed Soviet Army psychological operations in Afghanistan, I have, however, arrived at a few personal, but not scientifically verified, observations."

Link lifted a hand, indicating for the Russian to go on, by all means.

"I can tell you that I find you oppositionally defiant, although, curiously, without the usual attendant anger. Without such a release, the condition tends to build up, and it must in the due course of events find a method of release. Maybe this explains your artistic sensibility."

Link tried hard to remain impassive, taken aback by the accuracy of these characterizations.

"On a personal level, on matters of sexual relationship and intimate personal interactions, you are more likely to be attracted to somebody with whom you virulently disagree. This can be on matters of politics, art, social engagement, even personal hygiene. You are more likely to desire them, sexually, the more you find them aberrant."

"This is getting a bit private, doctor, but please continue."

"You are borderline obsessive, but you don't follow through on tasks that you find unimportant, even if the achievement of acceptable outcomes in such performance contains deep meaning for your potential intimate partners. This explains, for instance, your status as a single man, your failure to establish long-lasting relationship deep into middle age, your lack of a companion into the realm of senior citizenship. You like to see yourself as open to anything, but you are in fact the exact opposite – close-minded, selfish, egotistical. You are isolated, more or less by choice, in pursuit of self-centered commercial creations that you call art."

Link ventured no wisecracks to this one.

"You might be right," he said quietly

Karuliyak retrieved a Ziganov from a gold case. He struck a match to the Russian cigarette and let the smoke cloud around his head while he and Link peered at each other through international FaceTime.

"So, Mr. Adams, why not just carve the item we would like, and be done with it. Set your 'uncle' free. Set yourself free. Enjoy life. Can I send you some pictures of our young people in Novosibirsk? They are very pleased with their lives under the guidance of President Putin."

Link moved closer to the phone, to get a better view of a real live Russian organized crime kingpin.

"I've read a little about you, too," Link said.

"Your American press is famous for its 'fake news,' " Karuliyak countered, puffing on his Ziganov. "I am sure the portrayal was less than flattering."

"Not really," Link said, sitting back on the couch. "It was fairly neutral, really. You're just a crook. But you've always been smart enough to know that you couldn't do the time, which put you way ahead of the pack. You never would have made it in the prisons. You know you never would have survived inside, so you could never really be a *vor*. But you did have discipline, and you were willing to work, so you went into the military. You exercised your psychological brilliance. You established dominance over the weak-minded. You played your connections, and when your system devolved to the point where crooked opportunities were the best alternatives, the only alternatives, you took advantage of them. You've done well for yourself. I admire you for that. Come to think of it, I should do a sculpture of you, Mr. Karuliyak. You have far more substance than Angelina. But I won't. You are a genius, and your people are geniuses, but I can't abide your success."

"I am flattered," Karuliyak said.

"One more thing, if I can," Link asked. It was where everything was leading – Angelina's icy persistence, Rubiks' monomaniacal rants, Frankie's stalwart reporting. "All of this, how far up does it go?"

Karuliyak flicked his Ziganov and laughed. He was now seemingly resigned to a lengthier conversation with Link. It was possible he was even enjoying it

"I don't know how much I would believe from reading the American press about any Russian," Karuliyak began. "We are all, like you say 'bad guys.' I do not admit to any associations that have been reported, especially the ones in your local periodical. But I will say this – I do know people. I know people very well placed in our business and governmental hierarchy. I have maintained many of my contacts from the military, and many of them have spread throughout the key functioning points of our society. And I'll tell you this, too, Mr. Adams. I am a patriot. I am a Russian patriot, and you Americans need to know that we are not a nation to be trifled with or disrespected, as you have done with us for the past 27 years. I believe our president has made this point exceedingly clear to your leaders over the past number of years."

"He did even better than that," Link said. "He put Trump in the White House."

"Your American arrogance needed to be checked."

"So that's why you worked on Trump's behalf?"

"That was a secondary benefit. Primarily, our goal was to alter the international system. We desired the West to be left unsure as to whether it could ever again trust the leadership of the United States. We had hoped to leave the United States at war with itself. And you would have to agree, Mr. Adams – we succeeded."

"Maybe not, if Mueller has anything to do with it."

"It would not bother us if you impeach your Trump. He really matters nothing to us. We are finished with him. Like I told you, we have achieved our aim, Mr. Adams. Your President Obama made things difficult for us, but he was not so clever that we could not circumnavigate his policy goals. The money we made in our mortgage manipulations, the funds we obtained from your American credit card holders, and the funds that we are still obtaining through the accounts established in the names of your school children all across your country, in the pensions funneled by our government to our former employees who now work and live in your country – we have invested it all into ongoing political operation in the United States. We are talking about millions, to spend as we will. This includes the funds we have allocated for an original Lincoln Adams. The truth is, Mr. Adams, that we have enough resources remaining at our disposal – all culled from American sources banks – to fund our operations for generations."

Karuliyak flicked more ash.

"We have torn your country apart like it has not been since your Civil War," he continued, gaining momentum now, while Barghanyan and Chernekoff watched and listened like children trying to make sense of the adults' conversation.

For her part, the bored Angelina's attention seemed to have slipped to a TV just visible to the left of Karuliyak's head, which appeared to be showing the Russian soap opera *Bednaya Nastya*.

But Karuliyak was on a roll.

"Only we are smarter than the Confederates. We did all this without firing a shot," he bragged, his eyes lit with patriotic admiration. "And now, the irony, the beauty of the matter is, that the descendants of the forces who launched your Civil War, who turned in their guns at Appomattox, they now have millions of guns, and they run your country. They have manipulated the weaknesses of the system created by your so-called founding fathers. They are numerically inferior in your country, yet they control your presidency, your Congress, your Supreme Court. Your elites pour into your beautiful cities. They have created your urban renaissance, from New York to Chicago, even in your enjoyable little town of Sacramento. But they have abandoned the rest of the country, to what you call your 'forgotten Americans,' the ones easily swayed by Mr. Trump, who himself owed his power to your own Confederate descendants. What is your attorney general's name, Jefferson Beauregard?"

Karuliyak's laughter shook through the iPhone.

"Sounds right out of the 18th century, doesn't it? Now they are in charge in your country, and they will not surrender their power without launching a bloodbath. Of course, they needed our assistance to 'close the deal,' as you say. They could not have figured out a way to do it themselves. I don't know if they are smart enough, or courageous enough. They had retreated into the recesses of your country. All they needed was to be stirred."

"Manipulated, is more like it," Link broke it.

"All they needed was to be helped, and you cannot fault anybody who found the pressure points to highlight the divisions within your society that have existed since its founding. You have always been a hateful people, controlled by fear and racial animosity. These people have always had their representatives in your government. It was not too difficult to help them take charge, and now they control your legislatures, your presidencies, your state governments, your financial institutions, portions of your media. Soon, they will control your federal police apparatus, and your military. They have discredited your primary informational systems, your journalism. They will never control your academic facilities, but that is OK. Your universities, your professors, your intellectuals, have all been branded in the controlling Confederate mind as elitists, cut off from the thinking and concerns of the great heartland of your country. You place your faith in this Mueller, but the descendants of Jefferson Davis, of Nathan Bedford Forrest, of Breckenridge, of the likenesses of all the statues that they have fought to maintain, in Charlottesville and New Orleans and Memphis and beyond, they have very effectively challenged the objectivity of his investigation.

"You see, Mr. Adams, that no matter what Mr. Mueller might find, the disagreements between the factions in your country will remain for years, with or without Mr. Trump. In fact, many thinkers in our country would actually prefer to see your reputed progressive leaders in your Congress pursue impeachment proceedings, for that very reason. Who knows what such action might incite? What was it that Trump said about 'Second Amendment people'?"

Karuliyak laughed again.

Link realized that he hadn't really thought through all the implications of the political debate that was ravaging America. He saw, again, how Karuliyak might be right. He shook his head to shake off the confusion of the present, the chaos of his country, the tiredness in his bones.

"I can tell you one thing," he told Karuliyak. "You will never get a log out of me."

Karuliyak dropped his Ziganov. Angelina's attention, and iPhone camera handling, dipped just in time for Link to see him crush the cigarette with a tasseled loafer.

"That would be most unfortunate, Mr. Adams. For you, for your uncle, for relations between your country and mine."

Angelina turned the phone around. She went stone cold on Link.

"Make right decision," she said, sharply.

She clicked herself off.

It was at that moment that for the first time that Link glimpsed her essence, and that was her humorlessness. She was a damaged human. He felt a profound sympathy for her.

Saturday night evolved into Sunday morning. It was after midnight and the Russians didn't quite know how to let it all hang out, or what to do with Link.

He knew exactly what to do with himself. He was dead tired, having spent the day smoking dope and dancing. He pulled out the couch bed. He climbed in. He went to sleep in his clothes.

Barghanyan put in another call to Karuliyak.

"Let him sleep," the mob man told the spy in Russian. "Maybe he will find himself less obstinate in the morning."

"And if he is not?"

"We'll deal with that then."

"What about us?"

"What about you?"

"There is no place here for us to sleep. And we are hungry."

"I don't believe that your work at this moment calls for sleep. You are supposed to be keeping this man secure and making sure that he is within your custody at all times."

"And food?"

"I don't care what you do!" scoffed Karuliyak, patience wearing thin. "If he is asleep, I would imagine that one of you could find something close by. Send Chernekoff."

"But it's after midnight!"

"Even I was in America and Sacramento long enough to know that some places stay open all night long."

Barghanyan clicked the phone off.

Chernekoff agreed to make the food run.

He pulled on the studio door, which of course did not open, despite the sign on the glass. He turned directed a growl toward sleeping Link. Then he pushed the door open to the street outside.

When he and Barghanyan and Link first pulled up to the studio, the street was virtually dead.

Now, a human gathering had grown up around Link's studio. It was made up of the disheveled and deranged, the drunk and disorderly, the homeless of every category – the mentally deficient, the economically dispossessed, the inherently lazy, and the criminally inclined.

Some already had laid their sleeping bags around the studio. They stretched from Link's building to the curbless street.

Before Chernekoff's eyes, the homeless kept coming. They pitched their dome tents and practiced their disturbingly public bathroom habits.

Chernekoff first counted 40 to 50 people. By the time he'd finished counting, he had to count again. There were now 100.

They multiplied like loaves and fishes. Streams of homeless trudged down 13th Street from the north, from across Capitol Park, from beneath the Crosstown Freeway. They erected tarp tents. They laid out carboard boxes. They laid out newspapers. They pushed their belongings in shopping carts. The carried them in backpacks. They steered them on bicycles.

Link's studio was surrounded by homeless.

Some of them read books. Some of them played music. Some of them danced.

Most wore clothes, but not all of them, or not all of their clothing. They rolled in from river camps in West Sacramento where they had lived since the Gold Rush. They strolled in from campsites along the railroad tracks out to Sac State and back to the Yolo Bypass.

"Barghanyan!" Chernekoff implored. "You must see!"

Barghanyan came to the door. He stepped outside and saw and felt and smelled the social problem that confronted every major city in America.

"Disgusting," he told Chernekoff, in Russian.

"I can't move the car! These people, they are everywhere!"

"Maybe we should call the police."

"Great idea," sneered Chernekoff.

The Russians retreated into the studio. They tried to figure out what to do.

Link slept serenely.

"Should we wake him?" Chernekoff asked.

Before Barghanyan could answer, somebody walked through the unlocked door.

They looked up to see the Scrounger, who knew by now to pull on the metal bar rather than push it.

The henchmen stared in bewilderment.

Barghanyan asked, "Who are you?"

The Scrounger had been drinking heavily again, and he looked it. He was filthy, and he had a one-inch cut bisecting the bridge of his nose. His matted brown hair spilled from beneath a knitted Rastafarian cap.

"Who the fuck are you?" he countered. "Where's Link?" The crowd had by now grown to about 1,000. Swarms of humanity surrounded the Impala. There appeared to be no danger of it going anywhere.

Peering around the room, the Scrounger saw Link stirring from sleep.

"Scrounger?" Link said, surprised. "What are you doing here?"

"Don't you remember?" the Scrounger said, making his way over to Link and drunkenly examining the artist's face with his hands, as if to make sure nothing was out of place. Chernekoff and Barghanyan looked on, paralyzed by disbelief.

"Remember what?"

"This is your night."

"My night?"

"Yeah. The city's new voluntary shelter program. You signed up eight months ago, and now we're here."

"It must have slipped my mind."

"That happens when you get to be your age."

"What the – " Barghanyan finally sought to break in on the conversation, which the Scrounger found impudent.

"Why don't you shut the fuck up while we're talking?" the Scrounger told Barghanyan.

"Excuse me," Barghanyan said, strangely polite and demure in the face of this dirty, belligerent youth, "but I don't think you understand."

"Understand what? And you still haven't answered my question. Who the fuck are you? Link?"

Link rubbed the sleep out of his eyes.

"Well," Link said, answering for the Russians "these gentlemen have made me an offer I can't accept."

Knowing that the Witch Doctor played mandolin at the point of a gun about 150 miles to the northeast, Link decided to proceed with caution.

"We're in the midst of negotiations," he told the Scrounger.

"But you were asleep."

"I gave them time to caucus."

The Scrounger gave Link the fish eye.

Link looked at Barghanyan and shrugged.

"I think I've got to let them in," he said.

"Oh, no you don't," Barghanyan said, before Chernekoff broke in, in alarmed, quick Russian.

You could hear it coming from a block away, the piercing scream of the police sirens that moved slowly down R Street, through the homeless flash mob.

The sight of the cops approaching the studio induced panic in Barghanyan and Chernekoff.

"Where is back door?" Barghanyan demanded.

His English wasn't so good as it had been earlier.

Link showed them to the door in the back of the studio and unlocked it for them. The sign said "push." They pulled. It didn't open. They cursed in Russian while Link opened the door for them.

"Things really aren't that complicated," he said, as they ran through the back door and down the alley.

"You may never see your uncle again!" Barghanyan yelled back at Link, halfway to 12th Street.

Link accepted the truth of this. Such was always the case with everybody, every time you said goodbye to them. You never knew when you'd see anybody again.

Barghanyan and Chernekoff sprinted around the corner. They left their car parked in front of Link's studio.

The homeless army continued to grow, as two uniforms approached Link in the front doorway.

"Can you please tell me what is going on here?" one of them asked.

Link nodded toward the Scrounger and told the officer, "Ask him."

The two policemen stood back when the Scrounger took off his colorfully knit cap and scratched his head. With good reason – they worried about lice.

"I don't know," Scrounger said. "I'd heard about this new city program where different business types were going to be opening their doors at night to give us a place to stay. They told me it was going to start here, so I got the word out."

Link shrugged.

"First I heard of it," Link told the cops.

The cops looked at each other.

"It would be nice if somebody told us about these things," one of them, a young transgender female in pigtails, said to the other, an older gentleman with pink cheeks.

As they spoke, the homeless crowded toward the front door.

Link moved to the side to allow Scrounger and his friends inside.

"The bathroom," Link said, "is over there."

In orderly fashion, the homeless streamed into the studio and positioned their sleeping bags around the periphery of the room. They pitched tents outside. They occupied every square inch of space.

"One night – that's it," the older cop told Link. "We will be back tomorrow with the ticket book."

The officers explained that even the people who slept indoors were in violation of the city's no-camping ordinance. Link didn't understand how people who spent the night inside a building could be considered campers, but he also didn't understand how a foreign country such as Russia could have stolen an American election and delivered it to somebody like Trump.

He didn't make any promises to the police, but he did tell them:

"You might want to fingerprint that white Impala."

23. FIRE ON THE MOUNTAIN

Detective Andrew Wiggins rolled up in his unmarked a couple hours after the sunrise. He found Link handing out coffee and donuts to the homeless.

"The hell is going on here?" Wiggins asked, looking at the crowd, which by now had decreased to a hundred or less.

"We had a sleepover," Link replied.

"I see."

Wiggins appeared in his official capacity as a member of the Sacramento Local Russian Organized Crime Task Force, a wordy designation whose acronym, SLROCTF, was even worse. His was only the latest of a multi-agency law enforcement team to descend on the studio.

The FBI had been on the scene for hours already. They had already debriefed Link, who filled them in on the kidnapping of the Witch Doctor. Forensic examiners from his FBI partners worked the Impala as Wiggins spoke:

"I was hoping to go fishing this morning, down in the Delta. I worked all day yesterday, on the arrest warrant on Mrs. Uncle Nikita. Then I get roped into this."

"What did Mrs. Uncle Nikita do?"

"The false police report."

"Of course."

"Then we've got these guys," Wiggins said of Barghanyan and Chernekoff. "They got the break of the century when the feds didn't run them in the night they followed you. And they pull this crap?"

"I would like to press charges," Link intoned. "But I'm worried about my friend up north. Have you heard anything on him?"

The detective didn't know anything, other than that the feds were up in Mendocino County looking for the Witch Doctor, but that they still didn't have any information on him. Contributing to the problem: nobody knew where he lived.

"You sure he never took you to his house?" the detective asked.

"Never. He would just meet me at that bench in Round Valley. I would pick up the log and that was it. It was his schtick. Nobody could know where he cut his logs."

Wiggins nodded his head, as if he understood. As if there was any rationality to anything the Witch Doctor did.

As they spoke, the detective's cell phone rang:

"Yeah . . . Oh, really? . . . Where? . . . Beautiful . . . No, they're all yours . . . I'll let you know . . . Thanks."

He laughed when he clicked off the phone.

"They captured your guys," Wiggins told Link. "Police dog caught them in a backyard on V Street. They got tore up some."

A hard wind picked up from the north as the homeless crowd dissipated into Sunday with their morning treats. The Scrounger stuck around after Wiggins said goodbye to Link. The detective had to leave. The detective had to debrief the suspects.

The Scrounger lurked among the lingerers. Link shot him a quizzical look. It asked: what did you do and how did you do it?

"You're lucky I hadn't passed out yet," was the Scrounger's rejoinder.

It didn't surprise Link to hear that the Scrounger had been drinking all day before and into the night. He'd been hanging with some of his bum friends down by the river. He told Link he had just returned to his secluded campsite in the bushes alongside the Sterling when who should he see but his benefactor.

"I popped out to say hi, but then I see this goon trailing you, and then the car coming slowly up the street behind the two of you. So I crawled back into the bushes. I sure sobered up in a hurry. It looked like you might need some help, so I went out and got some for you."

The Scrounger said he reached for his cell phone as soon as the Impala U-turned away, only to find that it was out of power. This was a big problem for people living on the street, keeping your cell phone charged. He headed over to the Torch, where the doorman wouldn't let him in – it was a $10 cover on the Michael Ray Blues Band. The Scrounger knew not to press it. Fortunately, he knew Michael Ray. Fortunately, Michael Ray was his buddy. Fortunately, Michael Ray came out of the club during a break to smoke a cigarette.

Michael Ray lent the Scrounger his cell phone, for the cause.

"I called a couple of friends, and they called a couple of friends," he told Link. "I can tell you this – people know who you are. They like you, too."

"That's because none of you ever hounds me with ridiculous requests," Link said.

"I sent a couple people over to D Street, a couple more to Benny's, and I posted a guy on the 15th Street onramp," the Scrounger said. "I told a few guys to meet me at the studio. I figured you had to be in one of those places – you don't get around that much, you know."

"That's not entirely true."

"It's true enough. But I spotted that white car at the studio and I knew we were onto something. I got together with a couple of folks to figure out what to do."

"I guess you never considered calling the police."

"Are you kidding? And get you killed in a hostage situation? No, man. This was one we needed to take care of ourselves."

The Scrounger stood there with his hands in his pockets, waiting for Link to make the next move.

Link peeled off five twenties and handed them to the Scrounger.

"Oh, man, you didn't have to do that," the Scrounger lied.

"Hold on," Link said, reaching back into his pocket and fingering five more Jacksons. "Take care of some of your people, too."

The Scrounger smiled and accepted the money.

"Should be a very nice day on the river," he said.

The wind had been pretty stiff all morning, and now it gusted upwards of 30-to-35 miles per hour, fairly strong for the valley's bottomlands.

"No open fires down there today," Link advised. "I'm sick of reading about you burning down the parkway."

"I'll keep an eye on it," the Scrounger promised.

The sleepless night left Link exhausted. He was even more tired by the time he got home. Block by block, he fought a stiff north wind that blew in his face with rising intensity.

He was just walking up the steps to his front porch when Frankie called.

"What the fuck is going on?" Frankie asked.

"Well, I had some visitors last night when I was walking home from the train station."

"So I've heard. Are you OK?"

"Never better. But I'll be better than better once they find my guy up in Mendocino County."

"I'll let you know if I hear anything. You know I've got to interview you at some point. This is a huge development in the story."

"Can it wait a couple hours? I need some sleep."

"Of course. There's a lot of other angles to work in the meantime. I'm over at V Street now. I've already got the background on Barghanyan and Chernekoff. I need Wiggins to stop hating me for a second. Do you think you can help?"

"Not right now. But I can give him a shot later."

"He's the contact for the local details."

"I'll call him after I get some sleep."

"That'll work."

He splattered into unconsciousness the second he hit the pillow.

Calls of nature and hydration twice stirred him from his torpor. Another call from Frankie Cameron woke him for good.

"Have you been watching the news?" Frankie asked.

Link looked at his phone. It was 4:15 a.m.

"What day is this?" he asked.

"It's Monday morning."

"Monday? What happened to Sunday?"

"You slept through it. You haven't seen the news?"

"Not exactly. What's going on?"

"You might want to turn on your TV. Santa Rosa's burning. But that's not why I'm calling you."

It took a few seconds for the grogginess to lift from Link's head. He lumbered into his living room, in his underwear, his cell phone held to his ear. He found the clicker burrowed in the couch cushions.

Sure enough, the fire coverage covered every channel.

"But like I said, that's not why I'm calling you," Frankie repeated.

"OK. I give up."

"They found your uncle, or whatever that guy is to you."

"You mean the Witch Doctor?"

"Whatever. I mean, they didn't exactly find him, but they think they've got a pretty damn good idea where he is."

Frankie explained that in the hours since Link fell asleep, the task force confiscated Barghanyan's and Chernekoff's cell phones. The task force got a judge to sign a search warrant to fiddle around with them. The cops ran down Barghanyan's phone calls over the past 48 hours. They found one connection relayed off a cell tower in Mendocino County. They figured it had to be where the Witch Doctor had been FaceTimed.

"Where?" Link asked.

"They've got the tower isolated to a little town north of Ukiah – Redwood Valley," Frankie said.

Link knew the place well. It was the second to last stop before he cut off U.S. 101 on his way to Covelo. Frequently, he contributed a few dollars to the Coyote Valley rancheria, by way of their slot machines in a roadside convenience store/casino.

"So that's where he lives," Link said. "Makes sense."

"But you see the problem," Frankie asked/said.

"What?"

"It's on fire, too."

"Redwood Valley?"

"Si, señor."

For the next couple of hours, Link glued himself to the TV. By the time the sun came up, the fire had killed at least 25 people. The flames blew down a canyon from a wealthy neighborhood in the foothills above Santa Rosa to devastate a couple of suburban tracts. Reporters hadn't made the turn yet to Redwood Valley, but the aerial shots were terrible and the fire chiefs said they had an unknown number of fatalities there, too.

Link tried to call the Witch Doctor. He tried for hours. No connection – each call was met with the Witch Doctor's voicemail greeting, which sounded like a scream of agony. Link knew it to be the Witch Doctor's version of "hello."

Link didn't leave a message.

He needed to go to Redwood Valley.

He was in the midst of calls to rental car companies when his phone buzzed on his ear. Frankie Cameron's name flashed on the screen.

"I think I can help you out," Frankie said. "They're sending me to help out with the fire coverage."

"You? You're too old."

"It's all hands on deck. They're even calling in editors and reporters who they laid off."

"When are you leaving."

"Soon as possible."

"Where to?"

"I put in for Redwood Valley."

"That fits right in with my travel plans."

Frankie swung by Link's house within the hour.

The *Beacon* once maintained a fleet of company cars. These days, reporters had to rely on their own vehicles. Frankie's ancient Toyota Tercel wouldn't cut it on this mission. He rented a Jeep. He also rented a photographer, a former Beacon shooter, Patrick Bunch, a sardonic humorist who once nearly got Frankie killed when he drove two wheels off a thousand-foot cliff while the two of them were investigating the death-by-murder of a gold miner in a creek that feeds the north fork of the Yuba River.

The three of them no sooner got onto I-5 heading north when Patrick lit a reefer.

"Man, can't you hold off on that shit?" Frankie asked. "This is a serious situation."

"What do you think I'm taking a hit for?" Patrick answered.

He held in the smoke and tamped out the burning end of the joint with saliva he deposited on the tip of his right index finger.

"You want me at my best, don't you?"

Then he realized Link was in the car.

"Oh, sorry man. Did you want a hit?"

"No, thank you," Link said.

Patrick put on his headphones and closed his eyes. Link heard the muffled voice of Rhiannon Giddens set the groove for Patrick's ride.

The car fell silent as Frankie turned off the interstate on Highway 20 and headed west, toward U.S. 101, where they swung north.

Frankie pulled off the highway, on West Road, into downtown Redwood Valley. They stopped at the Redwood Valley-Calpella volunteer fire station. They needed to get their bearings. A hundred fire trucks protected the city core – a market, a bank and not much more.

Thanks to Frankie's press pass, the three roamed into the fire zone behind the firefighters' lines. They had the access, but they had no idea exactly where the Witch Doctor lived.

They drove up the main drag, East Road, to where it intersected with Tomki Road – ground zero. Oak and birch trees that canopied the drive wore overcoats of black. Burning embers lined their way past ruined shells of what used to be affordable ranchettes for NorCal blue collars in search of country living.

Piles of ash and rubble and the metal frames of incinerated automobiles and trucks were all that remained at every house on a two-mile stretch of road that led into the surrounding forest.

Frankie's car stopped at the first opportunity for everybody to get out and take a leak without offending these ghosts of houses.

They turned off the road into a cul-de-sac, Fisher Lake Drive. They exited Frankie's car, stretched, and Frankie and Patrick mapped out a plan to approach the people who had been burned out of their homes. The *Chron*, the *L.A. Times*, the Associated Press already had boots on the ground. Frankie and Patrick had to get snapping.

"I'll just wander," Link told them.

"If you come across anything good, let us know."

"Good? What good is there around here?"

Link caught himself. In the craven world of newspaper reporting, human pathos made for a good read. Reporters needed drama – a story. Although editors didn't call it that any more. They called it "content".

Frankie and Patrick took off, and Link took off on his own, hands stuffed into his jeans pockets and walking aimlessly. No destination or direction called him forth. He tuned into his gut, the fallback move every time he knew his brain couldn't or wouldn't get the job done. It told him to be open for anything.

He wandered up and down the road. He approached fire survivors who returned to view their destroyed half-acres. He described the Witch Doctor. He came up with nothing, except for a new take on the meaning of devastation.

He found the victims overcome by a searing sense of reverence, as if they were taking stock of their suddenly altered lives and lifestyles – liberated by disaster, momentarily, from the oppression of their daily routines. All of a sudden, they didn't have to be at work at 9 a.m. They didn't have to drop the kids off at school or pay the electric bill or tend the begonias. Of course there was anxiety and dread. Nobody liked living in a Red Cross shelter. Or in an RV. Now, they were back at the scene of their lives that really no longer existed except for the small parcels of the newly-blackened land that they had mortgaged or rented. They stood silent. Mostly, they searched for photos and trinkets that recollected loved ones and the past. Link came across one of them, a woman who appeared to be in her mid-40s, standing transfixed over an ash heap piled around a brick fireplace – all that remained of her home on Fisher Lake Drive.

At what used to be her threshold, she heard him approach, and looked up with serenity spread across her face.

"Can I help you?" she asked.

The question flabbergasted Link. Standing in the ruins of her destroyed home, she was asking him if he needed help.

"Ma'am," he said. "I am so sorry."

She shrugged, and said, "It's kind of a cliché that as long as you have your life, nothing else matters. It's also true. My husband's OK. My daughter's OK. We were all pretty shattered last night, and it was scary as hell getting out of here. But we're all still alive. There are some people from around here who are not."

Link nodded in a moment of silence. "Actually," he said, after what seemed a long time standing in the rubble, "there is something you could help me with." He told her he was looking for his close friend and mentor.

"And you don't know where he lives?" she asked.

"No, ma'am, I do not."

"But he's important to you," she said. "Your teacher. Your friend."

There was another pause. "There are lessons to be learned from everything that happens, in every breath taken," she said, half to herself. "The great challenge in life is to pick up the message and to figure out what it means, and who it's for.

"We talked about this last night, my husband and my daughter and me," she continued. "We've decided that this could be the greatest opportunity of our lives. Myanmar came up, I don't know how. I've never really thought much about Myanmar, or at all, really. But my daughter has, and she said that country needs some help. We talked about moving there."

Link could see the woman contemplating her new awareness. She went back to poking the ashes with her stick.

"I'm sorry I can't help you with your teacher friend," she told Link.

An hour into his search, and after several contacts that ended in an abject lack of information about the Witch Doctor, Link approached a man who slowly rolled his four-wheel drive onto Fisher Lake, to a house at the end of the cul-de-sac that backed down to an offshoot of the Russian River.

Blackened oak still simmered in his yard. Thick bark protected the trees' innards. Their kind had survived firestorms worse than this one.

What proved to be less impervious were the dozens of marijuana plants that the man told Link he had been growing in that patch of space behind what used to be his house. A barbed-wire fence circled the entirety of his modest little plot. A sign in front warned that trespassers were in danger of being shot, or eaten by the two Doberman Pinschers who now sat tethered in the back of the man's truck.

The large fellow wore blue overalls that covered the beach ball that served as his belly. A yellow hard hat protected his bald head while his reddened cheeks stuck out above a face covered by a black beard thick as an old-growth forest.

He welcomed Link to his charred world.

Link asked him if he knew where a crazy man who went by the name of "Uncle" lived.

"I've made it a point for about 30 years to know as few people around here as possible," the man said. "You're going to have to help me out a little bit. Like, maybe you could tell me what he looked like?"

Link did not like the man's usage of the past tense. He provided the Witch Doctor's basic description – medium height, grey hair, slightly Asiatic features, a distinctive stringy grey beard reminiscent of southeast Asian revolutionaries from the middle of the previous century. Pot head. One-time grower. Had to be 80 years old, at least. More recently, Link said, the man called Uncle might be accompanied by a couple of goofballs with Eastern European accents.

The beard nodded and smiled and laughed.

"I got him," he said. "Follow me."'

Link explained that he didn't have a car, that he hitched into the area with a couple reporter friends. Now he was alone and looking for the Witch Doctor.

"Jump in," the man told him.

They drove through the charred wreckage back towards town and swung left to East Road, and then east off of East onto County Road J. They swerved through vineyards overshot by the flames that still burned on the hillsides above them. Firefighters parked along the roads ready to jump.

They braked to a stop just before they turned off the county road onto a gravel pathway that bisected a vineyard. It was yellow crime tape that got in their way. A Sonoma County deputy stood inside it. Also inside the tape: an overturned Jeep Wrangler, exactly upside down, damage considerable. Outside the Wrangler: two lifeless bodies.

"They took the corner a little too fast," the deputy told Link and his bearded driver as they maneuvered around the wreck. He drove slowly down the gravel road through the vineyard. The road came to a halt at a barn with a massive metal vat attached to the rear.

"I've got some pals back here who do a little business," Link's escort said. "They grow grape. They sell leaf."

The grounds appeared well-ordered, with saws and tools stacked neatly under a tarpaulin. A 1967 midnight blue Volkswagen bug was parked to the side – the Witch Doctor's car.

"It looks like he's here," Link's driver told him – right when the Witch Doctor stepped outside to greet them.

"Hello, Ricardo," the driver said.

"Mr. Wayne, a pleasure to see you," the Witch Doctor said, before he noticed that the driver was accompanied by a guest.

"Ricardo?" Link said.

It dawned on him that this was the first time he'd ever heard the Witch Doctor addressed by a specific name.

It also dawned on the Witch Doctor that Mr. Wayne was not alone.

He spotted Link and greeted him with the usual term of endearment, although with an added, emotional emphasis.

"My son!" the Witch Doctor almost shouted, as he embraced his student. "What a surprise!"

"My uncle," Link replied. "My uncle Ricardo."

"Oh, don't worry about that," the Witch Doctor said. "It's just a name."

In their embrace, Link felt the Witch Doctor to be exceptionally fit. He'd always been healthy, spry, upbeat – his every day a Mardi Gras parade, a man who defied his 80-plus years by embracing them. He worked to stay trim. He stayed limber. He ate light. He exercised. He climbed hills. He hiked mountains. He exercised his mind. He read books. He sculpted logs. He did new stuff. He took up the mandolin.

"You are looking fine for a hostage," Link told him.

"You too, my son. Tell me about your night."

Link ran down the story of his own abduction, starting with the walk home from the train station through his being forced into the Impala through the human cocoon the homeless employed to spring him to freedom.

The chauffer stood and listened while the Witch Doctor provided details of his abduction by force:

"Well," the Witch Doctor said, "I drove down to the Roadhouse in Willits on Sunday, which was when, a week ago?"

"It was yesterday, my uncle."

"Yesterday? That was the longest yesterday I can ever remember. It seems a hundred years ago, today. I had always been interested in taking up the mandolin – I know nothing about how to play one, but I'd always been intrigued by its multiple capabilities, its use as both a driving force of nature, rhythmically speaking, yet at the same moment in almost the same stroke it provides an opportunity for melodic transcendability. The way these fellows hit the individual notes with such speed and ferocity, while never missing a beat. How do they play so fast? It must be that the strings are so close together. I also like the narrow neck. I think it will be much easier to master for somebody with hands as small as mine."

The Witch Doctor showed his hands to Link and to Mr. Wayne, the driver who was still wearing his yellow hard hat. The

Witch Doctor did not lie. His hands were almost as small as Donald Trump's. The range from the tip of his thumb to his pinkie finger could not have been more than a few inches.

Mr. Wayne felt he had accomplished his mission.

"I think I'll leave you guys alone talk about your hands," he said.

He nodded to the Witch Doctor's Volkswagen: "Your car is good?"

"Yes, brother. Thank you so much for delivering me my son. Here, let me show my appreciation."

"No, man, we're good," Mr. Wayne said.

"Please, just one second," the Witch Doctor said, hurrying into his hovel and emerging not 10 seconds later with a hand-crafted wooden doll doing some kind of dance.

"I am not Hopi so this is really not a kacina, but it is a creation that I recently completed, and I would like you to have it. We can call it the Fire Driver."

Mr. Wayne accepted it with almost a bow. He held it gingerly like something sacred as he got back into his truck and drove off.

The Witch Doctor watched him go.

"He has been my supplier on occasion," the Witch Doctor said, as the truck drove off. "Now, where was I, my son?"

"The mandolin," Link said.

"Ah, yes. The mandolin. I was just getting the feel for the mandolin," he continued. "My lessons were going to start this week. A young woman from the Roadhouse…"

"I take it that is a music store?"

"Yes. She was going to drive out here next week to give me my first lesson. Already I am getting its feel. I am sitting outside here in the early evening, enjoying the ferocious wind, but still being careful to watch for trees that might blow down on me, when these two men drive up in a four-wheel drive vehicle and they get out with guns and they point them at me and they force me inside. They spoke with very thick accents, and they were polite, but they informed me that I was being 'taken hostage'. They seemed apologetic. I told them not to worry, that I had never been taken hostage before, and I thought it could be a very interesting experience."

"Was it?"

"Not really. It actually was very boring. For having kidnapped me, I found these men to be very unobtrusive. They allowed me to do anything as I pleased. I made them tea. We talked. They mostly told stories about Afghanistan. They seemed to be very traumatized by their experience there. I told them about my work. They did not seem to be much interested. At some point I asked them what this was all about. The entire episode seemed to be as much of an inconvenience to them as it was to me. They did tell me that it had something to do with you, and how they knew somebody who wanted you to embark on a creation for them, and that you declined, and that made me laugh. I told them it was a hopeless situation for them, that they could not force sculpture. Not from you."

"I appreciate that, my uncle."

"So, we sat. For hours, until later in the evening, when they got the phone call, and they held up the phone to show me the pictures of you, on the sidewalks of Sacramento. It surprised me to see that you had been inconvenienced, too."

"And me, you."

The Witch Doctor continued:

"I got tired and I went to bed. I had no doubt that you would be fine. Truly, there was nothing I could do at that time to alter your situation, if it was a situation. So I got my rest. It was not easy. The winds at that time were howling like I had never heard them. They shook this place to its timber. I was concerned that my tree would snap. Yet there is nothing any of us can do about the wind, except get out of its way. I slept for a good while, a couple hours, maybe three. I assume they remained awake, and I did get some rest, until I awoke, and in the middle of the night, I immediately sensed a problem."

"The fire, my uncle?"

"Yes, I smelled it. I could detect from the level of smoke around my house that it was coming from someplace nearby. It had not engulfed me, but I could tell it was on the way. I went outside, and I saw the orange sky that had encircled me and that the flames had descended into the valley at the end of the road leading up to here. I felt it would be more safe if I stayed put rather than try and escape through the flames."

"Your captors, my uncle. Where were they?"

"I can only assume that they did not want any part of this blaze. They left in a hurry, a very high rate of speed."

"What were they driving, my uncle?"

"A four-wheel drive of some sort," the Witch Doctor said. "I believe it was a Jeep Wrangler."

24. GOING AWAY

Link had never seen Benny's more packed.

He scanned the room and concluded there must have been at least a hundred people crammed inside. They spilled onto the sidewalk. They packed the rooms to the front and side of the bar all the way out to the densely-occupied back porch on a cold winter's night in Sacramento.

Om and a couple sidemen pulled beer handles and poured shots. It looked like all 65 remaining members of the *Beacon* newsroom turned out. Dozens of alumni – the laid off and the bought out – also gathered.

The occasion was the last day at the *Beacon* for Frankie Cameron. His coverage of the Russian organized crime ring in Sacramento and its spillover effect on the presidential election got him some face time on cable news. The *Washington Post* and the *New York Times* took notice. The *Times* offered him a spot in the Staten Island bureau. The *Post* liked him for night cops. He went with the *Post*.

It also was the last Friday of 2017, and that brought in the regulars from the nearby auto body shops, same as it did on the first Friday of 2017 and every Friday in between.

Winds of change blew through the *Beacon*'s neighborhood. The paper sold its parking lot across the street from Benny's, and construction was scheduled to begin soon on an eight-story apartment building. Real estate developers bought the *Beacon* building itself. They leased it back to the paper for 15 years. Nobody had a clue on what would happen after that.

Link fought his way through the sidewalk crowd to the front door. He shoved his way inside. He recognized many of the older faces that peopled the bar in its prime, 20 years earlier. He recalled days of bookies and blue-collars and newspaper reporters who stood elbow to elbow and threw down Rubicon red amber ale. He saw a few faces from the old crowd that now worked as information officers for state agencies. Some flakked for human assistance, others on behalf of mass incarceration. A few hit it big as public relations whizzes. A few moved into the realm of political consultation. A few retired. A few were dead.

Plenty of the attendees took notice of Link and murmured to each other about his presence. He'd already been celebritized thanks to *People* magazine. Not very many of these people had seen him since he made the news two months earlier as a hostage of foreign spies. He hadn't seen any of them, either. Only a select few kept tabs on Benny's anymore.

Link didn't like the attention. He avoided eye contact. He spotted Mike Rubiks and the Scrounger engaged in an intense conversation in a far corner of the bar. He slithered past the high tables pushed against the front wall, to squeeze into some standing space next to Rubiks and the Scrounger.

Link was not surprised to hear them talking Trump.

Today's item was the *Washington Post* fact-check on the previous day's *New York Times* interview with Agent Orange. The *Post* found 24 false or misleading statements in the interview.

"I think it's a new one-day record," the Scrounger said.

It had been a lively couple of months since Link had been taken hostage.

Paul Manafort and a business underling, Rick Gates, had been indicted for money laundering. The same day the feds ran in Manafort, they announced the indictment and guilty plea on a fellow named George Papadopoulous, an operator who told the Trump administration he had a line on the purloined emails the Russians stole from the Democratic National Committee. Michael Flynn pleaded guilty to lying to the FBI, and now they were about to lock him up, unless he cooperated with Mueller – and it looked like Flynn chose the snitch route.

The flurry of stories over the past couple of months had left them numb. Rubiks, conveniently, logged them all into his cell phone on an updated email. He scrolled through them for the group – "The Secret Correspondence Between Donald Trump Jr. and WikiLeaks," "President Trump has made 1,628 false or misleading claims over 298 days," "CIA Director Met Advocate of Disputed DNC Hack Theory – At Trump's Request," "Secret Finding: 60 Russian Payments 'To Finance Election Campaign of 2016,'" "Trump White House Weighing Plans for Private Spies to Counter 'Deep State' Enemies," "Five Times Law Enforcers Could Have

Arrested Donald Trump But Didn't," "Kremlin Trolls Burned
Across the Internet as Washington Debated Options," "Election
Hackers Altered Voter Rolls, Stole Private Data, Officials Say,"
"Russia Tied to Funding of Tech Giants," "Mueller Reveals New
Manafort Link to Organized Crime," "Sessions Under Renewed
Scrutiny on Capitol Hill."

It was quite a litany.

"Each of them from legitimate news sources," Rubiks said.

Link spotted Frankie Cameron working the room from the
other side of the bar. Frankie looked up and made eye contact. He
swam through the sea of people into the Rubiks corner.

"What are you drinking?" Frankie asked the three.

Rubiks ordered a Racer 5, and the Scrounger made his a double
shot of Jack with a Budweiser back.

"That's all?" Frankie asked him.

"Better make it two Budweisers," the Scrounger said. "It's
pretty busy in here."

"What about you?" Frankie asked Link.

"I'll have a spritzer water."

Frankie countered with a fish-eye.

"A spritzer water?" he sneered.

"I am in a process of detoxification," Link said.

"The fuck are you talking about?" Rubiks broke in.

"Nothing major," Link said. "But I've been going stretches
recently without drinking – two, three days at a time. It's a bit
scary how good I feel during these brief dryouts."

There was a brief silence.

"Congratulations," Frankie said. "I'm getting you a Sierra."

Link shrugged. It was Frankie's night.

Frankie stood on his tippy toes and caught the eye of Om who
valiantly sought to keep up with the demands of a city that sought
relief from the dementia of 2017.

The bartender looked over his shoulder with a question mark
on his face that asked Frankie what he wanted. Frankie flashed a
series of hand signals – a point at Rubiks with one hand and an
upheld five fingers on the other. That means one Racer Five. A nod
to the Scrounger while holding up two fingers with each hand – a
double shot and two Buds. A point toward Link and to himself
with a left-right judo slash – a pair of Sierras. Om nodded, pulled a

handle, popped a pair of green labels and splashed a double dose of Dr. Daniels' spirits into a bucket for the Scrounger. Frankie wrestled his way to the end of the bar for the pick-up. He wedged his way back into the corner with a small round cocktail tray held high over his head.

"I said spritzer water," Link said.

"You got Sierra," Frankie replied.

Link rolled his eyes and tilted the bottle to his lips.

"I find myself on occasion to be a very weak man."

"Well," Rubiks broke in, "this is an occasion."

They didn't spend much time talking about Frankie. Everybody knew Washington was the right move. The *Post* had been in major hiring mode: the one good thing about Trump. The *Post* had a billionaire owner. The *Post* was a little dubious about Frankie's age, but they liked the Russian series. He was thrilled at the opportunity on night cops.

"Everything good happens at night," he said.

"Good in what respect?" the Scrounger asked.

"Nasty and newsworthy," came the reply.

"I thought you wanted to break in on Trump-Russia," Rubiks said.

"And I'm starting at midnight. I hope to work my way up to 1 a.m.," was Frankie's rejoinder.

Frankie drank up. He had to circulate – it came with being guest of honor.

It surprised Link to see Detective Andrew Wiggins in the house. If he distrusted reporters so much, why did he show up at the one bar that currently served every reporter in Sacramento, past and present? And why the friendly exchange between him and Frankie when Wiggins walked in the door?

It was an occasion.

Link took another sip of pale ale, but no more.

Rubiks and the Scrounger didn't notice when he set his bottle down and excused himself out the front door.

Outside in the still night air, the rumble of the crowded bar gave him a good feeling. He stopped and smiled, and felt happy for Frankie.

He headed toward the railroad tracks for the walk home when the clanging began and the gates dropped.

There were truths and ultra-truths in this world, and Link had a knack for knowing which was which. Of all people, it dawned on him that he got a major dose of it from, of all people, Anton Karuliyak – Link's Oracle of Delphi.

In getting to know himself after sharing the same skin for more than 60 years, Link arrived at a couple of understandings. He was:

Unclassifiable. Oppositionally defiant. Too self-consumed to engage in truly meaningful relationships.

He added it all up and came to a conclusion: none of the classifications mattered.

He had come to realize the reality of his own insignificance. The world finished last with him and it could finish last without him, same as the Pittsburgh Pirates with Ralph Kiner in the early 1950s.

Insignificance mattered.

He found the acceptance of his own insignificance liberating. Insignificance gave him power. Insignificance set him free. His insignificance never seemed more profound than in the steely roar of the 100-car parade that stopped traffic from San Diego through Sacramento all the way to Seattle. No matter what happens to you, the train's going to roll, he knew, just like it had been across his country for almost 150 years. No matter where you are, he thought, the train is going to slow you down, it's going to stop you in your own tracks. The question he contemplated is, what are you going to do with the time?

He was getting short on his. He didn't have enough of it left to waste a second. He realized he did not have the luxury of dormancy.

He also had a gift, and he knew he needed to put it back to work, against the forces of greed, danger, and untruth.

Tankers sped north with recently fracked oil. Covered hoppers headed for the rice silos of Glenn County. Empty center beams aimed for the timber mills of Roseburg. Automobiles were stamped for Seattle with fleets of freshly baked Priuses just off the boat from Japan.

Boxcars carried freights of young men and women.

The train passed, and Link stepped onto the tracks, toward D Street, toward home.

A half block down, he slowed his pace to a single tie at a time.

He came to a full stop.

He stroked his chin.

He reversed his field. He headed south. He got back to his regular pace. He hit three railroad ties for every step. He broke into a jog. He derailed at R Street.

He ran to his studio.

He felt a sense of joy with each step. He ran past the empty ice blocks, burned – possibly by arson – ahead of the construction of a work/live loft high-rise. He ran across 15th Street, past the Iron Horse Tavern and the R-15 and the Shady Lady. He ran all the way to 13th Street, all of them favorites on the occasions he felt a need for inebriation.

He felt for the key in his pocket. He unlocked the door, and pushed, just like the sign said. It didn't open. He laughed as he pulled the metal bar to open the door.

He flicked on the light. It flooded the room, and he eyeballed the log on the pedestal.

Acknowledgements

Thanks so much to Megan Anderluh (editor), Cindy Love (illustrator), and Dara Slivka (photographer).

91163271R00129

Made in the USA
San Bernardino, CA
23 October 2018